The Fraxilly Fracas

The Fraxilly Fracas

Douglas Hill

LONDON
VICTOR GOLLANCZ LTD
1989

First published in Great Britain 1989
by Victor Gollancz Ltd,
14 Henrietta Street, London WC2E 8QJ

British Library Cataloguing in Publication Data
Hill, Douglas
  The Fraxilly fracas
  I. Title
  813'.54 [F]

  ISBN 0-575-04403-9
  ISBN 0-575-04509-4 Pbk

Printed and bound in Finland by
Werner Söderström Oy

For Marjorie, especially

Part One

Highlight Pursuits

Chapter 1

When the call first came in from Fraxilly, I didn't accept it. Earlier I had told the Posi who runs everything on my ship to hold all calls. She records them, acknowledges them – unless I'm being incommunicado for some reason – and replays them for me later. That way I avoid being plagued by calls from obscure planets when I have important things on my mind.

What was mainly on my mind just then – in fact, preying on it – was another obscure planet. Our destination, named Ixyphal II.

We were down to Halflight, sliding through the tangle of the Lagoon Nebula interlink, making our way towards the secondary GalacNet lines that would get us to the sector containing the Ixyphal system. Many less well-equipped ships would have gone through that interlink only at Firstlight speed, and then nervously – because of the horror tales of ships that slid through the wrong slots and were caught in endless loops round and round the interlink for centuries. But Posi was performing superbly, as always. So I'd left my pouch-seat in the control area to take my troubled mind back to my personal cabin. There I tried to ease my worries by sipping a Freezobalm and thinking about the fee I could be carrying away from Ixyphal II.

If I could *get* away from Ixyphal II.

That planet is populated by millions of little blue paranoids who have many arms and legs and absolutely no inhibitions. Especially about avenging insults, real or imagined. They are among the most hypersensitive exters – extraterrestrials – I've ever encountered, and I almost refused their commission for that reason. But they offered a very tempting fee simply to transport an art object, a sculpture, which they'd bought as a centrepiece for a planetary arts festival they were staging. And I had foolishly thought it would be the easiest fee I'd ever earned.

Instead, as I sat in my cabin moodily pouring another Freezobalm, I was facing a good chance of losing my valuable reputation as an interplanetary courier. And maybe my even more valuable life.

The job had started well enough, with the receipt of half the fee up front, then the receipt of the sculpture. It had been made by a galactically known artist – an ancient, smelly and mostly blind human living on a renovated asteroid near the Home System where Old Earth still spins. The artist had fussed around while the thing was being loaded on my ship, babbling about how important it was and how delicate it was and so on, until I'd just stopped listening.

I'd also stopped looking at the sculpture. I don't know anything about art, but I know what turns my stomach. It was about room-sized, and bright blue, which may be why it appealed to the Ixyphalians. It seemed to be a conglomeration of small shapes, looking vaguely like humans and exters, who were all suffering extreme torment in deeply disgusting ways. Supposedly a weird image of an afterlife. And it seemed to be made from millions of tiny fibres, like coarse hairs, all twined and braided and knotted, fixed firmly together by the artist's special secret process, which I think he called Solidity Polarization.

Except that the solidity didn't stay polarized.

It was my partner, Mala Yorder, who first noticed it. Mala is small and trim and dark-haired, with luminous blue eyes, the lissom body of an Ondilian angel-dancer – and the mind and soul of a policewoman, which she once was. She has all the skills as well as the attitudes that her police training gave her. So she is highly observant, good at noticing things. Particularly small errors and omissions on my part.

In this case, some time before we reached Ixyphal, she had

gone back to the storage and cargo area to look at the sculpture again, murmuring things like "masterpiece" and "magnificent" and the usual art-appreciation noises that people murmur. And then she came running forward, shrieking.

"Curb! Quick! It's *fraying*!"

I went back to look through the view-panel, and felt my stomach go into zerograv. There was a scattering of blue fibres on the floor – a large scattering – and some of the outer figures looked different. Just as repulsive, but different. Smaller, and distorted.

Then Mala shrieked again. "Curb, you pinch-headed moron!" She mostly calls me by my last name. It's her way. "You've left it in *atmosphere*!"

I suppose I should have been paying attention to the old artist, when he was telling me that the thing had to be carried in near-vacuum with traces of helium and neon but definitely *no* oxygen, which would destroy it. But then the old fool should have been a little less unwashed and boring. Besides, I didn't see why I should do everything myself, and said as much to Mala, tersely.

"I thought you'd seen to it, dribble-brain!" she yelled, when she'd finished directing Posi to alter the gases in the cargo area. "What are we going to say to the Ixyphalians?"

"Nothing," I told her. "I'm going to fix it."

"*You?*" Disbelief and scorn were heavy in her voice, but I put it down to stress. And eventually I convinced her – or anyway caused her to throw up her hands in rage and dismissal and stamp off to her cabin.

Then I fixed it. With one of my better inspirations.

I put on a spacesuit and went into the cargo area, where I found that while the main part of the sculpture was now solidified again, the fibres on the floor were disintegrating and useless. But it didn't matter. I simply went and fetched a squeezer of magi-glue and a pair of my socks, in a pleasing electric blue. They were among my favourites, but the sacrifice had to be made. Back in the cargo area, ruining two pairs of gauntlets in the process, I ripped fibres from the socks and glued them here and there, in and around, more or less filling out the places on the sculpture that had been affected.

11

It took a long time, it was tedious and tiring, but in the end I thought the repair looked almost unnoticeable. Yet when I coaxed Mala out of her cabin to have a look, she stared through the view-panel with her normally rosebud mouth compressed into a thin line.

"It's horrible," she declared. "The Ixyphalians will tear our bowels out and hang us with them."

Then she flounced back into her cabin. And it was shortly after that when I retreated to my own cabin and the comfort of a Freezobalm. But throughout the delicate passage across the Lagoon interlink my mind kept replaying Mala's last graphic remark — with the growing conviction that she'd understated the Ixyphalians' probable reaction.

As it happened, the Ixyphalians were overjoyed.

They greeted us royally, oblivious of the fact that we were sweating and trembling. Or I was, anyway. Mala just goes pale when she's anxious, with a slight darkening of her eyes. Perhaps the little blue exters thought humans are always like that. Perhaps humans *are*, around Ixyphalians.

Anyway, they unloaded the sculpture with reverence, popped it into a transparent showcase filled with the right gases, made a number of loud noises expressing awe and admiration, and wheeled it away without having noticed a thing. Some of them remained behind to tell me at length how the object was a perfect focus for their festival that was being held in memory of one of their multi-armed folk heroes. It probably *was* perfect, at that, with all its images of pain and suffering. But I didn't listen too closely, being busy trying to stay upright despite slightly rubbery knees.

Then they clapped me on the back with too many hands, thrust upon me the plastiform wafer that confirmed payment of the rest of my fee, and proclaimed that they would create a song for the festival in praise of "the most safe and reliable Delmore Curb, master courier". I stammered out a fairly acceptable reason for declining their invitation to make a personal appearance at the song's premiere, and very shortly

Mala and I were back on our ship as Posi took us off-planet, with much relief all round.

So much for art appreciation, I thought. But when I said as much to Mala, as a joke to ease the tension that still showed in her eyes, she merely called me an unrepeatable name and stalked away to her cabin again.

Then, finally, as we hit Highlight in deep space beyond the Ixyphal system, I asked Posi for a playback of any comm messages. And I lay back in the cradling pouch-seat, enjoying the feeling of being safe and relaxed – and financially secure for a while, with that fee safely tucked away in my Fedbank account. It was a moment to be savoured, when danger was past and I was wholly at peace.

It was the last peace I was to savour for quite a long time.

Just then, though, the Fraxilly message looked very interesting. Even Mala said so, when she emerged again. (I'd had Posi put the message on the commscreen in her cabin, as well as on the one in the control area where I was. I don't hold grudges.) Mala did point out that she found elements of the message suspicious. I reminded her that she finds a great many simple, normal things suspicious, as the police mentality does. She ignored me, and told Posi to repeat the message.

It was from an employee of the Grand Emissary from the planet Fraxilly to the Sentient Federation. It said that the Emissary would soon be travelling to SenFed Central, and that en route he wished to communicate directly with me, face to face, on a matter of immense delicacy. It politely requested that, for security reasons, I bring my ship down to Underlight speed at specific co-ordinates, at a specific time, and prepare for rendezvous with the Emissary's ship.

"All this security, matters of delicacy," Mala said. "That's what's suspicious. Someone as important as a SenFed Emissary creeping around in secret."

"Why not?" I replied. "An important man needs privacy and security more than anyone."

And now he seems to need *me*, I said to myself. It was a

13

pleasing thought, that I might soon be moving in more exalted circles. I was not going to let Mala spoil the anticipation.

She was frowning. "You said *man*. Is Fraxilly a human planet?"

"No idea. Just a figure of speech."

She turned to Posi. "Give us a full rundown. . . ."

"Wait," I interrupted quickly. "We don't need all the details. It could take *hours*."

It was true enough. Posi is equipped with the most advanced call-beam facility, which lets her link up with other servo-mechanisms and artificial intelligences, nearby or distant. From just about anywhere on the GalacNet she can access systems on other worlds including the all-inclusive Encyclo-banks of SenFed Central. There was no knowing how much might be there about Fraxilly. Or how much would be useful to us as background. But I knew that Posi was quite capable of droning on forever with useless stuff about gross domestic product and tertiary natural resources.

That's often the trouble with thinking machines. They're like people. They sometimes just don't *think*.

Still, Posi is the best that creds could buy. By far the most advanced type of Intelloid – artificial intelligence in non-human form – and more capable even than the latest model of all-purpose, human-form mandroid. Also a *lot* more expensive. In fact it's usually planetillionaires and the like who can afford a Posi. But I had bought mine at a time when I'd luckily accumulated some nice big fees, and she is just what I need, in every way. Her name-classification stands for Polyfunction Organizational and Service Intelloid – and it's always useful to be organized and served. Though Posi can be deeply irritating at times – she has the pedantic self-esteem of a precocious child – I often feel I'd be nearly helpless without her.

"Synopsis, Posi – just the main headings," I directed, ignoring Mala's stony look.

Posi obliged, revealing that Fraxilly was a small human planet, a member of SenFed for less than three hundred years, remote and poor and backward. Poverty kept everything depressed including the birthrate, so that the planet held only a few million people, mostly low-tech agricultural. And the

14

place was ruled by an absolute monarch named y'Iggthradgi-pile the First, known as the God-King. Many legends were told about this ruler, not very credibly, including (I allowed Posi one example) tales of his improbably heroic virility. But it was proven fact that the God-King was unusually long-lived and overwhelmingly rich.

"He and his court live in a luxury that is as excessive as his subjects' poverty," Posi concluded, in one of her most disapproving tones. A tendency to editorialize seems to come with higher-level Intelloids.

"Stick to the facts, Posi," I told her firmly. "Anything more?"

"No, Del," she replied, "unless you wish me to provide the subsidiary data. . . ."

"Definitely not," I said quickly. I then gave her the co-ordinates from the Emissary's message, instructing her to drop down to Underlight as we neared that point. Then I leaned back and smiled at Mala.

"See? That's all we need to know about Fraxilly."

She grimaced. "Posi's right. It sounds sickening. People starving while their 'God-King' wallows. . . ."

I sighed. She gets these surges of anger now and then, against injustice and evil and so on, no matter how often I try to remind her about the facts of life. But I don't stop trying. It's the least I can do.

"Mala love," I said patiently, "Fraxilly is a faraway place of which we know little. We can't make things different there. We simply provide a service, transporting things. It's not our business if the people who hire us aren't *nice* people. We can only require them to pay us, and not to get us into anything dangerous or illegal. . . ."

"You've never worried about illegal," she snapped.

"I may cut a corner or two, now and then," I said stiffly. "Anyone does, in business, if it helps to provide a better service. . . ."

"Curb," she broke in, "I should tell you that I'm never closer to getting *out* than when you start being sanctimonious about how you operate."

"Fine," I snarled. "You could probably get back into the FedPol. For about an eighth of what you're getting here."

"It might be worth it!" she yelled, and flung herself into another flouncing departure for her cabin.

I settled back into the pouch-seat, smiling to myself. That was the third angry walkout in one biological day, and the second threat to resign in less than a bio-week. We were getting interestingly close to setting a new record. But, I told myself, I shouldn't provoke her too much. That would be cheating. And I suppose it did upset her.

All the same, I was confident that her threats to leave me were mostly empty. When she joined me – after we'd met while she was still an undercover FedPol investigator – she sternly announced that she was coming into the firm for the sake of the money, and because the job offered interest and challenge without the lethal risks that a FedPol agent often had to run. I'd accepted all that, just as I accepted her usually sharp-edged attitude to me during the nearly two years of our association. Because I was certain that other things lay beneath the surface.

It seemed to me that beyond the superficialities of our relationship there was a growing rapport, a strengthening of feeling. She never even hinted at it aloud, of course, probably because such emotions ran counter to the veneer of toughness imposed on her by her FedPol training. But I sensed it within her. And I was sure that, given time and patience on my part, it would eventually emerge and flower to give a rich new dimension to our partnership.

Meanwhile, I had to accept that she was probably not consciously aware of the true nature of her feelings. Women often aren't. So she had to express them, and relieve her tensions, with these stormy little displays of temper.

But it made things difficult for me, at times. Just as it was difficult to be alone so much of the time with such an attractive young woman, despite the size of the ship and our separate cabins. In fact, I had once or twice let myself be tempted into making overtures to her. But when they had been greeted with expressions of total derision and distaste, I realized that she was still not ready to come to terms with the full womanly depth of her unacknowledged feelings. So I backed off at once, and resumed my patient waiting.

16

At least there was nothing to prevent me from enjoying a fantasy or two, now and then, while waiting. As I began to do while reclining there in the pouch seat. And intermingled with my usual imagined scenes of Mala and me together were other images – of Grand Emissaries and God-Kings, what they might want of me, what they might offer in return.

I had only once or twice done jobs for high SenFed aristocrats, or for royalty. It seemed at the time that meeting the Fraxillians could create some sort of major turning point in my career.

If I'd been able to guess at the future, the turning point would have been right there – wheeling the ship around and moving as fast as possible away from anything to do with Fraxilly.

Chapter 2

It was going to be well into the next bio-day, I knew, before we made all the Netline interactions that would bring us to the rendezvous point. So I had a quiet dinner – alone, for Mala was still sulking – followed by a refreshing sleep. I even enjoyed an inspirational dream in which a God-King, radiant and fatherly, conferred wealth, honour and titles upon me. But when I awoke, it was time to put dreams aside and get hold of reality.

That meant a substantial breakfast, followed by a word with Posi to confirm that everything was on course and on line. Later, in my cabin, I treated myself to a long, languorous Omnipure sauna before turning at last to the task of choosing my outfit for the meeting with the Emissary. Something discreet, quiet and slightly formal, I thought. Probably the dusty-green tunic-and-leggings ensemble, with the pink-and-gold collar and cuffs and the pink-trimmed gold boots.

And when I had laid out the clothing, I began the even more important business of transferring my personal armament.

Among my acquaintances there are some who like to seem amused or amazed by my weapons. They call them excessive. They make remarks about an unmanly attitude, and they pretend to look for yellow streaks. But I never rise to their teasing. I see my weapons as reflections of a sensible, realistic caution – that of a true professional.

I've worked at a number of occupations that put me into positions of possible danger. As a private investigator, for instance, or earlier as a guide on the giant planet Wörbali'n, where the smallest life form had teeth as long as my arm. I know all too well that it's a big rough galaxy out there, full of more surprises than the human imagination can conceive of. And I've always liked to be ready for surprises, especially the lethal sort. That means approaching my work realistically. Not for me the reckless, romantic heroisms that make obituary writers reach for phrases like "untimely end" and "cut down in his prime". I don't consider that I've *reached* my prime. And I intend to get there, with the help of professional caution and my range of weaponry.

The weapons are made for me on Clabidacia V, the home world of spidery exters with delicate filaments instead of limbs who are among the finest micro-engineers in the SenFed. For me they have miniaturized an array of defensive and offensive armaments, which I carry in disguised form here and there on my clothes, accessories and body. I've gathered them slowly over the years, because they're cruelly expensive. So is the constant need to maintain them, and to re-energize or replace some of them. But it's worth it, because they've never let me down. As is to be expected from the work of such notable craftsmen. Crafts-exters.

Anyway, when the complete transferral was done, I dressed myself with care and switched on a full-length mirror for an inspection. The mirror showed me a youngish man, perhaps a little thin and no more than average height – whatever average is in a galaxy overflowing with exters and mutant humans. There was a suspicion of extra flesh at hip and belly, but that's to be expected on an adult male. All in all, the image that looked back at me was not displeasing.

I've heard people say disparaging things about my looks – a narrowness of shoulder, thinness of face, pointedness of nose. But I try to be indifferent to the slurs of my enemies. My hair may be ordinary brown, a bit wispy and thinning – but it's all hidden under a thick wig that is tawny-blond and artfully tousled. Why not? Everyone goes in for a little enhancement, one way or another.

In any case, my wig is more than just a wig. And the jewelled headband that encircles it, the rings on my fingers, the studded belt around my waist, my other jewellery, other bits of my clothing and of my very self . . . all are more than they seem.

Most importantly, everything – mini-weapons, clothes, mood and spirit – seemed just right, perfectly ready to meet an important personage.

So then I spent a few hours quietly relaxing, until finally Posi reached the rendezvous point, reduced speed and gave the "spacecraft sighted" warning. I sauntered along to the control area, trying to be at ease. But what the screens revealed was not likely to make me feel easy.

The Fraxillian ship, displayed on the perceptor screens, was breathtaking. I'm proud of my own ship, a good-sized and costly Starstream Mark 8 cruiser. But the Grand Emissary had swung up in the very newest model of the Novablast Personaluxury Liner, making me feel like a meteorite next to an asteroid.

The immense dumbbell-shape drew closer, almost languidly threw out a wide-focus tractor beam, and anchored our two ships together. Then from one of its airlocks something began to be extruded, like a giant worm stretching out – an expanding Manport passage, to connect the airlocks of the ships. No clumsy spacesuited crossing for the Emissary. The Manport reached my ship's airlock and clamped on, with puffs of vapour as it formed its insta-seal around the join.

"Spoken message being transmitted," Posi said brightly.

"Let's hear it," I said, still staring at the liner, a little dazed.

A hearty human voice emerged from a speaker. "Greetings from the Grand Emissary Lord y'Fiprehaude of Fraxilly to Curb the Courier. Requesting permission to send Manport passageway to bring you aboard."

"A little late to ask," Mala said sourly. She had just emerged to frown at the Manport, wearing a plain dark coverall that made no concession to dressing up for important company. Except that her figure made it look good anyway. "And why should we go to them?"

"Because they're the clients, with the money." I keyed my comm into action. "Greetings from Del Curb to the Grand

Emissary Lord y'Fipre ... y'Fip ... to the Grand Emissary. We will come aboard with pleasure."

Mala sniffed, but I grinned and opened the airlock. "Come on, smile," I told her. "How else will you ever get to see inside a Novablast liner?"

We floated quickly across – no artificial grav even in a Manport – to be greeted by a small pale human wearing lushly decorated robes, who abased himself in the manner of a true flunkey and then blandly introduced himself as one y'Pripio. He guided us along a functional passage or three, then finally into a large open area where he halted – obviously to let the full impact hit us. And it did *hit*, so that I did a suitable amount of gasping and goggling and even Mala drew in her breath with a hiss.

I wasn't so overwhelmed, though, that I forgot to raise a finger to one of the jewels in my headband, as if idly adjusting the band itself. Then I slowly turned full circle. Facing forward again, I touched the jewel again, seeming to brush at a lock of hair. Only then did I properly examine what lay before me.

I'd seen the Illusochamber advertised – for the rich – on the galacvid. But I'd never seen the real thing. Except that there *is* no real thing: it creates illusion. I knew that the area where we were standing was sizeable enough. But I was looking at immensity. A fantastic chamber from a fairy-tale palace, staggeringly wide and dizzyingly high, gleaming marble floor and walls, snowy-white fluted pillars, glossy draperies and glowing works of art. Towards the centre of the chamber was the reality in the midst of illusion – real pillowy furniture, a real fountain and pool in rainbow colours, real near-naked nymphs playing in the water. . . .

Only by then the nymphs were retreating at speed, in a flurry of droplets and giggles, so I got only fleeting views of slender backs and rounded behinds. In any case the flunkey, y'Pripio, was moving again, leading us to the largest of the cloud-soft couches, where a man was reclining.

He was small, scrawny, hairless and quite ugly, aside from his teeth when he smiled, which were gleaming re-gens looking sixty years younger than their wearer. He wore a rich robe so encrusted with precious metals and stones that I wondered if he could stand up under the weight. And his eyes were tiny, wet and somehow avid as he looked me over – wholly ignoring Mala – from head to foot.

"The Lord y'Fiprehaude of Fraxilly," the flunkey intoned, "Grand Emissary of His Divinity the God-King y'Iggthradgipile the First."

"Del Curb," I said briskly, unwilling to appear any more overawed than was diplomatically useful. "Nice to meet you, Lord y'Fip . . . y'Fipre. . . ."

"Come, dear boy," the Emissary said in a high, affected voice, with a languid wave of the hand. "Come sit by me, where it's comfortable."

With some wariness I lowered myself on to the front edge of his couch, while from one side more flunkeys appeared, guiding a hover-table laden with delicacies and fancy drinks. The Emissary gave me another view of his new teeth as I glanced round.

"Do take refreshment," he purred, "and tell me what you think of my environment."

In fact I thought the whole fairy-palace effect was a long way over the top and painfully unoriginal. A total waste of the fantasy potential of the Illusochamber. But I wasn't about to voice either that thought or any of the others that were gathering in my mind. I simply took a glass of Ephractian feather-wine and nodded. "Very nice. Very luxurious."

The gleaming smile widened, then vanished under the onslaught of a large, sticky confection of some sort. During that pause I realized that Mala had not been offered a seat, nor any food or drink. The Emissary and his people were behaving as if she simply wasn't there. I could see that she was scowling and stiffening into a Mark 2 temper, so I gave her an encouraging smile – which raised her, as I expected, to a Mark 3.

"So this is the great Del Curb," the Emissary was saying through a mouthful of stickiness. "The famous interplanetary investigator, lately turned courier. I suspect there is a story behind that change of vocation."

I shrugged. "Just a search for new challenges, new horizons, that sort of thing." And new ways to make a living that didn't threaten to put an *end* to living, I might have added.

"Mm." He seemed to have slid over nearer to me, though I hadn't seen him move. "I would have expected you to be bigger."

I sighed inwardly. If I had a decacred for every time someone has said that . . . But I put on a bright new grin. "I *am* bigger," I said jauntily. "Bigger than lots of things. Than a Melorivicish tree-dwarf, for instance."

He laughed so hard I thought he would dislocate his dentures. "How *droll!*" he finally gasped. "And how *modest!* But then modesty is your key-note, is it not?" Again his hand waved languidly. "The unassuming garb, the inexpensive little ship . . . all signs of a man who knows his own worth and has no need for display."

Mala's vigorous snort stirred up a few echoes, but no one looked around. And I felt a bit rankled. Unassuming? Inexpensive? The condescension was beginning to go too far. So was the Emissary, whose airy wave had brought his hand finally to rest, with elaborate casualness, on my knee.

I shifted away minutely. "What I *do* have a need for, your lordship, is your reason for contacting me."

"*So* business-like," he murmured, moving his hand up to my thigh. I was by then realizing something that had eluded me before, about the fleeing nymphs. All that slim, rounded, unclothed flesh I'd seen – from the back – had not been *girl* flesh.

I could also see that Mala was near to exploding, which might have been disastrous. You don't want to antagonize rich and powerful Emissaries, especially not on their own ship in deep space. Not if you plan to soak them for a very large fee.

So I retained my grin, a bit strained, and slid minutely away again. "Business before debauchery, lord, as they used to say on Old Earth."

"Mm. So. Very well." With a sigh he withdrew his hand and struggled to sit up. "To business, then. Explain, y'Pripio."

The flunkey bustled forward self-importantly. "The Lord y'Fiprehaude wishes to commission you to convey – with the *utmost* discretion and security – an object to Fraxilly. And place it, with your own hands, into the hands of *no one* except the Most Sacred Body-Servant of His Wondrousness the God-King."

I waited, but he had stopped as if he thought he had said it all.

"I'll need more," I said patiently. "What kind of object? Why all the secrecy? Why have you come to me? And – most important – how much?"

The flunkey hesitated, then responded by answering the last question first – with a figure that was nearly four times larger than the largest sum I had thought I might try asking. I stared, open-mouthed, hardly even noticing that the Emissary's hand had crept back on to my leg.

"In return for that amount," y'Pripio went on, "we would expect you to maintain total discretion and loyalty for the duration of the contract. And to accept only the minimum of information necessary for you to complete the task."

"But we can answer some of the dear boy's questions," the Emissary put in, massaging my quadriceps. "The object is a prized possession of the God-King's, *very* valuable. Perhaps his *most* valuable acquisition, worth more than a planet's ransom. But to you, my dear, it will simply be a small cylinder of Balbazian steel, that wonderfully unbreachable metal. And *you* are taking it, rather than any other, because our . . . *usual* carrier service has regrettably gone out of business. And because we *know* we can rely on your experience and skill to convey it safely."

I took a sip of wine, gathering my responses. If the thing was so valuable, then the secrecy and the size of the fee were understandable. And if how the Emissary lived was any indication of life at the top on Fraxilly, presumably the God-King did like to own things worth a planet's ransom. So I nodded and smiled and agreed, while part of my mind began to toy with the question of whether Balbazian steel *was* as impregnable as its well-advertised reputation insisted.

I asked for the usual guarantees – that the object wouldn't endanger my ship or anyone on it, and that carrying it would breach no SenFed laws. Instantly y'Pripio produced a document with those assurances already signed and sealed. I know that such guarantees aren't really worth the plastiscrip they're printed out on, but they have at least a token legal value if there's any trouble. Then I asked for half the fee in advance, and was given a wafer confirming the immediate transfer of that amount to my Fedbank. And finally I asked where the object was.

"Vadinamia," the Emissary said merrily.

That was reassuring. The "safety-deposit planet", as it was called, prided itself on being the most secure place in the galaxy – and also one of the most law-abiding. It had its own unique ways of safeguarding objects in its care, and its own ways of keeping the galaxy's criminal predators at bay. If Vadinamia had the Fraxillian cylinder, it looked like I'd be making a safe and secure pick-up. As long as I maintained my own security.

So it was all settled; y'Pripio smiled blandly, Mala's temper subsided to a Mark 2, and the Emissary's hand slid smartly up into my groin. Where it ran into the special ceramic-and-leather codpiece that is tailored into most of my tights and leggings, a useful protection in many situations.

A very few moments later, Mala and I had firm hold of the contract for the job and were taking our leave of a decidedly miffed Emissary. We hurtled at speed back to our ship, and Posi got us away about two nanoseconds after the Manport had withdrawn to the Fraxillian liner. By then Mala and I were sunk into our pouch-seats, awash with laughter. Or anyway I was, while Mala struggled to keep her giggles from swamping *all* of her outrage.

"Foul little *lizard*!" she said, half-choking.

"Wasn't he just?" I agreed, mopping my eyes.

"I mean *you*, Curb! Sitting there grinning while he groped at you . . . What would you be doing at this moment, if I hadn't been there?"

I sat up, glaring. "I'd be doing exactly this – sitting here laughing my head off. Only if you weren't here I'd be *enjoying* it!"

She sniffed, then switched the subject as she does when she knows she's wrong. "Well, you needn't be so pleased with yourself. No matter how much he's paying. There's something slimy and crooked involved in this whole thing."

I shook my head. "Mala, we're transporting a container. That's it. If there's slime, I don't care, as long as it doesn't come off on me. Us. And it won't, as long as we do the job and keep security. Which reminds me – Posi, sweep for bugs."

With no apparent pause, Posi replied. "All internal perceptors show no intruding devices, Del."

I nodded, and sank back. So far, so secure. The Emissary's Illusochamber had also been free of bugging devices, as I'd found when I'd been fiddling with my headband, activating a mini-ceptor in one of the jewels. We were clear, and we were going to be rich. Not even Mala's temper or suspicions could diminish that.

"I still have my doubts," she said, almost as if she'd heard my thought.

"Then waive your share and let me do it alone," I suggested.

She merely snorted, as I knew she would, and stared moodily at the blank screen of the comm.

"You don't like the job because you don't like the Emissary, because *he* doesn't like women," I told her. "Never mind. I do." And I reached over to slide a hand along her upper arm, then down the trim length of her back.

But she shook it off angrily. "If you want to fondle someone, go fondle the Emissary. And listen to what I'm saying, Curb. There's a smell of nastiness about that Fraxillian, nothing to do with what he likes to fondle. There's nastiness and too much mystery. Which could add up to serious trouble."

"It adds up to more Fedcreds than we've ever earned for one job," I said lightly. "That's all. We simply have to be sensible and professional, and we won't have a speck of trouble."

And with that monumentally fate-tempting remark, I gave Posi the new course to follow, and settled back peacefully in my pouch-seat.

Chapter 3

At that time our position was most of the way across the galaxy from the sector where the planet Vadinamia lay. Even at top levels of Highlight speed it would take us a few bio-days to get there. But that didn't trouble me. I always enjoy the restful times of interstellar travel. I can take it easy, relax with the galacvid – which is networked throughout the sentient worlds along another form of call-beam following the GalacNet lines. But on the journey to Vadinamia I also spent some time giving a little thought to security.

It's a problem people are always thinking about, but never wholly solve. Whether in the SenFed or in the Freeworlds that haven't joined, there is simply no such thing as one hundred percent security. Within the SenFed almost every one of those million or so planets is vying with at least some others – for influence, for position, for trade and aid and income. To manage the vying successfully, they need information. So information becomes a valuable commodity, and the gathering of it a labour-intensive industry.

The gatherers proliferate like the Yechotinic Polyp plague. I know because I was one, once, as an investigator. So was Mala, as a FedPol agent. They labour away, digging up the secrets with every bit of up-dated and often extra-legal technology they can get. They scrape up gossip and rumour and myth, when hard data is thin, to keep their salaries coming in. And they strive non-stop to thwart, misinform or actively eliminate one another.

They particularly infest the important places where secrets might abound. Like the planetary cluster that makes up SenFed Central. And like the wealthy worlds, the high-tech industrial worlds, the larger resort worlds, the popular cross-roads worlds. . . .

And Vadinamia. Where I was going to have to keep a secret about an incredibly priceless mystery belonging to a God-King.

But I felt fairly confident. Vadinamia has its own ultra-tight security that has been frustrating spies for a long time. As for the other end, Fraxilly, I doubted whether it was important enough to have any spies watching it.

"Maybe," Mala said, when I said as much to her. "But we need data."

So she went off to go doggedly through the full factual screening of Posi's data of Fraxilly. I managed to avoid a lot of it by having some tasks of my own. I made some comm-calls to contacts on planets here and there, pretending to some that I was looking for commissions, to others that I was in different parts of the galaxy transporting things for different people. All a casual but effective smokescreen, neatly blurring our back trail.

But Mala did insist, with some steeliness, that I look at some of the data. So I had to watch an earnest and over-long documentary, first made for one of the vid's information services, about the ruler of Fraxilly. It showed a few shots of the God-King's residence, called the Divine Sanctum, which looked from the outside as big as some planetoids and not much lovelier. I was impressed, though, by the Sanctum guards – those specialized, monstrously expensive, human-form soldiers called killdroids. And I was interested to hear – the film-makers weren't allowed *in* the Sanctum – about the God-King's lavish lifestyle, which included a large stock of harem girls.

"At least it proves he's hetero," I muttered to Mala. But she merely looked at me, coldly, and fast-forwarded.

We found no security tips in any of that film's material. Just more specifics, tediously detailed, of the contrast between the God-King's immense wealth and the miserable poverty of the people. And more legends and lies about the God-King's supposed longevity, divine strength and other supernatural powers. It seemed to me that if the Fraxillians were docile enough to put up with their misery, and stupid enough to believe in their ruler's divinity, they weren't likely to offer much of a threat to him or to my delivery.

So, ignoring Mala's reproaches, I took myself back to my cabin and the galacvid's more entertaining screen material. And there I was, nearly a day later, when the call came from the Ardakkeans.

There was nothing unusual about getting either that call or the earlier one from Fraxilly. That was how prospective clients often made contact, since Mala and I made the ship our home and office, in space, much of the time. The comm-link details for reaching us are available in a number of professional-directory data banks. But it *was* unusual to have another caller ask for another highly secret, ship-to-ship rendezvous.

"Everybody's getting clandestine and paranoid," I complained to Mala.

"Everybody always was," she replied. She was also busy, through Posi, acknowledging and agreeing and setting up co-ordinates for this new meeting.

Then, of course, she turned to the task of getting from Posi all available data about the planet Ardakke.

I was about to stop her, expecting another turgid flood of brain-numbing data, but Posi surprised me. There was very little information available – even on the SenFed Encyclo-banks – about Ardakke. I didn't have to ask Posi for a synopsis because that's just about all there was.

Apparently Ardakke was one of those cranky "closed worlds" that exist here and there. It was a human world, we learned, theoretically part of the SenFed but only just. Its emissaries were seldom seen at SenFed Central, and it received no diplomats from other worlds. In fact it allowed very few off-worlders on to the planet, and they were mostly technicians with special skills – who were required to live restricted lives in special compounds, hardly ever mixing with the local population.

But other off-worlders had now and then wheedled their way on to Ardakke, claiming to be academic researchers. A few were legitimate, but most were spies. Yet they had all come up with very little. The real researchers found themselves as restricted as the employed technicians, and soon left in frustration. And the spies all seemed to have been the clumsy types, exposed and expelled almost at once.

Not that anyone seemed to care very much, according to the data. The conclusions were that Ardakke was small and remote with nothing much to offer, where dull people led uneventful lives. The accepted theory said that within their closed society they probably practised some exclusivist cult religion. Everyone seemed content to let them get on with it.

Yet now some of these standoffish people from an introvert world were out on the GalacNet lines, coming to meet Mala and me.

I wasn't looking forward to it much. All the indications were that they would be a stern and forbidding lot, which is my least favourite type of person. They'd definitely sounded that way on the comm – and there was another hint about their nature in the fact that they were too withdrawn to make a *visual* link. Which seemed odd, since all the data had agreed that they were an unusually fine-looking race.

'They're dragging us a long way out of our way," I grumbled to Mala, indicating her note of the co-ordinates for this new rendezvous.

She shrugged. "It'll add a few more days to our hop to Vadinamia. But the Fraxilly package isn't going anywhere. And I'd go farther for a chance to have a look at people from this planet of mystery. Aren't you curious?"

"Not very," I muttered.

"Then just think of it," she said with a superior smile, "as a few days extra for you to go on pulping your brain with galacvid garbage."

"The vid has a lot of very educational and cultural programmes," I said stiffly.

"I know. And you're very selective. You watch everything else."

I knew then that if she was in that kind of mood there was no point in staying around. I withdrew to my cabin, to find that I was just in time for a repeat episode of *Garry Garrison, Para-space Pilot*. So one bio-day placidly followed another, the ship plunged on through Highlight, and nothing at all of importance happened. Until the Ardakkeans came on board.

They came to us, which was something. And they came in an old-model passenger pod, out of a slightly battered Stellablaze cruiser – a line that had been discontinued before I was born, and a ship that was markedly smaller than mine, which was gratifying.

But nothing else about the meeting was.

Expecting them to be dull and puritanical, I'd worn one of my most conservative outfits – pearl-grey blending into iridescent blue, with glitter-silver trim at wrists, collar, belt and headband, and plain-contrast boots (one grey, one blue). But I was surprised by their looks, as they came through the airlock – enough to keep me from being puzzled, then, about how they had crossed from their pod to my ship without space suits.

There were four of them – three men and a woman, as was later revealed, though I couldn't tell in that first glimpse. I could see, though, that they were tall and broad of shoulder, and walked with that kind of lithe confidence and grace seen in GalactiGames athletes in peak condition. They were wrapped in long, midnight-blue capes that disguised most of their shapes, but their uncovered faces were strikingly hand-some. Thick dark hair, large dark eyes, pale unblemished skin, sculpted planes of the face, straight noses, strong mouths. All four looked quite different, yet slightly the same, like distant relatives with an underlying family resemblance.

Mala had come out in one of her crumpled dark coveralls. But as the first Ardakkean strode through the airlock she went wide-eyed, whirled and vanished back into her cabin. Even before the fourth one had entered she had reappeared –

in a flimsy thigh-high tunic of translucent Tructollean cling-silk. Almost at once she was aiming her brightest smile at the nearest Ardakkean, who proved himself to be a male by grinning back at her and swelling his chest manfully.

By then the Ardakkean who appeared to be their leader was approaching me, throwing the cape back. And it was my turn to go wide-eyed, for the leader was a woman, possessing every anatomical aspect of femaleness in glorious Amazonian splendour. She and the others – when they let their capes fall open – were wearing one-piece outfits of a lighter and duller blue than their capes, with black boots and belts. Not so much conservative, I thought, as repressed. The outfits were not particularly tight-fitting, yet they revealed much of their splendid physical development and amazing muscle definition.

I found that I was mostly focused on the leader's chest, where the blue cloth was more taut, stretched by the magnificent swelling mounds beneath it. But in truth I didn't have much choice where I focused. She was standing directly before me, and her bosom jutted not too far below my eye level.

"I am Sergia, of Ardakke. You are Curb?"

She spoke Galactic with an exotic accent and in a voice that was strong, melodious and full of authority. With difficulty I raised my gaze to her face, staring dazedly at the soft abundance of her mouth, the petal-perfect skin, the powerful femaleness that radiated from her eyes.

"I'm Curb," I said in a voice that sounded rusty.

A small frown creased the smoothness between her eyebrows. "*You* are the one who brought down the spymaster of Aldebaran? Who rescued the Callitee princess? Who put an end to Rimeq the Renegade?"

For people from a closed world, I thought dimly, they're well-informed – if a few years out of date. "That's me," I said. "Or it was."

She pursed those edible lips. "I had imagined you would be bigger."

Here we go again, I thought. But I found a bright smile. "I *am* bigger . . ." I began.

The frown deepened. "It is no matter. We wish to hire your

services. And those of your . . . partner?" She raised an inquiring eyebrow towards Mala.

Mala tore her gaze away from her grinning Ardakkean male. "Mala Yorder," she said. "His *business* partner, only."

"Ah," Sergia said. The two women looked at each other for a moment, no doubt exchanging one of those wordless communications that women contrive now and then. At last they both smiled faintly as if to say message understood, over and out. Then Sergia turned back to me, her smile regrettably fading.

"A crime has been committed on Ardakke, most serious and treasonable. But we cannot identify the criminal. Crime is nearly unknown among our people, and we have none of the means or experience to pursue it. We need an investigator of your reputation, Curb, to seek out the criminal, so we may punish him."

Lost in the contemplation of her beauty and the music of her voice, I just went on looking, waiting for her to speak again. But then the meaning of her words, and the thickening of the silence around us, came home to me.

"Investigator?" I echoed. "I'm not. I haven't done that for two years. I'm an interstellar courier now. Curb the Courier. . . ."

She made a gesture with a graceful hand that shut me up as if it had turned a tap. "You *were* an investigator. Your skills still must exist. And we are in need of them."

"Why not go to the FedPol?" Mala asked.

Sergia shook her head, dark curls quivering. "We have no experience of them. We are a closed world, having little contact with Federation authority. We would not wish groups of policemen on Ardakke, prying into our lives. We seek only one person, or perhaps two – to conduct an investigation that we could oversee."

Another time I might have bristled at the idea of being overseen, at work. But I'd let my gaze slip back down to the wonderfully outthrust cloth over Sergia's chest, so I wasn't picking up every detail.

"Can you tell us anything about the crime itself?" Mala asked.

Sergia glanced at the others, as if for confirmation, then told the story. Or some of it.

Ardakke has a native shrub, she said, called *phet* in their own dialect. It produces berries from which comes a juice called phetam. To the Ardakkeans, every tiny drop of phetam is immeasurably, heart-breakingly valuable. So every tiny drop is carefully gathered and even more carefully stored.

But somehow the ultimate betrayal had been committed. Someone on Ardakke had managed to *steal* a small amount of phetam – and, probably, to spirit it off-planet.

"Why?" Mala asked. "What makes it so valuable?"

"We prefer not to reveal that," said the Ardakkean man next to her. "We hope that you and Curb can investigate without that data."

"I don't know . . ." Mala said doubtfully.

I said nothing, being still in rapt contemplation of Sergia's magnificence. But I slowly became aware that they were all looking at me – just about the time that Sergia became aware of the direction of my gaze. With another frown, she took a step back. Weirdly, the step turned into a kind of floating movement, so that she seemed to be somehow poised in the air for an instant.

I blinked and looked up at her face again, to find that it held an icy glare. "We are naturally prepared to offer payment for your services," she said tightly. And she named a sum.

It was small enough, compared to my usual fee, to make me smile. Compared to the Fraxilly fee, it made me laugh aloud.

Sergia acquired a slight flush to go with her glare. "We are not a rich people. Our world strives to be self-sufficient, and there are few resources to spare. We offer you what we can afford."

One of the men chuckled. "As an extra inducement, Sergia, we could allow him to stare at your breasts for a while each day."

They all burst out into rich, musical laughter, Sergia included – and joined, I'm sorry to say, by giggles from Mala.

To my annoyance, I found it was my turn to flush. "Just the sort of remark I might expect," I said coldly, "from an uncivilized closed-worlder."

Their laughter faded, and Sergia's glare returned. "It is not *we* who are uncivilized," she snapped. "I begin to wonder, Curb, if your reputation as a brave and successful investigator may not be falsely inflated, undeserved. . . ."

That did it. Though I'm cautious by nature and habit, I have a temper that can flare up if I'm rubbed the wrong way. Perhaps I did have a few lucky breaks as an investigator, now and then – and some useful assistance, here and there. But what this Amazon had said was downright slanderous.

"Then forget the whole thing!" I rasped. "I don't need your dull little job, or your pathetic fee!"

"In that case, they are no longer on offer to you," Sergia replied coldly. With a nod to Mala, she whirled away in a sweep of dark cape, the men following – until Mala stopped them.

"Here's an idea," she said. "I was in the FedPol once, and I have a friend there who has worked undercover, named Chertro. I could ask him to contact you. He'd work alone and be as discreet as you'd want."

Sergia nodded. "That might serve well. You are kind. Our thanks."

Then they stepped into the airlock, after a last lingering gaze between Mala and her Ardakkean. As the lock slid shut, she turned to me with a merry grin.

"You might at least have *sold* them that information," I snarled.

She laughed. "What are you all heated up about? You've been telling people for two years that you'll never be an investigator again. Or would you have gone back to it, just for the beautiful Sergia?"

"No chance," I said firmly. "I meant what I said. Anyway, I'm not interested in some petty crime involving a weird drug or whatever. And the fee was miserly. We're better off giving our time to things like the Fraxilly job."

She smiled wickedly. "But isn't it a shame that the Fraxillian Emissary wasn't a woman with an over-developed bust?"

I might have made an angry reply about her own flaunting of herself at the male Ardakkean, but there was nothing to be gained by it. So I turned on my heel and stalked away to the control area. It was time to forget about Ardakkeans and their mysterious phetam, and get back on course for Vadinamia and the problems that would surely be waiting for me there.

Chapter 4

Shortly Mala joined me in the control area, losing no time in calling her FedPol friend, Chertro, to suggest that he contact Ardakke and offer his services. From the warmth in her voice, as she spoke to him on the comm, I began to suspect that she and Chertro might have been more than friends at one time. But I told myself sourly that that was in the past, while here in the present a living was to be earned. So I left Mala to it, went back to my cabin's screens and terminals, and set Posi to probing the data banks for something about phetam. And drew a blank.

"There is a listing of the shrub, the phet," Posi said, "in the galactic Bioregister contained in the Encyclobanks. But there is no reference to a by-product."

"Odd," I mused. "Aren't all life forms and bio-resources supposed to be listed?"

'That is the supposition, Del," Posi said. "But the Bioregister is a service, not a requirement. If a home world chooses not to include an item in its listing, that item will not appear in the Bioregister. Although it seems contrary to all logic. . . . "

"Right, Posi, thank you," I interrupted. And in the welcome silence I pondered awhile.

I'd begun hunting for data on phetam to see if it really was as valuable as the Ardakkeans claimed, and if so, why. But now . . . If there was no listing for it in any of the available data stores, I had stumbled on a case of data suppression. A secret.

Which meant, my instinct told me, that phetam really *was* valuable, and those caped puritans didn't want the whole galaxy to know about it.

So I fell into one of my enjoyable reveries, examining the problem from every angle, looking for the key point where I might provoke a few kilocreds to tumble into my lap, by acquiring a bit of phetam. Perhaps, I thought, I'd been too hasty in rejecting Sergia and her muscle-bound cohorts. But if so, I felt that I had a chance of retrieving the situation, once I'd made the Fraxillian delivery. I was sure that I could smooth over our little misunderstanding, and that Sergia would then be glad to have me on the job – so to speak – instead of some heavy-footed FedPol type. And my reverie had begun to include some delightful visions of how Sergia might make me welcome when I was interrupted.

"Del!" It was Posi, of course. They're just pure-intellect machines, as we all know, but I swear that it's not only out of humanizing sentiment that we give them female names and pronouns. Posi has the most *womanish* ability to choose the worst moments to disrupt a man's thoughts – usually with something trivial. As in this case.

"I have accessed an ancient fragment of a data store," she told me proudly, "recovered from the dead planet Ichael, whose star went nova 157 years ago."

"So what?" I said sourly.

"It contains sections of a report assembled by a self-employed intelligence agent from Ichael, who made a study of the planet Ardakke."

That made me sit up. "Anything in it?"

"Of course," Posi said, sounding surprised. "I could not have accessed it if there had been nothing in it."

I ground my teeth. "I mean anything of interest, to me, about phetam."

"Nothing about phetam," she said.

"Then why bother me with it?"

"Because it contains material about the Ardakkeans that might stimulate your sense of humour. Although I may be mistaken. Even an advanced Intelloid cannot be properly programmed with an inclusive appreciation of human laughter-stimulation. . . ."

She was speaking with the usual tone of insincere humility that she puts on when talking about human qualities that Intelloids lack. (There aren't many. Not useful ones, anyway.) It's another thing that makes me wonder if the crazed geniuses who developed the first Intelloids weren't perpetrating some subtly painful joke on the human race.

Eventually I got her redirected, and she told me what she'd found. It was a mostly garbled, semi-literate report put together by the free-lance Ichaelan spy, largely based on idle remarks and hints and speculations picked up from technicians who had worked on Ardakke. When the free-lance added them up, he came to the remarkable conclusion that Ardakke was nothing less than the setting for the next evolutionary step for mankind.

According to the spy's theory, the Ardakkeans had been transformed – by some beneficial mutation, he theorized – into *super-beings*. And he noted some of the superhuman attributes they were supposed to have developed – like unnatural strength, invulnerability, the power of flight and some others. Along with being very impressive physical specimens.

I laughed, of course. Though admittedly I did feel a brief uneasiness when I remembered that odd floating movement of Sergia's. Not to mention the peculiarity of their lack of spacesuits when crossing from a passenger pod to a ship's airlock. But then I told myself that those were idle fancies. I had no doubt that this Ichaelan free-lance, probably some spindly droop with acne and myopia, had found himself on a world where nothing but good old genetics had spawned a race of tall, handsome, muscular people. So he'd started shouting, "Supermen!"

To my knowledge, cranks and dreamers have gone around talking about and looking for *Homo superior* ever since the primitive times when writers still used paper. And with precious little success. I always say that there are planetillions of humans in this galaxy who haven't even come to terms with being *sapiens*. *Superior* still looks a long way off.

"This fragment from the dead planet Ichael," Posi then

added, "is part of a nearly forgotten data package held at a university on Quarley's World, a planet located on the Rim Beyond the Rim."

I scowled. "So?"

"In my search of all *other* Federation data stores, it has become clear that the data on Ardakke has been tampered with. Portions have been erased. Since it is an Intelloid's ability to perceive matrix-links between apparently discrete items and extrapolate . . ."

"Get *on* with it," I snapped.

". . . beyond them," she went on imperturbably, "I can speculate that someone may have overlooked the Quarley's university, when removing from all data banks material akin to that gained from the Ichaelan agent."

When I'd sorted that out, I shrugged. People going around wiping data stores – all except one – because they said Ardakkeans were super-beings?

"More likely," I told her, "the Ardakkeans have been erasing every mention of their very valuable phetam. To keep the vultures from learning about it."

Except, I thought, now some vultures had learned about it, and had got away with some. Which showed how wrong that mud-brained Ichaelan spy had been. All right, the Ardakkeans seemed fairly naïve about some things, like crime. But even so, if they really were super-beings, how could anyone manage to steal from them?

By then Posi was asking me to explain the connection between Ardakkean phetam and the carrion bird of Old Earth called the vulture. I'm convinced she knows all about image and metaphor, and just does it to annoy. And she succeeds. Feeling a headache coming on, I switched off the terminal, stretched out on my bunk and returned to my interrupted reverie, mingled with more speculation about why phetam should be so valuable.

And the ship, meanwhile, rushed relentlessly along its interrupted course to Vadinamia.

*

Days later, we were only a few bio-hours from the Vadinamian system when we received a call from Mala's pet FedPol, Chertro. He had already visited Ardakke and seemed very full of himself. I was in the control area with Mala at the time, so I had to suffer through it. The fellow's smugness and unnecessary familiarity with Mala made me dislike him at once. Just as much as I disliked the lean, tanned, grinning face that he presented on the comm screen.

"Hallo, little Fuzzy!" he began. Later I asked Mala the origin of that unlikely nickname, but she merely told me, with a faint blush, that it was none of my business.

"You put me on to a good thing," he went on, "with Ardakke. Nice simple job, perpetrator in custody, everybody happy. Or nearly."

"That was quick," Mala said, and gave an odd little chuckle. "Not like you at all."

Chertro's grin altered to a distasteful leer. "Some things I *like* to do quickly, Fuzz," he said. And when they'd finished gurgling and sniggering at each other, he went on. "Can't understand how those people couldn't find the thief themselves. I spotted him right off. One of the off-world technicians, taking some kind of massive bribe from other off-worlders to steal phetam. The Ardakkeans were amazed – and shocked. I think they just couldn't believe that anyone would do that to them. But closed-worlders are often kind of naïve, and gullible."

He added that Sergia's people had been grateful, though they'd ushered Chertro and his prisoner off-planet as soon as they could. But they weren't totally happy – for it was confirmed that the stolen phetam was also off-planet. Chertro had hopes, though, that the interrogation of the prisoner – going on at that moment – would reveal where the stuff had gone.

"One other thing might interest you," he added. "I was mostly reporting to that woman leader, Sergia. . . ."

"I met her," Mala put in. "Lucky you."

Chertro laughed. "She's spectacular, right enough, but not my type. I'd say she's a bit of a fanatic, and just as naïve as the rest of them. I like women who're small and neat and who *know* a few things. Right, Fuzz?"

He widened his moronic grin into another leer while Mala went into a revolting spasm of tittering. But in the end the repro-brain got his story told. It seemed that when he had arrested the thief, and reported to Sergia, she had been sitting in an ornate chair made of a local high-gloss hardwood. Hearing confirmation that a trusted employee had indeed turned thief, she had gripped the chair-arms in white-knuckled rage.

And the arms had been crushed to splinters and sawdust.

Mala laughed. "Well, she's big and strong, just like the men. . . ."

"I thought you'd have noticed the men," Chertro said with an echoing laugh. "But it was weird. I had a look at a chair like it, later, and the wood was hard as chunki-crete."

"Probably there was a flaw in that one chair," Mala said, in the voice that women use when they think men are being fanciful little boys. "Think of it as another reason for you to stay away from big gorgeous women with enormous boobs."

"I'd always stay away from them, Fuzzy," he said earnestly, "if you were around."

And they went back to their chucklings and grinnings while I made a scowling withdrawal. For a second the echo, in Chertro's story, of the notion that Ardakkeans were super-beings tugged at the edge of my thoughts. But I pushed it away. I was through with thinking about Ardakkeans. I would spare not one more thought for their closed-world mystery, their mythical super-powers . . . all of it. I had to turn my concentration now on to the Fraxilly job.

Though I still thought, when that was done, it might be worthwhile to sniff around here and there for any leads worth following that might turn up the stolen phetam.

Alone in my cabin, then, I got comfortable, put all trouble-some thoughts out of my mind, and switched on the vid to one of the best of what the vid expressively calls its Everlasting Serials. And by the morning of the next bio-day, Posi had brought the ship's speed down to Firstlight and we were sliding through the system that contained Vadinamia.

In a while we had drawn close enough to sight the planet itself – a slowly enlarging spot of brightness on the ceptor screens – by which time Posi had contacted the spaceport. I knew that the Vadinamian Intelloid who was the entry controller would guide Posi to an orbital position where we would wait for our turn to land – for only one ship at a time can make the approach to Vadinamia's unusual port. I was leaving all that to Posi, as usual, and paying more attention to the lateral and reverse ceptor screens around the control area.

Most visitors to Vadinamia are aware that, as they approach the planet's territorial space, they will have to pass through what might be described as a sort of gauntlet. I was waiting for it to show up and confront us. It didn't keep me waiting too long.

Posi gave the warning – spacecraft approaching – and the screens flashed up the images. Three long, lean gunships, the latest model of the Nebulance 40 GTF (that is, each one carrying forty fusitron energy weapons). I watched the screens unblinkingly as the three wheeled into triangular formation around my ship – their guns trained in an unmistakable attitude of menace.

Chapter 5

Even if I hadn't expected the gunships, their colours would have told me what they were. Matt black relieved by knife-thin white stripes, with a broader stripe of white down over the nose. Everyone in the galaxy, probably even in the closed worlds, knows what those colours mean.

Famlio.

The galaxy is full of criminal organizations of every sort – from gangs of juvenile hot-jetters who storm through the Netlines and vandalize the odd moon to groups of hard-bitten specialists in banditry and terrorism. But the biggest, best organized and just about the nastiest was Famlio.

It's a long-established human set-up, whose name comes from the Old Arcturean quickspeak for "Family Organization" – because they like to affect a patriarchal system and because they demand the same absolute loyalty and devotion that one would show to close kinfolk. I'm told that the word also occurs in the local exter dialect of the planet Milifinil-il, where it means "there is a smear of faeces below your fourth ventricle". No one ever reminds a member of Famlio of this coincidence. Famlio members tend to be touchy. As well as large, ugly and violent.

I'd expected to be met by Famlio gunships because they're always there. The organization gathers to the smell of credits like Vygeantic blood-worms to a corpse. Like all criminal gangs, Famlio specializes in profiting from human weaknesses such as pleasure, greed and fear. For instance, they have near-total control of the manufacture and sale of *bliss*, the illegal drug that induces brief comas filled with incalculable pleasure, and that rots a user's brain inside seventeen weeks. Famlio also has its tentacles around many legitimate businesses, including large chunks of the galacvid – which, as Mala likes to say, has the same effect as bliss but takes longer.

Similarly, Famlio has found a way to make a profit from Vadinamia.

Over the centuries the "safety-deposit planet" developed and refined all its amazing ways of maintaining the security that is its primary resource. So Famlio and other criminals have never felt able to plunder the place directly. But Famlio didn't take long to see other possibilities, in the established tradition of what is ironically known as *protection*.

A visitor to Vadinamia is greeted, just outside territorial space, by the black-and-white gunships. They announce that the visitor must pay a certain sum, Famlio's fee for protecting the visitor and his valuables from robbery. Anyone who doesn't pay gets robbed. By Famlio.

Sometimes they even rob a visitor who *has* paid – if the cargo, being brought to or taken from Vadinamia, is valuable enough to tempt them. But then no one should ever expect a criminal organization to be trustworthy.

At the same time, I feel, no one should be too over-awed by Famlio's own belief that they're all-powerful.

The three ships swirled around my ship, neatly bracketing it as they matched its speed. I felt the usual clench of tension in the bowels, and could see pale anger in Mala's face, but there was nothing we could do. My ship might just be able to outrun theirs, but it couldn't outrun the fusitron blasts that would be fired if I tried it. And while my ship does have useful guns of its own, in nose and tail, they were hardly a match for the hundred and twenty flamers ranged against me.

So I just waited for the contact, and hoped that my voice would sound calm and easy as I told Famlio my lies.

When the comm blinked into life, I saw a face that I vaguely recognized – a Famlio enforcer named Pulvidon, who had lately been rising rapidly through the ranks. It was odd to find him in charge of such a low-level enterprise as the Vadinamian protection racket. I wondered idly if he had done something wrong and been demoted. Anyway, he was a lean and hot-eyed human, wearing the usual Famlio garb – a roomy over-tunic and trousers of dull black with white pinstripes and a black shirt with a wide white necktie hanging down the front. The outfit is supposed to be traditional in some way, but I've never bothered to find out how.

"Thought it was you," Pulvidon said, flashing sharp eyeteeth in a carnivorous grin. "What brings the great Del Curb to Vadinamia? Delivery or collection?"

The sneering was heavy but unavoidable. I get it from most of his kind, who remember that I was once a private investigator, and so to them not far removed from law.

I simply gave him a cool look. "Neither," I lied. "Just touching down briefly, scouting for work."

Mala gave me a quick startled glance, but wisely said nothing. She knew that what I said was believable enough, since Vadinamia was a highly likely place for a courier to drum up a job conveying something somewhere. It was also a likely place for lies told by a courier to be exposed, by the host of spies that gather there, Famlio and otherwise. But I believed that I could avoid them, with some help from the Vadinamian processes themselves.

Pulvidon narrowed his eyes. "That better be true, Curb. You wouldn't like what happens to people who try to cheat me."

"Why would I lie?" I said, putting an injured tone in my voice. "If I get a client down there, you'll be the first to know."

"That's for sure," he snarled. "And if you don't bring anything off-planet, I'll let you off with the minimum."

"Why should I pay protection," I asked irately, knowing the answer very well, "if I'm not carrying anything to protect?"

He produced his carnivore grin again. "Insurance, Curb. Deep space can be dangerous. Think about it."

The screen shivered and cleared as he cut off, which allowed me to offer him a few choice epithets that he couldn't hear. As we watched the striped killer-ships peel away, for once Mala and I were in total accord – both anxious, both angry. Except that her anger was mostly aimed at me.

"What do you think you're doing now?" she wanted to know.

I shrugged. "I don't see why I should pay them if I don't have to."

"You *do* have to," she snapped. "You'll never con Famlio."

"I've done it before, other places," I told her. "It's not hard. They're too confident, too certain that we're all terrified of them. So they aren't a hundred percent efficient. They have little blind spots – places where the system is out of phase, holes in the structure where a person can slip through if he's sharp and quick enough."

"Like a rat?" she inquired innocently.

I scowled, but let it go. "The main thing is that we have no choice. At the least we'll have to pretend we're carrying nothing. But really I want to try to slip past them. Or would you like to announce to Pulvidon that we'll be carrying a priceless but unidentified object for a God-King?"

She shook her head slowly. "He'd hijack us before we were out of planetary speed."

"Exactly. So we have to try to avoid them. And we can do it. We'll just have to be very alert and very low-profile."

"Like a pair of rats," she murmured.

But then Posi gave the "imminent entry" warning, and we sank deeper into the enfolding embrace of our pouch-seats as the ship tipped over an unseen edge and began to fall all the way down to the planet.

We swept over the surface of the planet without a glance at the perceptor screens, for Vadinamia's surface is of no account. It's permanently overcast, with frequent squalls of rain that burns like acid, more deadly even than the stuff that history says helped to kill Old Earth. But the rain has no effect on the tireless hostility of the local life forms. Accounts by the first space-travelling visitors to the planet say that they found even the rocks and plants coming after them, but that has since been shown to have been normal travelogue exaggeration.

But the first visitors did find intelligent life *within* the planet, in a vast hollowed-out area that has as much land area as some smaller worlds. Life presumably evolved there because it was safe from the horrors on the surface. Most of the access points from surface to interior are quite small and easily guarded or blocked up. So the intelligent Vadinamians developed their underworld civilization, under an artificial sun, in peace and safety.

And that very excess of safety inspired some bright Vadinamians into a galaxy-class piece of lateral thinking. They recognized that they were living in an immense natural *vault*, with many extra security features also built in. And in the SenFed there were people and governments willing to pay fortunes for the promise of near-perfect security.

So Vadinamia became the safety-deposit world. It also became a very tedious place, since you can scarcely blow your nose there without going through a security check. As for getting *in*. . . .

There is only one entry point for spaceships into the world within the planet. It's known as the Vadinamian Valve, and it's big enough for only one ship to pass through at a time. At that entrance, every ship goes through a painstaking security-check examination right down to molecular level, which can seem endless. In fact they had Mala's and my molecu-prints and other data from our previous visits, and that helped to speed up the process to a slow crawl. But we knew that the *real* checks would come when we left. The Vadinamians don't much care what you bring in – but they'll go to any lengths to stop you taking things out that you shouldn't take.

Vadinamia's claim to fame, in its vid adverts, is as "the bank that can't be robbed". In fact I know about one occasion when it *was* robbed, though they've mostly hushed it up. It was when a thief of some brilliance spirited away some micro-miniaturized documents hidden in a pimple on his chin. He'd had a real pimple when he arrived, but during the time he took to find and bribe an official to provide the documents, the blemish had healed. So he simply made a convincing artificial one to hide his miniaturized booty, and the Vadinamians missed it – because when he left he was just the same as when he arrived.

That, however, was in earlier times, before molecu-tech searches and all the rest. Now things are different. Vadinamia has spent lavishly on all kinds of state-of-the-art technology.

There are no longer any bribable Vadinamians in direct contact with the stored valuables – just servo-mechanisms, including mandroid guards and Intelloid overseers with multi-phase fail-safe levels of programme reinforcement that make them incorruptible. And at the Valve, as ships enter, there is also a small army of Intelloid screeners operating the scanning technology that record every detail of visitors. As they did to Mala and me. Nothing was disassembled or even disturbed, but in the end they had complete molecular images of us and the ship – which we would have to match perfectly upon departure. No chance of sneaking a false pimple past them now.

It all took just over a bio-day, after which we drifted down from the Valve and touched ground at the spaceport. But even then there was no acceleration of the process. Things happen in their own time, on Vadinamia.

I trudged along and paid the usual fee to the port collector, then presented myself to a Vadinamian Warden, one of the high officials overseeing the Intelloids that do the real work. As usual, he laboriously studied my various credentials, including the plastiform wafer from the Fraxillian Emissary. He knew I was no impostor, from the screening at the Valve. But he had his own procedures, and he seemed to enjoy them. Finally, after a comm-call to the Emissary brought Lord y'Fiprehaude himself on to the screen, to simper a confirmation, the Warden grudgingly gave me clearance. But he had saved one further little irritation for the end.

"We are twenty-seven *dous* from Recovery, Visitor Curb. You arrival is not well-timed."

The average Vadinamian looks like an over-sized larva, boneless and segmented. Half of the body moves along the ground on many little legs – the front half rears up taller than a man, with many little arms. The head, if that's what it is, is crowned with a tuft of rubbery antennae serving various functions. There is no expression on the face, because there is no face. But I swear that when a Vadinamian tells an off-worlder that he's going to have to wait around even longer, the joints between the upper segments curve into a number of smug smiles.

I wasn't smiling, but I wasn't particularly troubled. That's life, on Vadinamia, as I said to Mala when I told her the news.

"Twenty-seven *dous*. . . ." She had to pause to work it out, having had only one brief experience of Vadinamia before. "Nearly three bio-days!"

I shrugged. "We'll find ways to pass the time."

"Which means you'll fall back into the vid," she said. "Not me. I hardly got off the ship, last time. This time I'm going to go sightseeing."

"I'll go with you," I said, which surprised us both a little. But I was feeling a bit tense and restless, and didn't feel like being alone or sitting still.

So we picked up one of the little floaters provided at the port, and went exploring. Off-worlders are restricted to the spaceport and the small city that has grown up around it, but that was all right. While Vadinamia will never be a rival to any of the known holiday-resort worlds, it has a few things to offer by way of amusement. Even better, Mala was being fairly close to friendly towards me, making her very good company. So I didn't even raise an objection when she insisted on touring the Story of Vadinamia museum, which included a lengthier account of the planet's development than I could ever want – plus an equally detailed, and gruesome, study of life and death on the planet's surface.

Later on, though, we found a little bar on the edge of the port city, with acceptable food and drink. And before long Mala was actually responding to some of my witticisms with that flashing smile which alters her from being pretty into being staggeringly beautiful. Back on the ship afterwards, she flashed the smile one more time – and then whisked away to her own cabin. I might have felt a little downcast at that point, only the evening had made me feel more encouraged about my prospects with her than I'd felt for some time.

Miraculously, her mood hadn't altered the next day, as it often does. We took up our time-killing almost where we'd left off. I showed all the tolerance and good humour that a woman might want of a man when we investigated the range of shopping offered by the spaceport city. Though I admit that Mala bought nothing during our slow trawl through the available outlets, while I picked up two reasonably priced shirts in a subdued canary-yellow-and-indigo, and an irresistible pair of boots made from the filmy hide of the Rexol'rian flutter-snake.

And then, as we drifted back to the ship after a placid midday meal, a shadow darkened our cheerful day.

Chapter 6

It didn't seem so at first. The shadow was in the form of a vast
spaceship resting near ours, and the last thing it looked was
shadowy. The surface was gleaming with pure white and even
purer gold. You might have thought that no meteor shower,
no space dust had ever touched that brilliance. And within the
rich glistening shine were a million intricate decorations, a
million subtle shapings and carvings, so that the whole thing
began to resemble some giant confectionery, the ultimate in
the art of a crazed master pastrycook.

Mala shrieked with delight, and stopped the floater to stare.
"What *is* it?"

"One of the compact versions of the Astropalace liner.
Someone's got carried away customizing it."

"More money than taste," she said with a giggle as we
floated around the thing, shading our eyes from its glaring
brightness.

"There's something," I said slowly. "Something it reminds
me of. . . ."

And then the memory leaped into life as the liner's spotless
white airlock opened, and some figures emerged.

Most of them were small, gnarled, dark-furred exters, but I
scarcely glanced at them. In their midst was a man, a human,
who would certainly catch any eye in nearly any crowd.

He was built a bit like a male Ardakkean – that is, tall,
broad-shouldered, lean-hipped, muscular. But otherwise he
was quite different. He wore a pure-white sleeveless jerkin

casually open at the front, white tights that left not the slightest doubt about his gender, thigh-high white boots. His hair curled in a thick golden tangle, his skin stretched taut and golden-bronze over his rolling muscles and over his high-cheekboned, demonically handsome face. Framed in the air-lock, he seemed like his ship to have his own light source, shining white and gold. And his smile, appearing slowly as he looked down at us, gleamed with a whiteness that almost hurt.

I knew, then, who he was. And what. And the knowledge was dampening my shirt with the clammy sweat of anxiety.

Mala was motionless, eyes wide, lips parted a little, as if hypnotized. Then the gnarled, furry exters began pointing at her, chattering in their own dialect with guttural noises that sounded like laughter. At that Mala flushed slightly, but even so seemed unable to tear her gaze away from the man in gold and white.

He, however, after making a very close inspection of Mala, was looking at me.

"Curb, isn't it?" His voice was golden, too, a melodious baritone that carried effortlessly down to our open floater. "The courier? With a *very* lovely companion. . . ."

"You know me?" I said harshly, feeling the worry-sweat burst out afresh.

"I believe we know of each other, you and I," the golden man said, his smile and his voice taking on an edge of mockery. "Are you visiting this world in the course of some . . . employment?"

"That's my business," I snarled. "Or will you tell *me* why *you're* here?"

He chuckled resonantly. "We will keep our own counsel, then. But we will surely see each other again during our stay. And perhaps I can invite your lovely friend to visit my ship, so that she and I might also become acquainted . . .?"

Mala looked about ready to climb up the side of the ship towards him, if she had to, so that I felt it necessary to grasp her by the arm. That drew a fiery glare from her and more resonant chuckles from the golden man, until – flushed and annoyed as well as uneasy – I got the floater away from there.

It wasn't until we were in our own ship that Mala asked. "Who . . . *was* that?"

"You don't know?" I said, surprised. "The FedPol must have a file on him to fill a room. That's Gharr. Gharr the Gherpotean. One of the most notorious and obnoxious criminals in the galaxy. Calls himself the prince of bandits."

Her eyes looked a little dreamy. "Really? *That's* Gharr? Why didn't you introduce me?"

"You should be glad I didn't. He may look a bit glamorous, in his overdone way, but he's poison all the way through."

She was licking her lips thoughtfully, not paying attention. "And those exters, with the fur?"

"His followers – or crew. I forget where they're from. People call them the Gharrgoyles. They say he recruits them so he can look even more golden and gorgeous by contrast."

"He doesn't need to," she murmured.

I scowled. "When you've finished drooling over him, you might re-activate your brain and help me think of how to find out why he's here." When she looked at me blankly, I went on. "We're about to pick up a very valuable thing. Suddenly one of the best-known bandits in existence turns up, parks near us, and starts giving us big knowing grins. Is that coincidence?"

"That's over-reaction," she said. "He could be here for any number of reasons. . . ."

"And it would be a great relief to know what they are."

She smiled. "I could go and visit him, as he suggested, and ask him."

"You keep away from him," I told her. "He's as likely to feed you to the Gharrgoyles."

That was when Posi broke in, to announce a comm-call. It was from another officious Vadinamian Warden, informing us that the next Recovery – which would release the Fraxillian package – would occur at exactly the mid-hour of the following bio-day. I thanked him and switched off rather brusquely, since right then I was more concerned about that evening and night, and what I wanted to do during that time.

Mala agreed with surprisingly little hesitation to stay behind and protect the ship, while I went back out into the spaceport city. I wanted to sniff around a little, and I always do that better on my own, without distractions. In a way, I was thinking, Gharr had done me a favour. His arrival had jolted me back into a proper appreciation of my problems, which I'd pushed aside in my enjoyment of Mala's warmer mood.

So I was mentally on my toes as I took a floater into the city and then left it, mingling with all the pedestrians thronging the walkways. Naturally I knew that I wouldn't be wandering unnoticed. Famlio would have people watching me wherever I went. And there might well be other watchers. Though in that crowd of humans, mutants and exters there was no way of telling who was watching who.

After a while, though, I began to feel sure that I'd spotted a Gharrgoyle – or maybe a different one at different times – wriggling through the crowds behind me. Which just strengthened my suspicions of Gharr. And I had a feeling that a certain exter with spiky reptilian skin and several eyes was also appearing too often in my wake. I might have tried a few quick manoeuvres to lose those shadows. But Vadinamia's spaceport city is a compact place, and any tails would have picked me up again soon enough. So I just kept on my way, letting them all come along for the ride, while I hunted for confirmation of what I suspected and feared about Gharr.

I didn't try asking any Vadinamian officials, because they would have sent me angrily on my way. On Vadinamia secrets are kept secret, and visitors are left strictly alone as long as they keep the peace. Vadinamia doesn't care if you're a criminal or a captain of industry (not that there's much difference). Nor do they care how you might have come by your possessions, off-planet. If you bring something to them, they assume it's yours, and they keep it safe for you. No questions asked – about anything.

So as night fell I looked for information elsewhere. I haunted bars and lowish dives, entering into innocent-seeming conversations, turning them to talk of new arrivals, waiting for hints and rumours about Gharr. And – nothing. Most people were aware that Gharr was there, but the news seemed to be mainly of interest to human females. You'd have thought the man was a vid star rather than a murderous bandit.

Eventually I decided to give up. If Gharr was there for any

reason to do with me, I'd have to wait and find out. Besides, I'd begun to think that Mala had been right. Perhaps I was over-reacting. There hadn't been any lapses in my security that I knew of. And the Gharrgoyle trailing me needn't have meant anything special. I was a known courier, on Vadinamia, possibly there to pick up something valuable. Just seeing me there would trigger the thief responses of someone like Gharr.

That's the trouble with this work, I thought. It does attract the villains.

But I'd eluded them before and I could again, I told myself, almost jauntily, as I ambled into the bar that I decided to make my last stop for the night. It was fairly crowded, but I found a place at the side and bought a beaker of No-tox Fungi-beer – which tastes like mouldy bread but leaves your head clear. Raising it, I glanced at the door to see if my tails had arrived. And nearly choked on the drink, which it probably deserved.

The spike-skinned exter who had been following me was coming through the door, in company with several other exters, none of them very humanoid. But it wasn't their appearance that had shaken me. It was their watchful defer-ence towards the even more unusual exter in their midst.

That one was squat and immensely wide, with a sleek moist skin and an upper body sprouting ten powerful tentacles, two of which were extra-long and whippy. Cephalopoid, he'd be called. And I had no trouble recognizing him. The tentacles, the skin – with its patchiness that spoke of increasing age – were clear giveaways. But so, most of all, was the faint trickle of what looked like black smoke or mist from his slit-mouth. It was a protective capability, I'd heard – a black mist that could suddenly be blown out in a huge, blinding cloud.

But I wasn't recalling the data so clearly at that moment. I was simply staring. Because the tentacled exter was a living legend – of crime – as he had been for longer than I'd been alive.

Ten-huc, known as Blackbreath, the cruel and ruthless pirate chieftain from the Alkaline Asteroids.

It was too much. Gharr was on Vadinamia, and a Gharrgoyle

had tailed me. Now Ten-huc was there – and one of *his* crew had tailed me. It couldn't be any kind of coincidence.

And if it wasn't, it was terrifying.

As I shakily set down my glass, with a new attack of the clammy sweats seeping into my shirt, things grew more terrifying. The group of pirates had clustered in one corner of the bar, and were all staring directly at me in an unblinking, blood-icing way. Then Ten-huc said something, with a tiny puff of blackness. Two vaguely serpentine exters detached themselves from the group.

And began to move slitheringly in my direction, keeping their metallic black eyes fixed on me.

I'm glad to say that I never found out what they intended. I could guess that he might have asked me what Gharr had asked – what I was doing on Vadinamia. And I'd heard enough about the grisly ways in which he liked to make sure his questions were answered. But thankfully the two exters never got to me.

As they approached, there was a loud clumping of heavy boots at the door of the bar, followed by an almost quivering hush. Then a great many of the bar's occupants began to behave as if they had just remembered urgent appointments. They all headed for the door, with that slightly stiff gait of people who are in a tearing hurry but who are trying not to break into a run.

The reason for the rush – and for the retreat of the two serpentine pirates – was an armed and armoured squad of FedPol Forcibles, that elite branch of ultra-combat heavies, who had pushed their way into the bar.

I stayed where I was, trying to look indifferent, though I did set my beer aside and asked the bartender for a calming shot of Hypergrog. The Forcibles stood silently by the door, studying the departing customers – and exchanging particularly cold stares with Ten-huc and the pirates as they sauntered out.

Well, no one expected arrests. The trouble with powerful

interplanetary criminals is that they are powerful and inter-planetary. Everyone *knows* about Ten-huc and Gharr and Famlio and the rest – but proof is something else. Whenever the FedPol think they've built up a case on one world or another, they find platoons of sharp lawyers appearing, kilo-creds are spent, evidence vanishes, witnesses have strange accidents. . . .

So the criminals move freely around the galaxy, pursuing their profession, and the FedPol must swallow its frustration and hope one day to be in the right place at the right time to catch a big-time wrong-doer in the act.

And those watching Forcibles swung their empty stares around the nearly deserted bar, then wheeled their tight formation and clumped out.

I sat still, sipping slowly and thinking hard. The FedPol don't have a permanent presence on Vadinamia. No SenFed world is *required* to have them, and the Vadinamians prefer to manage their own law enforcement. But the FedPol can and do visit any SenFed planet whenever they want, in pursuit of an inquiry or a suspect.

And there they were on Vadinamia, the night before a Recovery. Along with Gharr and Ten-huc and Famlio. And no doubt other dangerous folk who might not have been known to me.

For a moment I toyed with the idea of getting back to the ship, lifting off and going a comfortingly long way away. But I couldn't do it. A very large number of kilocreds has a loud voice, and the Fraxillian fee was still shouting in my ear.

I had to go through with it, I thought. And be quick, watchful, clever, like a wild creature that must elude the hunters. I seemed to hear an echo of Mala's tasteless remark – "like a rat?" – but I ignored it. More like the *perril* of the Richian moon – sleek, fast, perfectly camouflaged, armed with an array of defensive weapons. Let the predators gather, I thought. Can't catch me.

I moved to the door of the bar, stepping lightly, warily. No one paid any attention to me. Outside, I registered the fact that the walkways were almost empty. It was getting late, and not many folk would stay up carousing on the night before a

Recovery. I glanced around me, then slid with *perril*-like stealth towards a nearby bank of shadow.

It turned out to contain an unseen, jutting corner of the building, and as my shins crashed into it I barely managed to stifle my cry of pain. No one noticed that, either.

So I hobbled away, my shoulders involuntarily hunched against the thought of eyes behind me, watching. Within a few moments I was on a floater, crossing the fairly well-lit spaceport, still with no one in sight anywhere around me. As I passed the palatial ship of Gharr the Gherpotean, I saw that it was shut up tight, with no sign of activity. Then I was at my own ship, dismounting from the floater – and abruptly halting.

There had been a definite rustle, behind me. Or maybe beside me, I thought, as the tension built. I saw that there were a few patches of shadow around me that could have been crammed with evildoers. I flexed my arms slightly, trying to stop my hands from trembling, readying the mini-blazers in my wristbands.

Then I whirled, so quickly that I nearly ricked my neck, as I caught a movement at the edge of my vision. From one of those shadow-pools a small, semi-spherical object came sailing towards me in a high looping arc.

As it glimmered with reflected light, I recognized it. I was carrying several just like it, in miniature. But the recognition didn't flash along my neurons in time to activate my legs before the thing exploded in my face with a breathy *puff*.

A half-visible haze billowed around me, sweet and soft. Laboriously, my mind formed the words GAS GRENADE in large capital letters, then underlined them and began to colour them in. I didn't feel the ground when I hit it.

58

Chapter 7

I awoke, and found myself on a cold hillside.

On the planet's surface.

It had been one of the kindlier gases, so the after-effects left me feeling only as if I had swallowed barbed wire and my brain was battering at the inside of my skull. At least I could move, breathe, stand up – and be sick. That made me feel a bit better, so I tottered to the top of the hill and stared bleakly around, in the equally bleak daylight.

For as far as I could see, the surface was bare, grey dirt – rocky, bumpy, ridged, pitted. I wasn't sure whether a distant haziness was dark vegetation or my vision being hazy. Nor did I look too closely at a scummy pool nearby, which rippled ominously. I simply stared across the empty greyness while my headache rattled my brain cells like a QuaAvian earthquake.

I was vaguely aware that my death was imminent. Luckily, the gas had left me feeling so foul and depressed that I was almost looking forward to it, feeling faintly curious about what form it would take.

Not immediate suffocation, anyway, for the surface of Vadinamia has a thin atmosphere with some oxygen. Like most SenFed worlds. It had very little warmth, but the chilly air was helping to clear my head. So did a Metastim capsule when I finally managed to fumble one out of the tiny pouch in my belt. But as I began to feel better, I grew more terrified.

No one could survive that surface for long. It was a miracle that I was still alive at all. Clearly I had arrived between downpours of the searing acid rain, while none of the local wildlife had come looking for a snack in my vicinity. But it was only a matter of time.

Unless I could find the place where my would-be killer had brought me out, and get back in.

Everyone knew that there were plenty of smaller access points from Vadinamia's interior to its surface. The Vadinamians keep some open and make forays on to the surface for obscure sorts of research. I'd never met an off-worlder who knew where they were, or cared. Yet now someone had found one of the openings, and was using it to kill me.

Only that someone had done a stupid thing, from his point of view. It indicated that he didn't know me well – for which I was deeply grateful. He had dumped me on the surface just as he had found me. Fully dressed, including accessories and jewellery.

With a slightly shaky hand, I took hold of the pendant hanging around my neck and pressed its jewels in a certain way.

"Hello, Del."

Posi's cheerful voice, clear and welcome over the mini-comm in the pendant. I wished I could direct her to bring the ship to my rescue. But leaving through the Vadinamian Valve the ship would have to go through another full molecular security check. I doubted if I had the necessary day or so to spare.

Instead, I directed Posi to pinpoint my position with her ceptors, then to access – discreetly, for it was probably illegal – Vadinamia's central data store to find the nearest opening to the interior. Which would presumably be the one I'd been brought out through.

It had to be possible, for someone else had obviously located that opening. But then I found that they hadn't done it that way.

"Vadinamian data stores are protected by multiface security codes," Posi reported almost at once, "with reflex fail-safes against code-break attempts. Set up and reinforced by advanced Intelloids who are Posi-sisters."

I might have known, I thought, feeling suddenly much

colder. The Vadinamians are usually a step ahead. Now they had acquired Posis to improve their security – and to provide a barrier that my Posi couldn't breach.

In panic, my mind went blank. Fortunately, Posi's didn't.

"But it will be possible," she said happily, "to access the data you seek from another source – in 3.47 minutes from now."

I was about to ask her how, when I was distracted, and silenced, by a double-edged shock.

A *thing* slid hugely over the crest of a nearby ridge, and gazed at me from several eyes.

And a blazing-hot drop of wetness fell precisely on to the top of my head, and began to sear its way down into my hairpiece.

In other words, one of the surface denizens was deciding I looked edible, while some large drops of acid were arriving as forerunners of another lethal shower.

"Posi!" I shrieked. "*Hurry!*"

"Only 2.51 minutes now, Del," the maddening mechanism replied. "I am waiting until one of the spaceships orbiting this planet passes over your position. Then I will form a call-beam link with its perceptors and use them to locate the opening that you seek."

I worked out, later, that a ceptor from orbit may have been how my enemy had found the opening in the first place. But I wasn't thinking about it then. Attracted by my outcry, the *thing* was flopping towards me for a closer look. It resembled a huge, tubby fish, about three times as long as I was tall, with thick appendages like fins trying to become legs. The top of it was covered with a thick, slabbed hide like pliable armour, with all the eyes jutting from the front. But I was more focused on the row of large sucker-mouths along its less armoured underside. Mouths that opened and closed hungrily as it advanced, showing lots of saw-teeth within the openings.

But it didn't move too swiftly over the rocky soil, and I began to doubt if it would reach me before the deadly rain finished me off. By then large drops were falling all around me, another landing on my wig and one splashing on my shoulder, making me jump as if I'd been prodded with a therm-knife. I was vaguely aware of my voice repeating "hurry – hurry – hurry" into the pendant. And then the part of my mind that is concerned solely, single-mindedly, with my personal survival saw what it needed to see.

Drops of acid rain were also falling on the monster. To no effect, because it belonged there.

From the thought to the deed, instantly. Pure terror-driven reflex brought the mini-blazers in my wristbands into action.

But the monster's armoured back was impervious to that as well. And another drop of acid rain left its scorch-trail down my arm.

Almost sobbing, I dragged off one of my rings, automatically adjusted the stone, and tossed it into the path of the creature. As it flopped its way forward, the vulnerable underside came down on the ring just as the mini-grenade in the stone erupted into satisfying flame.

I slid a slim vibro-dagger from my right boot and stepped grimly forward.

"Del, I now have the data," Posi's voice announced from the pendant. "If you turn thirty-eight degrees to your right, I can direct you to. . . ."

"In a minute, Posi," I said. "I'm just getting an umbrella."

In fact it was slightly less than a minute. My work-rate was speeded up by the further drops of rain that fell on me. So I had crudely skinned the dead creature, and was holding its armoured hide above me, before the shower began in earnest. Totally sheltered as the vitriolic stuff teemed down, I walked swiftly away – on a line provided by Posi, watching me through the ship ceptors that she had temporarily borrowed by means of her call-beam.

And that's one reason why I spent a middle-sized fortune on the most advanced form of Intelloid in the universe.

But I wasn't exactly strolling along enjoying myself. The acid rain was splashing around my feet, rapidly dissolving my boots. And the creature's blood was dripping heavily down on me – harmless, but repulsively slimy and smelling like rotting Detrovyllan haemo-cheese. I tried to ignore both discomforts, but I wasn't happy.

Soon Posi guided me over another bleak ridge to an innocu-ous-looking depression, with a broad flat slab of stone lying at its centre. Blithely she informed me that the stone was covering an access port to Vadinamia's inner world.

It was firmly fastened, of course, so that no floppy monster could flip it up and wander underground for lunch. So I sourly jerked off what was left of my acid-seared wig, activated it, and let its compact thermic bomb blow the cover to flaming fragments. Then I skipped down the entry ladder with indes-cribable relief. Dumping the monster hide as I reached the bottom of the shaft, I hurried away along some disused-looking passages, by then moving on bootless, bare and blistered feet.

When I pushed open a door leading to a better-lit corridor, I realized that I was on an upper level of the main administra-tive building of the spaceport. I also found myself facing an astonished mandroid guard, who began to reach for his hols-tered stun-gun. I suppose my experiences and my burns made me both irritable and hasty, for I responded by flicking a sonic grenade at him, from another ring, that scrambled all his synapses.

Whereupon a sizeable squad of his fellow mandroids came around a corner and arrested me.

It all eventually got straightened out, despite the Vadina-mian distaste for the unusual, and suspicion of off-worlders. My appearance showed that I *had* been on the surface – and the officials were kind enough to put some healants on my (superficial) burns while they sent mandroids to check my story. They came back with the monster's hide and a report on the blasted stone cover at the opening, and with these verifi-cations the authorities grew friendlier.

But they adamantly refused to listen when I insisted that someone had been trying to kill me. It was all most puzzling and distressing, they said, undoubtedly some mysterious acci-dent that could never be explained.

I got the message. They weren't going to become involved in one client's intent to murder another. If they did, they would have to investigate. But this was Vadinamia, where no ques-tions were ever asked that didn't concern anti-theft pro-cedures. So . . . it hadn't happened.

Angry but resigned, I stamped away from their bland assurances. Or I would have stamped, except that my feet hurt. By then I was wearing a pair of mandroid's boots, a size too large, and a lot of small medi-strips and healant salve on my other burns. My clothing was drenched in monster-gore, where it wasn't tattered in the places charred by the acid rain.

And when I finally appeared in my ship's airlock, the only thing that Mala could find to say was, "Don't you look a *mess!*"

She showed a little more concern when she learned what had happened. And she seemed flustered when I demanded to know where she'd been when I'd been gassed right next to the ship. After all, she might have seen it on the ceptors and come out to help. But she finally admitted that she hadn't been in the ship at the time. She'd gone for a walk.

Suspicion rose up in me like bile. "And was Gharr at home?" I snarled.

"No, he. . . ." She stopped, bit her lip, then tossed her head. "As far as I could see, his ship was closed up tight."

I would have questioned her further, except that she finally grew solicitous and began paying attention to my injuries. So I pushed suspicion away and enjoyed being fussed over. And at the same time, I pondered a little over who had tried to kill me, and why.

It made no sense, like many things on Vadinamia just then. What had brought Gharr and Ten-huc and Pulvidon to the planet at the same time? Why were all of them so interested in why I was there? And if they somehow suspected that I was picking up something valuable, why would any of them try to kill me *before* the pick-up?

"Maybe," Mala said, after I'd shared some of these speculations with her, "it was just someone who doesn't *like* you."

And that annoyed me enough to drive me to my cabin, to clean myself up and choose fresh clothing. Because despite the mysteries and attempted murder, it was then getting on towards the mid-point of that Vadinamian bio-day. Which was the time of Recovery.

*

The process of Recovery is not one of the galaxy's most fascinating spectacles, but if you're an off-worlder on Vadina-mia you have to be there. So we arrived in good time, Mala and I, and I was pleased that in a new hairpiece and fresh clothes – a long-sleeved short-robe over loose trousers and soft boots, in shades of chartreuse and cinnamon – my injuries didn't show at all.

Not that anyone was looking at me. Most of the others in the off-worlders' viewing gallery seemed important people, or anyway self-important, who were occupied with looking com-petitively at one another. There were humans of all shapes and sizes, richly and ostentatiously dressed, and a large mingling of equally impressive exters. It grew quite crowded, since many of the guests had retinues with them, or at least bodyguards.

Then a realization struck me, unnervingly. As far as I could see, every one of those off-worlders was an *owner* (or the employee of one), there to claim or deposit some personal valuables. No one there was the kind of person who would be offering a transport or courier service.

No one but me.

That disturbing thought made me even more glad to have dressed soberly and inconspicuously. But Mala had gone some way towards the opposite. She was wearing – barely – another creation in cling-silk, which drew many approving eyes. Still, they were looking at her rather than me.

Until the moment when every single guest turned to stare avidly towards the door, with murmurs and gasps, at a series of startling arrivals.

First was Ten-huc, tentacles rippling, and a few of his more presentable pirates. The frisson that he caused was still sweeping through the gallery when it paused and then redoubled. A black-clad Famlio contingent had marched through the door, with Pulvidon in its midst, blank-faced and hot-eyed. And then, stagily delayed till it was almost too late, came Gharr the Gherpotean, with Gharrgoyles.

His entrance stirred up an even larger excitement, and the crowd surged forward – Mala among them – for a closer look. So they all got a good view as Ten-huc rasped something with a whiff of black mist, and Gharr whirled with teeth bared. But he controlled himself – there was a force of mandroids that would have done the controlling, otherwise – and merely snarled a reply that left the old pirate fuming. Literally.

Their rivalry was almost a solid presence in the place. The aging pirate king facing the youthful bandit prince – patriarch against upstart – monarch against usurper. I wished they would go somewhere and fight a duel to the death, and that it would end in a draw.

Then Gharr, wheeling away, spotted Mala. He smiled dazzlingly and looked her up and down as if fondling her with his gaze, while she returned his smile and somehow without moving made her cling-silk dress ripple and shimmer. In unthinking annoyance I moved towards her, one of the Gharr-goyles saw me and pointed, and Gharr looked my way.

His smile vanished as if it had been peeled off. His face went as hard as the bronze it resembled, and his eyes said things I preferred not to hear. And that was all the evidence I needed.

By then Ten-huc and Pulvidon and their followers had seen me, but hadn't looked at all surprised. Gharr had. So it must have been the Gharrgoyles who had put me on the planet's surface to die.

I stared around, sweating, wishing I could go and lock myself in my nice safe ship. But that was impossible. And Gharr glowered at me once more, then stalked away into the throng, while Ten-huc watched him balefully and Pulvidon grinned his carnivore grin.

Then the crowd shifted around me, thankfully taking me away from their gazes. Though not from Mala's, who rejoined me with a startled expression.

"I saw how Gharr looked at you," she said. "Do you think *he* . . .?"

"Yes, I think he," I croaked. "And I think. . . ."

But I had to stop. The mandroid guards had come to usher us along, herding us to our seats.

It was Recovery time.

The Vadinamians like to stage Recovery as if it was some kind of major ceremonial – with the required assembling of all the off-worlders, the exact timing and so on. Many first-time visitors are taken in, and expect exoticism. They are disappointed. The off-worlders are all required to be there so that the Vadinamians can know where they are and can watch them, at a time when the stored valuables are a little more vulnerable than otherwise. And the exact timing is simply the Vadinamian way.

In fact nothing much happens. Within the vast vault-like inner world of the planet there are thousands of caverns, small or large, which are also like vaults. No off-worlder has ever been inside any of them, but we are told that there are caverns within caverns, vaults within vaults, like those ancient puzzles where every opened box reveals another, smaller box. Each outer cave or vault can only be entered through a small version of the iris-like Vadinamian Valve. The openings are controlled by incorruptible Intelloids, and only they know which inner vaults hold valuables, and which valuables are stored where.

At a Recovery, the Intelloids guide mindless servatons into the caverns. They emerge with large silicaplast containers, all exactly alike. Guarded by mandroids, the servatons are sent off to the spaceport to deliver a container to each ship. While the off-worlders are sitting in their gallery, watching the process on screens, being closely watched in turn. Some of the containers placed on the ships contain valuables, others are empty. No onlooker, during the process, can know which is which.

So, tediously, it was done. The servatons at last emerged from the off-world ships, whose airlocks had been remote-controlled by the overseeing Intelloids. The locks were closed again, the process ended, insipid Vadinamian refreshments were served in the visitors' gallery. And a short time later, Mala and I were on the safe side of our own ship's airlock, staring at what lay nestled within the opened silicaplast container.

A small, bright, metal cylinder, a bit shorter than my forearm, a bit thicker.

The first thing I did was ask Posi to scan its contents. But Posi couldn't. I'd forgotten a point in the vid adverts for Balbazian steel. It's not only unbreakable and impervious to heat or cold or acid or anything. It's also impermeable to any kind of perceptor or X-ray scan. Even at the spot on the cylinder where there was a hair-thin slit, half a millimetre long, obviously for a pre-shaped molecular key.

In short, the cylinder's contents were a mystery. So I set it frustratedly aside, to concentrate on another mystery.

Which was how we could get away from Vadinamia, unmolested by any of that cavalcade of criminals.

Chapter 8

I put in the usual request for official clearance through the Valve, and was pleased to find that we had got lucky. A number of ships were leaving at the same time – presumably with what they'd come for, after Recovery – but we were slotted into the readiness pattern at fourth place. Even so, it gave us plenty of time to kill. And the first thing I did was to set up a security precaution that had occurred to me when I'd seen the cylinder.

Balbazian steel is a rarity, because it's about three hundred times harder to make and costlier to buy than even high-tech accelsteel. (That's why it gets used for only small and special-ized purposes, not for things like spaceship hulls.) But the Balbazian stuff doesn't *look* all that special. In fact the cylinder looked just like one segment of the pedestal that anchors the personal work surface in my cabin.

So while Mala was attending to Posi as they plotted our course to Fraxilly through the primary and secondary Netlines – a bit complex, since we'd be shifting through eight sectors even if we took the direct route – I took charge of the cylinder. It needed only a few moments, and a touch of magi-glue, to insert the cylinder as part of the pedestal. The unwanted segment that it had replaced went into the disposal unit to be jettisoned during Highlight.

Then we waited, as the ships ahead of us lifted off one at a time to make their laborious way through the Valve's exit-security process. It took about a day and a half for each of them, during which time my nerve-ends were pinging like a Du-gnorian soniharp.

And when we were only a few hours from our turn to lift off, we had last-minute visitors. Who tightened up my nerves a few more turns.

Six large FedPol officers, steely of expression and watchful of eye.

I tried to tell myself, as they invited themselves in, that there was no need for anxiety. I had committed no crime on Vadinamia. Even if the contents of the cylinder were illicit, it would be the Fraxillians' crime, not mine. But a FedPol presence can unsettle even the innocent. So I fretted and sweated as they stalked in and stared around with that disapproving, accusatory look of all cops everywhere.

But then I nearly laughed. It turned out that they had come to *consult* me. Mala and me, that is – for they knew something of my investigator background, and Mala's FedPol career.

"We figured," their leader said in an almost respectful tone, "that if anyone might have heard a thing or two on this world it'd be you, Mister Curb, Miz Yorder."

"Possibly," I said. "Depending on what about."

The leader nodded as if I'd said something deeply wise, confirming his faith in me. "About a valuable object gone missing from the planet Ardakke. Sir."

That tightened Mala's back muscles – and mine too, though I was more concerned with keeping my jaw from falling open. "Ardakke . . ." I said lamely.

Mala intervened. "As I'm sure you know, Curb and I had a brief contact with some Ardakkeans. That resulted in my contacting a friend named Chertro, one of your officers." The FedPol leader was listening stolidly, giving nothing away. "I've heard nothing about Ardakke since then."

"Nor have I," I put in quickly. "Are you thinking that the missing object is on Vadinamia?"

Everyone knows that the quick way to make a cop end an interview – with an innocent party – is to start asking *him* questions. "We're just pursuing enquiries, sir. If you say you've heard nothing. . . ."

I frowned and rubbed my jaw, looking thoughtful. "One

thing did come to my notice," I said. They looked alert and encouraging. "Someone in a bar was talking about Ardakke in connection with Gharr the Gherpotean."

The six officers nearly snapped to attention and saluted. "Yessir," the leader said, "we intend to interview that person before he leaves. Did you hear anything about the *nature* of the connection?"

I went on frowning and rubbing. "Only that someone said, isn't it lucky for Gharr that he could just about pass as an Ardakkean if he dyed his hair. . . ."

"*Could* he?" the FedPol leader nearly shouted. "Thank you, sir. We won't detain you any longer."

I've never liked that turn of phrase – "detain" – but I ignored it and relievedly closed the airlock behind them. "Well, well . . ." I began.

Mala was glowering. "You didn't really hear that about Gharr, did you?"

"Hardly," I said. "But they'll keep glamour boy busy till we're well away from here. And I owe him that, at least, after he and his Gharrgoyles tried to kill me."

"Mm," she said. "It really infuriates me!"

"That he tried to kill me?"

She looked surprised. "No – I mean that Chertro! All his promises about being as discreet as the Ardakkeans wanted, and now there are FedPol squads clumping around half the galaxy!"

"He didn't look all that reliable," I said, less than soothingly. "But it's not our problem. Our problem involves us getting into deep space past a patrol of Famlio gunships."

"I'm still worried about that," she said. "Maybe you should pay them. You'll just get Famlio trying to kill you as well as Gharr."

Famlio would try to kill us *both*, I thought, but didn't say it. "It's not that risky," I told her. "I've done it before. Posi calculates a window that leads to a gap in their patrol, and we shoot through."

"And they've never come after you?" she asked dubiously.

"Never. The Famlio patrol doesn't admit it or record it when

71

ships get past them. It makes them look bad. And the personnel of the patrol doesn't care that much, or for very long.
They're fairly low rank, and are always being shifted to other
jobs. Or being killed, because in that profession life expectancy
is fairly low."

"But now Pulvidon's there," Mala said. "A top enforcer."

"Maybe not any more, if he's been demoted to running the
Vadinamian racket." I reached over and patted her arm. "Just
remember what I said before, about Famlio's blind spots. Trust
me. It's a calculated risk, but it can be done."

"If you say so," Mala said shortly. "But why is it the only
time you take risks is when you're likely to make a profit?"

"When else?" I asked, baffled. But she just shook her head
and went back to her pouch-seat and Posi's course-setting. In
good time, too, for a moment later a Vadinamian voice
announced over the comm that our lift-off slot was now open.

Of course that was just stage one, when we moved gently up
into position at the Valve. There the Vadinamian permanent
station gave us their usual, painstaking, molecular once-over.
I was pleased to note that since they'd acquired Posis they
were getting almost quick about it. Very little more than a
bio-day later they had established that our exit molecules
corresponded with our entry molecules, save for those of the
cylinder that we'd acquired and that was accounted for in their
scanning. We were free to go.

Except we weren't. With very poor timing, Posi announced
that her perceptors showed a Famlio gunship sliding by within
visual range of the Valve.

That was unsettling. I'd expected Famlio to be patrolling in
deep space, as usual, giving me room to manoeuvre and avoid
them. But this ship was down in Vadinamian territorial space,
directly in my way. As if Famlio had become *very* intent on
intercepting someone, or something, leaving the planet.

A second later, a Vadinamian official came on-screen and
irritatedly pointed out that the Valve was about to open and I
should be moving.

"Don't rush me," I snarled over the comm. "I've got a thrust
problem with one of my planetaries."

"Make *haste!*" the official spluttered, segments wobbling. "The scheduling requires. . . ."

"I am making haste," I interrupted. "Shut up and leave me to it. Or do you want me to go through the Valve at Firstlight speed?"

That shut him up. It probably would have shut the Valve up, too, all that power boiling through its stasis energy field. I could almost hear him fuming from his inspection station. Not that I cared, for I was doing my own fuming. No way was I going out with a Famlio ship in my flight path. Not even if I had to block the Valve for a week. . . .

At that point Posi chimed in to say that another vessel had come into visual range just beyond the Valve. I was sure she meant another Famlio ship. But, blessedly, she didn't.

"It appears to be a ship of the Federation Police, Del," she said.

I laughed aloud with relief. Probably the FedPol contingent visiting Vadinamia had left a backup ship in orbit, as they often do. And it had come down to the Valve to see what the Famlio ship was doing there. So I gave Posi the go-ahead, and we surged out through the Valve, coming almost face to face with the two ships. But Famlio wasn't about to enforce any demands for "protection" payments with the FedPol watching.

Posi then told me that a comm-call was coming in from the Famlio ship, but I told her to ignore it. And neither of the other ships changed position as we fled past them towards deep space.

I lounged back in my pouch-seat, smiling with satisfaction. In a few minutes we would be ready for Firstlight, and then we'd be clear. Because no matter what suspicions the various crooks might have about my purpose, no one knew where I was going next.

That thought prompted me to ask Posi for a routine sweep for bugs. When she pronounced us clean, I lounged and smiled some more, thought peacefully about the Fraxillian fee, watched peacefully as Posi took us into Firstlight. Until Mala reached for the comm-switch.

She was calling Chertro, her FedPol friend of the lean and grinning face. I was pleased to see his grin vanish when Mala gave him the vicious edge of her tongue for ignoring the Ardakkean request for discretion, causing the FedPol squad to visit Vadinamia.

"You've got it wrong, Fuzzy," he finally said, when he could get a defensive word in. "You're out of touch. Didn't the squad on Vadinamia fill you in?"

"They weren't giving anything away," she said tightly. "What are you talking about?"

"They could have told you," Chertro said, still defensive. "Too late now for being discreet. All the Ardakkean beans have been spilled."

And before Mala could lash at him again, he explained, and terrified me right down to my boots.

First he reminded us that it had taken him no time at all to find the Ardakkean thief – an off-world technician working in one of the phetam refining plants. The man had been secretly hiding away tiny portions of phetam, a drop or two at a time, until he had saved up about a half-litre. Which he then sent off-planet, by various well-disguised and roundabout routes, to an unknown recipient. Probably his huge bribe was paid to him along the same obscure channels. It had all been going on for years, Chertro said, and apparently earlier technicians had been doing the same for a long time before.

But just recently a stage in the delivery had broken down. One of the carriers dropping out, Chertro thought. That caused a series of hiccups in the process, and the ripples allowed the Ardakkeans to get wind of the theft. Which brought Chertro in to catch the thief.

"And the one who's paying the bribe?" Mala asked.

Chertro shook his head. The routes were impossible to trace back, he said. But he had a feeling that they included some diplomatic folk, employees of Emissaries and the like.

A small chill, like a seedling of absolute-zero ice, congealed in my stomach.

Mala was frowning. "Didn't the thief himself tell you anything, when you questioned him?"

Chertro, oddly, looked a little sheepish. "He said some things. We broke him down fairly fast. But he didn't *know* who was paying him, or who got the phetam in the end. And then. . . ."

"Yes?" Mala demanded, as he paused and gulped and looked more sheepish.

"Well . . . He was taken."

"*Taken?*" I think that was the first time that a chill hit Mala, too, for she seemed to grow a little pale.

Chertro was nodding embarrassedly. "Someone got through our security and got him out. A couple of days later we found his body in a disposal. He'd been tortured."

Neither Mala nor I bothered to ask who could have done it. Probably Famlio – but it didn't matter. Some criminal organization, anyway, with informants inside the FedPol, learning that a prisoner from Ardakke was talking about a priceless substance he'd stolen. So the organization kidnapped the prisoner and squeezed him dry.

And obviously other criminal organizations with spies in the right places would hear about it. So several sets of criminals might go looking, at the same time, for the priceless substance. . . .

"They wouldn't have got more out of him than we did," Chertro was saying. "He really didn't know who was paying him, or where the stuff went. Too many cut-offs in the operation. Must have cost someone millions."

"He must have known where the phetam went in the first stage," Mala said.

Chertro shrugged. "All he knew for sure was that the stuff went off-planet. But he'd picked up hints that, at some point along the way, it'd be left on Vadinamia." He peered from the screen. "Where you and Curb have been. . . ."

Mala blinked, and grew paler, but quickly assured him that as far as she knew it was just a coincidence. I could tell, though, that she was beginning to have some uncomfortable suspicions – like the ones that were spreading the chill all through me. Then I thought of another question – just as Mala asked it.

"Chert – did you tell anyone that it was me who got you involved with Ardakke?"

He frowned. "I probably mentioned it here and there. Is that a problem?"

A *problem*? I would have yelled it if my throat hadn't tightened up. No wonder there'd been so many major criminals on Vadinamia. No wonder Famlio had sent a top enforcer. No wonder they were all watching me. They had gone to Vadinamia to look for phetam and had found a well-known courier – the *only* courier there – who also had a known connection with Ardakke. It was a miracle that *my* tortured body hadn't been found in a disposal somewhere!

I wanted to be sick. Or scream. Or shoot someone. Preferably Chertro with his stupid grin and all the crooked FedPols who let someone walk away with the Ardakke prisoner.

But Mala, looking paler still, was assuring her friend that there was no problem. I realized that she wasn't going to tell him about events on Vadinamia so that he wouldn't jump to any conclusions and complicate things. And that was when he grinned and offered one more piece of terrifying information.

"One funny thing that technician said, about phetam. About why it's so valuable. Must be like those miracle elixirs and things that people pay fortunes for. But it's a joke."

"*What* is?" Mala asked warily.

"What the prisoner said. Seemed proud of himself for having found out, because he said it's supposed to be the planet's big secret. He told us ... well, what he said was that phetam makes the Ardakkeans super-human."

When Mala switched off, there was none of the intimate cosiness of her last talk with Chertro. That might have pleased me, but by then I was in an advanced state of fear-chill, feeling nothing much except numb. Even so, some brain cells were still working, as I stared inwardly at the nub of the problem.

Phetam had been stolen from Ardakke by someone who had no shortage of credits to spend and who had access to the secretive practices of diplomats and Emissaries. And phetam was supposed to have magical medicinal powers, or something. I sat unmoving, adding up all the factors over and over, getting

76

the same answer, while Posi took us up into Highlight and on to the first Netline of our route. Then I took a deep breath.

"Posi," I said carefully, "give me a list of what the old data-package you found says are the special powers of the Ardak-keans. And a comparison list of the so-called divine powers of the God-King of Fraxilly."

Mala, who had been doing some thinking of her own, looked at me uneasily. "I see you've grasped the implications."

"The implications have grasped us," I said.

Then Posi replied, and the lists confirmed every scrap of my dread. Not that they corresponded exactly, but they were close enough. The Ardakkeans were said to be superhumanly strong and invulnerable to most life-threats. They supposedly could even live a while in space without life support. I grew colder, remembering their visit to my ship. They had the power of flight, super-effective senses, X-ray vision, heat-ray vision. They were also amazingly healthy, immensely potent sexually, and unusually long-lived.

The listed powers of the God-King, assembled from among his worshippers, tended to be more flattering and less specific. But the echoes were clear. He was said to be super-strong and super-virile, invulnerable to mortal harm, and had once been seen to fly. And if the records were right he had occupied the throne for more than two centuries. While his predecessors had been ordinary royal humans.

"So," said Mala quietly, "the God-King has been bribing technicians on Ardakke and stealing phetam all that time, to make himself godly. And bleeding his world to death, to finance. . . ."

But the rest of her sentence was lost, as Posi interrupted with a note of puzzlement in her voice.

"Del – my perceptors show a spacecraft presence in this Netline."

Now most travellers know that Highlight isn't really a velocity, nor is a Netline a place. It's a different plane of existence, where normal space and time are somehow bypassed. The physics baffles me, the philosophy bores me – but I do know that it would take about seven years for me to write out all the digits in a statement of the odds against encountering another ship in Highlight.

If we had done so, it meant. . . .

"The other ship," Posi said, confirming my thought as it formed, "has been locked on to our energy-field infrapattern, by means of the advanced Intelloid that controls it."

My fear-chill magnified unbearably. If the ship was locked on to us, it must have been following us from Vadinamia.

"Posi, down to Firstlight!" I yelled.

Posi moves at speeds that make a neutrino seem like a Habectric salt-snail. But this time she was too late. Even as I spoke, we were reduced to just about no light at all.

A terrible grinding *crunch* struck at us like a solid barrier. The ship leaped and juddered as if trying to turn inside out. My pouch-seat automatically deepened and clutched me like an egg. As a reddish darkness gathered in my vision, I waited, breathing with difficulty, to die.

Because that's usually what happens when your ship has been blasted in space by fusitronic guns.

Chapter 9

"I have stabilized at Halflight speed," I heard Posi say – and found myself almost babbling with relief that she was still functioning. And that I was.

"Where's the other ship?" Mala asked, her voice as raw as I'm sure mine would have sounded, if I'd been able to speak.

"In pursuit," Posi said, with mild disapproval. "I am taking evasive action."

I found some of my voice. "How badly have we been hit?"

"Damage survey," Posi replied, "shows disruption of outer fabric at a midship location. Automated mechatons have already set a temporary patch and seal. Further damage . . ."

"Oh, please," I mumbled.

". . . as follows. Eight perceptors partially disrupted. One thruster of planetary drive shut down. . . ."

For a moment I wondered if I'd brought the bad luck down on us by pretending the planetaries weren't working, at the Vadinamian Valve.

"And," Posi went on, "sections of the interfield links within the guidance systems are becoming unstable. At the moment, however, I still have lightspeed impulse power and navigational capability."

"And life support?" I asked urgently. "And the guns?"

"And your own systems? And the comm?" Mala put in just as urgently.

"And the vid?" I added.

Posi's voice sounded weary, like a parent pointing out the

obvious to troublesome children. "If the ship had sustained damage in any of those areas, I would have included the data in my damage survey." She paused for an instant. "I can offer a conclusion, on a high probability level, that the enemy ship intended to immobilize us, not destroy us."

Immobilize us, board us, rob us, I thought miserably. But then all thought was dispersed. The pouch-seat clutched me again as the ship suddenly bounced sideways with another grinding crunch and shriek of stressed metal.

"*Posi!*" I was shrieking as well.

"The enemy ship has fired on us again," Posi said easily, "but my evasive action was effective and the blast did not strike us."

"Are we just going to go on evading?" Mala asked, her voice even more ragged than before.

"You want to go sub-light and shoot it out?" I snarled.

"That would be unwise," Posi said, with her usual refusal to perceive irony. "My suggestion would be to use the Highlight Flicker, to effect an escape."

My mouth opened, but I said nothing. The Flicker is a navigational trick used by ships in a hurry to make planetfall. They go straight from planetary speed to full Highlight, then back again – and back and forth, time after time, in little jumps. Each jump crosses a few light-hours in a bio-second or two. It helps to get a ship through crowded places like solar systems without running into a planet.

But the Flicker is used by freighters with full-automatic Intelloid navigation. Not by ships with human passengers. Because a prolonged series of such jumps can seriously unhinge a human nervous system.

"It'd kill us," I said at last, faintly.

"A brief use of the Flicker would merely cause pain and unconsciousness, with assurance of full recovery," Posi said. I swear I could hear amusement in her voice. "And the element of surprise could allow us to break away, or could bring us into a position to fire on the other ship."

"What if it doesn't?" I asked.

"Then they fire on us," Mala said grimly. "Shut up, Curb. Posi, do it."

Posi never wasted time obeying orders. The leap to full Highlight plunged me deep into the pouch-seat. But then the shattering instant fallback into sub-light speed felt like something was trying to pull my bones out through my flesh. I howled with the pain, howled again when something like a mountain fell crushingly on me as Posi hurled us straight back up to Highlight.

The reddish darkness returned to my vision, and I dived into the anaesthetic of unconsciousness with a welcoming sob.

"Right," Mala said, with more crispness than she should have been able to produce. "What now?"

"My head hurts," I said weakly. So, for that matter, did every nerve-ending in my body. True, I seemed to be alive and intact. But I wasn't sure that was enough compensation for the pain.

"Come on, Curb," Mala snapped. "I'm hurting too, but we're not going to get anywhere sitting around moaning."

"I don't much want to get anywhere," I mumbled.

She sniffed. "Yes, you do, and so do I. So we have to figure out who's after us and how we can avoid another attack."

With some justifiable complaints, I struggled to sit up. It was just like her, to be super-efficient after an emergency, when normal people are wanting to curl up somewhere soft and ease their battle wounds. But I knew that Mala would allow me no peace until I joined in her speculations.

The trouble was, that's all we could do – speculate. Although Posi had perceived the *presence* of the other ship she had never had a clear sight of it. Being in Highlight tends to distort her direct sensory modes. And even when the other ship tried to follow us into Flicker, so that both of us were in sub-light together for a millisecond, Posi had only glimpsed it. Because in that instant she had fired the ship's rear guns and had blasted the other ship's nose section into particles. So all she could report was that it seemed dark and cruiser-shaped.

"It could have been anyone," I grumbled. In fact I was sure that I knew who it was, and I thought Mala must be too.

"Anyone from Vadinamia," Mala pointed out, "or they couldn't have locked on to us."

I nodded, then flinched as my headache flared. "It could have been lover-boy Gharr."

"Not in a *dark* ship," she said coldly. "Anyway, he wouldn't."

I was tempted to make some sardonic inquiry about how Mala could sound like she was defending Gharr, when he had so obviously been the one who had tried to kill me on Vadinamia. But I decided against it, not entirely sure that I'd like the answer.

"All right," I conceded at last. "This time it was almost definitely Famlio. Maybe we should have paid the protection fee."

Mala snorted. "And you said it would be easy to get past them. A calculated risk."

"I didn't expect . . ." I began.

"No," she broke in, "you never do. But anyway, I don't think they came after us just to get their little fee."

Unhappily, I knew she was right. Especially in the light of what her friend Chertro had told us. Which all meant several unpleasant things.

That the cylinder we were carrying probably did contain the Ardakkean phetam. Or at least that many dangerous people thought it did.

That the phetam was unguessably valuable, a rich prize for criminals. Perhaps because it was some kind of miracle elixir. Or people thought it was.

And that Famlio had come after us to get it.

Even worse, all the other unspeakable villains wanted it too. Gharr had already tried to get me out of the way – probably thinking that Mala would collect the phetam with me gone, and he could then collect it and her too. And Ten-huc was no doubt hatching his own plots. And who knew who else?

Mala had clearly reached all the same conclusions. "If we really are carrying the Ardakkean phetam . . ." she began.

But I interrupted her. "Posi – cancel the course setting for Fraxilly."

As Posi complied, Mala looked startled. "What are you doing?"

"Keeping us alive," I said flatly. "The only edge we have is that the Ardakkean prisoner, the thief, didn't know the final destination of the stolen phetam. So Famlio can't know it either. Which means that even if we *do* have the phetam on board, our enemies don't know where we're going. But they'll know – from the ship that attacked us – where we are now. And they'll come looking for us."

She nodded slowly, grasping the point. The ship that had followed us would have left a record of its course, and ours. So Famlio would send more ships along that route, searching for us. And not just to take the phetam, either – not now. We had done the unforgivable, striking back, disabling a Famlio ship, maybe killing Famlio people. They'd have to hunt us down or suffer a severe loss of credibility.

The hunt might demand a huge allocation of ships and personnel, but Famlio had the resources. The odds, in the short term anyway, favoured them. Especially if we kept going on the course we'd established.

"We'll have to hide out," Mala was saying thoughtfully. "Turn the phetam over to the FedPol and disappear for a while. Maybe out on the Rim Beyond the Rim."

"You're partly right," I said. "About disappearing."

Not forever, of course – not with the usual turn-over of Famlio personnel. In a few bio-years, the decision-makers of the organization would mostly be new appointees, their predecessors dead or retired, old vengeances losing importance.

"Partly right?" Mala echoed, frowning.

"We're not turning over the phetam to the FedPol," I told her. "We're going to deliver it to Fraxilly. We'll need the creds when we go into hiding."

Her frown deepened. "We can't just deliver the phetam now we know it's *stolen*. It belongs to the Ardakkeans."

"We can't be absolutely certain," I said quickly, "that there *is* phetam in the cylinder. We're just guessing – like Famlio and all the other crooks are guessing. And there's no way we can find out. But we *do* know that delivering the cylinder, whatever is in it, will bring us a lot of creds. And I want them."

"But it's *crazy*, going to Fraxilly now," Mala said. "We have to find a place to hide, and get dug into it."

"Not me," I told her as I struggled painfully up from the pouch-seat. "I'm not spending the time ploughing the Chac'li fever-steppes, or herding Tyyrkyn mountain pigs. If I have to disappear, I want to do so in comfort. With Fraxillian kilocreds to smooth the way."

Her frown eased back a little. Maybe it was the thought of the mountain pigs. "Well," she said, "if we make the delivery quickly. . . ." Then she remembered. "But you just cancelled the course to Fraxilly!"

My nerve-ends were even more painfully ablaze now that I was vertical. "We need a different route to Fraxilly – more tangled and roundabout, to throw off any pursuit," I said tersely. "Start Posi setting a course that will take us on to a parallel Netline, doubling back the way we came. Then she can work out a different course to the Fraxilly sector."

"And what are you going to be doing?"

"I am going to my cabin," I told her. "Where I'm going to have a relaxing soak in AmnioEze, and a drink or two. Or more than two. And during that time I am going to work out a way to keep us safe while we complete the job that will make us rich."

She sniffed. "With a damaged ship, and a Famlio fleet scouring the galaxy for us."

"Those facts make my task harder," I said loftily, "but not impossible."

And I took myself away, feeling pleased with my parting shot, to my recuperation.

Recuperation went well, as modern science ensures that it will, especially after a nap deepened by some well-aged Ilwiiin smoke-ale. But the thinking proved less successful. A way to combine the two goals, safety and riches, eluded me. Perhaps my brain hadn't fully recovered at the time, despite the sleep. And my concentration wasn't helped when Posi intruded to tell me there was a comm-call of some urgency.

For one sweaty moment I was sure it would be Famlio, about

to issue dire threats and promises. Not that it would really have been a problem, other than psychologically. Famlio or whoever could fling out all the comm-calls they wanted, along the Netlines, but they couldn't get a fix on our position until or unless we responded.

Yet Posi seemed to think that I'd want to respond to this call. And when I saw the face on the screen, I agreed. It was y'Pripio, the little flunkey of the Fraxillian Emissary, looking as bland as ever, informing me that the Lord y'Fiprehaude desired a moment of my attention.

This time the old Emissary was not in flirtatious mood. Tension was plucking at his aged tendons like lute strings, mottling his complexion into an approximation of Sefcredian clay-lizard skin.

"*So* glad to find you well, dear boy," he said, wheezing slightly. "It seems so *long* since we . . . I seem to have grown a trifle anxious."

If you only knew, I thought. "What could be troubling you?" I asked with careful innocence.

"One hears things," he said vaguely. "Tales of . . . unusual sorts of activity. On Vadinamia."

"Oh, that," I said, knowing that he would have acquired fully detailed accounts of everything that had happened, from a number of free-lance information vendors. "A flurry of excitement, nothing to create anxiety." I gave him a smile with perhaps a little cruelty at its edges. "Not anywhere as exciting as another bit of what you call 'activity'. The murder of a man who stole a priceless substance from a world called Ardakke."

He was an experienced diplomat, skilled at revealing little. But the comm-screen exposes faces in the harshest detail, and for an instant I saw something move at the back of his wet old eyes, like a creature threshing in a net.

"How interesting, I'm sure," he wheezed at last. "But more to our point – you do have the cylinder safe? And you can make delivery?"

"I've contracted to do so, and I will," I said firmly. "But if I'm delivering what I *think* I'm delivering, your lordship, I'm an accessory to theft and corruption. More immediately, I'm also a target for every bandit and assassin out on the Netlines. Which means – since I didn't know about all that when we drew up the contract – there will be a surcharge."

He snarled and whined and grizzled, admitted nothing, pretended to be insulted, tried to bully me or bluff me or charm me. Eventually, when I voiced the thought that it might be better if the FedPol took charge of the cylinder, he gave in. Moments later Posi confirmed that a further pleasingly large sum had been transferred to the holding facility of my Fedbank, to be released to my account when the job was done. I knew the Emissary wouldn't cheat me, because then I wouldn't deliver. And because I knew too much.

But the prospect of even more income from the delivery, now, made it all the more imperative that I got on and off Fraxilly safely.

And in that moment I realized that by some deep-rooted instinct I was already doing the right thing. Almost automatically I'd told Posi to shift Netlines and double back. We were heading away from the Fraxilly sector, so Famlio could search in that area all they wanted. And we were heading *towards* a sector containing a world that seemed a beneficial place to be, for a while.

It was closer, for one thing. And it was also a place where I could get my ship repaired by skilled persons whom I more or less trusted. Which was a fairly high priority, if I was going to elude the hunters.

I knew there were risks in going to that planet, but there were risks wherever we went. And increasingly, as I thought about it, that planet seemed the best idea. While Famlio was looking for us near the Fraxilly sector, we'd be elsewhere. By the time they left that sector to search elsewhere, we'd be heading for Fraxilly, with a fully functional ship. It all underlined what I'd always believed – that Famlio had grown too big, scattered and over-confident, and could be eluded by someone who was small, concentrated and clever. They'd never know that we'd been and gone. Then, with a little luck, we'd find a comfortable hiding place and wait for Famlio and everyone to forget about us.

Quick, smart and lucky, I said to myself. Practically my motto. Then I went to tell Mala.

"We're going *where*?" she said, her voice rising.

"Home," I repeated.

"*Uulaa*?" Her voice rose higher. "Everyone knows that's our base. You've located there for *years*. . . ."

"And I have friends there," I said. "Like Frejji, who'll fix the ship better than anyone."

"But Famlio . . ." she began.

"Famlio is looking for us in other sectors. By the time they think of looking on Uulaa, we'll be gone, with the ship fixed."

"So you say," she replied, looking a little dazed.

"Mala, love." I patted her arm encouragingly. "Believe me. Uulaa is the *last* place, right now, that anyone would look for us."

Chapter 10

"Everyone's lookin' for y', Del," Frejji said. "What y' been up to?"

I didn't answer right away. I had gone into partial shock.

We had arrived in Uulaa's system a few moments before, and as we drifted down to planetary speed I'd contacted Frejji on the comm. Frejji is a big, bulky exter, very humanoid aside from her glossy dark-purple fur and the eight fingers on each hand. She is a brilliant mechanic and engineer, especially in spacecraft structures and Intelloid analysis. She is also something of a friend. Which has never stopped her charging me painfully large sums.

Nor had it stopped her from giving me news that struck me dumb with panic.

After assuring me that her comm was entirely secure – no one tampers with Frejji's machinery – she had told me that odd things were happening on Uulaa. Strange people arriving, singly or in groups, all with something in common. They were all criminals.

And they were all looking for me.

Mala was glowering at me, an angry gaze that could have melted accelsteel, not needing to voice her opinion of my error of judgment. For a moment, in my panic, I thought about swinging the ship around and getting out. But there was a problem.

On the flight to Uulaa Posi had reported a growing unreliability within sections of the guidance system, mainly the interlinked network of perceptors that served as Posi's external senses. If we didn't get the damage repaired, we could end up with a blind ship and fly ourselves into a black hole.

In short, I *had* to be there, at Uulaa. Where a host of crooks was looking for me.

"Who . . ." I stopped, cleared my throat, tried again. "Who's looking for me?"

"Quicker t' say who ain't," Frejji said with a sharp-fanged grin. "Lessee. Place is fulla Famlio, fer a start. Top people, too. Saw with my own eyes that hotshot Pulvidon."

I gulped.

"Then there's the golden boy, what's-his-name, Gharr, an' all his little devils. . . ."

I moaned.

"An' a buncha other folk. Ayril ka Ti, remember her – the robber baroness? An' con artists like Retaa've an' ol' Perrisharikk. Then there's. . . ."

I whimpered, as the recitation went on. It was as if Uulaa was hosting a PanGalactic Convocation of Criminality. With me as the guest of honour, and pièce de résistance.

"Why," Frejji was saying, "somebody tole me they saw just about the nastiest bunch, come in lately. Y' wouldn't believe it. Oversize exters bulgin' with weapons – an' in the middle of 'em, lookin' a thousand years old, Ten-huc hisself. Ol' Blackbreath."

I shuddered.

"An' there's more spies pourin' in, too," Frejji added. "Never been so many, here. An' all of 'em, crooks an' spies an' ever'body, sniffin' round after ol' Del Curb."

"Frejji," I said weakly. "Help."

But when I quickly explained our problem and made my request, her large furry face wrinkled with doubt.

"I c'n see why y'd want me t' come make repairs in space," she growled. "But I don't like it. Slows the work down, makes it dangerous."

That wasn't true and I knew it. Frejji is completely at home in zerograv, having spent many years building magni-freighters among the moons of Cytostom. Anyway, she'd have the help of Posi and the ship's auto-mechatons. And her own delicate manual skills could never be hampered by the customized membrane-thin spacesuits that she works in. Especially when she has a little TK ability that can perform many manipulations beyond the reach of her hands.

So, I thought, she's after something too. Like all the others. But when I accused her of that, she firmly shook her head.

"Not me, Del," she said. "I want nothin' t' do with what's got killers after y'. I jus' want a fair rate fer a hard job."

I relaxed a little. She was just using the fact that I was desperate to hold me up for an outrageously high fee. I'd have done the same myself. I winced a little – well, a lot – when she named the sum. But eventually we haggled out an agreement. She would shuttle up with her equipment as soon as I got established just outside Uulaa's territorial space. And she'd work day and night, as I wished, for only a small extra payment.

"'Course y'll hafta get off the ship," she said.

My throat tightened again. "Why?"

"Y' got interfield problems, I got t' shut things down, check through. No ceptors or life support or nothin'. Y' won't wanta hang around."

"We can't go down to the *planet!*" I said, perhaps a little shrilly.

Frejji snorted. "Y' want t' stay in y'r ship after I shut down y'r ceptors an' everythin'? What if Famlio sends up a ship t' make a sweep? Y'd be trapped, never see 'em comin'."

I flinched, feeling trapped already. She had a point about how vulnerable the ship would be. But even so. . . .

"All those *spies*, though, Frejji," I began to say.

Her laugh was boisterous. "Del, c'mon! This's *Uulaa*! It's fun time here, like always. This's the Three-Moon Festival, or maybe the Ceremony of the Inner Spiral, I ferget. *Fancy dress* time! Get y'rself up as a Geho'quein spine-toad or somethin', come on down an' mingle. Who's gonna know it's you?"

So, fretful and fearful, I had to give in. I felt even worse after I transferred a lot of kilocreds to Frejji's bank as a down payment. Meanwhile Posi was sliding the ship forward, slowly and carefully because of the malfunctioning guidance system, to the co-ordinates Frejji had chosen. Just beyond a world teeming with terrifying folk who wanted to find and dismantle me.

How fast news travels on criminal grapevines, I thought miserably. Especially when it concerns something pricelessly rare, like phetam.

But in the end I saw that Frejji was right – that Mala and I *could* probably stay unrecognized in the midst of a typical Uulaan carnival. And there were a couple of other things, I told myself reassuringly, that helped to tip the balance back a little towards our side.

First, I knew that they were on Uulaa – but they wouldn't know I was.

Second, Uulaa was my home. So I probably knew it better than most of my enemies.

I called Uulaa my home, but of course it isn't my planet of origin – or anyone else's. It is a warm, mostly oceanic world with only rudimentary forms of life, whose few land masses had been restructured and reatmosphered as holiday havens for the rich. It has gone through several more face-lifts, and is now a thriving resort world, especially popular among the fast-moving, free-spending hotburners of the galaxy. Who include hustlers and tricksters and lawless folk of every sort.

I suppose that's why I like it. With its reputation, Uulaa is an important crossroads. If everyone who is anyone doesn't actually touch down on the planet fairly often, at least their activities come to be known through Uulaa's favourite indoor sport (after making money) – trading information, along with rumour and scandal.

Best of all, Uulaa is a Freeworld, without local sentient population and so outside the Federation. The FedPol had undercover agents there, naturally, but no official presence. Even better, people like tax inspectors didn't visit even undercover, unless they were feeling suicidal.

So all in all it's a great place. And it likes to make itself more attractive to the hordes of fun-seeking visitors by holding an almost endless series of Festivals, Carnivals, Games, Ceremonials and so on. During which the Uulaan authorities relax even the few laws and rules that normally exist. At festival time nothing is illegal or forbidden as long as you have the price. Everyone puts on an identity-erasing disguise and leaps uninhibitedly into no-holds-barred, orgiastic delight.

Which, I was beginning to think, might be just what I needed to ease a few tensions. And if the gathered criminals could find me on Uulaa at its most chaotic, they were sharper than I imagined.

By the time Posi had established the ship at the specified position, Mala seemed to be thinking along similar lines. She had stopped giving me murderous looks and seemed quite bright-eyed as we got ourselves ready to leave the ship. By then we'd decided to go down separately, in the little passenger pod. Mala chose to go first, saying that she would check out the landing area for dangerous watchers and warn me if necessary when she sent the pod back up. I didn't argue.

But I did argue when she insisted that we *remain* separated while on the planet. I'd had visions of various Uulaan delights that I hoped she might join me in, above all the free-fall Orgitunnel, among whose heaving tangle of bodies in simulated zerograv I've had many a memorable experience. And Mala had put on a figure-hugging neck-to-ankle suit of Luxipelt, which together with a whiskered and sharp-eared mask made her look like one of the slinkiest, most enticing Clovellyan felinoids I'd ever seen.

But she was insistent. "People are looking for us down there, Curb. Think. They're looking for a man and a woman, our sizes and ages. Disguises or not, if we're together they'll look at us harder."

I agreed, naturally. Avoiding throngs of killers did strike me as a higher priority even than fulfilling my Mala-fantasies. So off she went, while I got on with transferring my mini-weapons to my own costume.

I felt I was looking quite authentic, in the guise of one of the nearly extinct Grislewings of Egertro. (They're primitive, semi-humanoid exters who haven't given up being cannibals despite a sharply reduced birth rate. Hence near-extinction.) I was wearing a tight black one-piece, with hands and neck coloured Egertroic green, and artful smears of scarlet down my front to simulate the usual bloodstains. As well as the long-muzzled, black-fanged mask, I had a swirling ankle-length cape in black and green to represent the wings.

I was examining the effect in the mirror before putting on the mask, vaguely wishing that I could levitate a little to improve the illusion. But flight, I thought idly, would be a useful ability any time. And that led me to think of phetam, and to wonder again if it really did confer super-powers. Toying with that idea started a train of thought about some of the other activities probably open to super-beings, which led me to conjure up some images of myself with Sergia, the Ardakkean, minus her costume, in the Orgitunnel.

So for a second it seemed the most natural thing in the world when the ship's airlock suddenly opened, and I stepped out of my cabin to see Sergia framed in the lock, with two male Ardakkeans behind her.

She still filled her boring blue costume wonderfully, I noted – while part of my mind slowly realized that my ship's damaged perceptors probably had kept Posi from spotting their approach.

Then the same part of my mind registered that the Ardakkeans had again come to my ship without spacesuits, and had opened the airlock manually despite its seals. And that part of my mind seemed to whine faintly, and go very cold and still.

But the rest of me was running a bluff, of the outrage-at-intrusion sort. "What do you think you're doing?" I demanded. "Breaking in here. . . ."

"Curb!" Sergia interrupted, moving towards me with a stern gaze. "Can you truly be a thief and a liar? Do you dare to help those who robbed us?"

I drew myself up, looking offended. "What are you talking about?"

"We have learned things about the galaxy," she replied grimly, "and we will be greatly glad to get back to our Ardakke. But out here we have searched and looked and listened – and we have heard things. We have heard about a planet called Vadinamia, where our stolen phetam may have been taken. And we have heard that Del Curb was on that planet, along with numerous evil people who seek the phetam.

93

Now all the evil ones seem to be on Uulaa, pursuing Del Curb. As are we."

"How did you find me?" I asked, my bluff crumbling a little.

One of the men smiled mirthlessly. "The criminals look for you amid the filth and decadence of this world. But Sergia believed that you would be fearful, would skulk in space beyond the planet. So we have waited out here, watching. And here you are."

"With our phetam," growled the other man.

I tried a light laugh. "Everyone thinks I have the phetam, just because I'm a well-known courier."

"Or because you are a well-known trickster driven by greed," Sergia snapped.

That stung me. "And what are you driven by?" I demanded. "A bighearted desire to give phetam to the galaxy?"

Then I flinched as they took a threatening step towards me.

"Phetam belongs to us," Sergia said stonily, "not to any other planet or people. Others who lack our inborn ethics would use it for evil ends. No doubt it has been so used by the unknown one who has been arranging the thefts. We are *driven*, Curb, by a need to retrieve the phetam – or destroy it. Then we can return to Ardakke and take steps to prevent further thefts."

"Fine by me," I said, managing a shrug. "But I can't help you."

They all scowled. "Why should we believe you?" asked one of the men.

I thought fast. "Because," I said cleverly, "you know that my partner has a close connection with the FedPol. Don't you think the FedPol would have checked me out, since Vadinamia? But I'm not under arrest. . . ."

Sergia's frown deepened for a moment. "It may be so. The man Chertro seemed honest and reliable."

Old reliable Chertro had rightly called them naïve and gullible, I thought. And I smiled winningly, while the sight of Sergia's abundantly filled costume gave me an idea or two.

"No hard feelings," I said. "I can understand your concern. Tell you what – why don't you come down with me to Uulaa? We could see the sights, have some fun, and maybe I could think of some ways I could help you." I looked at the two men. "Sorry, though. I've only got a two-person pod."

The men glanced at Sergia. For a moment I felt hopeful, since she had begun to smile and was moving closer to me. But then her smile twisted as her hand reached out to grasp the front of my costume – and lifted me smoothly into the air, at arm's length above her head. She hadn't adjusted her stance or braced herself or anything. Just hoisted me up, with the strength of her arm alone.

"Curb, your thoughts are plain. I have looked at your planet Uulaa, and I know what sorts of *fun* you would seek there. I can see the lust-gleam in your eyes when you stare at me. You are a fool. Ardakkean women have their choice of Ardakkean men when they wish to mate." Her gaze swept slowly over me, up and down, lingering for a moment on my groin while her smile grew mocking. "I do not think *you* have ... much to offer."

What was most humiliating was the odd glint that showed in her eyes as she studied me. It made me recall the list of supposed super-powers of Ardakkeans. Including X-ray vision.

As her companions bellowed with laughter, she tossed me aside. As someone might discard an empty mixifoam container. I landed in a heap, bruised and furious, thankful only that Mala hadn't been there. She probably would have been laughing too.

"It occurs to me," Sergia went on, "that Chertro and the Federation Police might also have been deceived by you. So we will search, for our phetam."

I expected them to start flexing their muscles in a wrecking, ransacking assault on the ship. I did not expect anything like what happened.

The three of them moved through the ship at a speed that I can hardly describe. And that I could hardly see. They became three blue smears of light on the air, flashing from control area to cabins to cargo spaces to everywhere, every centimetre of the ship's interior. They didn't wreck anything, they hardly disturbed anything, but they examined everything. In seconds, and with that strange glint in all their eyes.

But when at last they halted in front of me, their eyes also held disappointment. Because even if they did have X-ray eyes, they had failed to spot and to penetrate the cylinder of impervious Balbazian steel in my cabin.

"It seems you do not have it," Sergia said grudgingly.

I had only barely struggled to my feet. "I told you," I snarled.

Her mouth twisted again. "It may mean only that you do not have it *here*," she said. "We still believe that you are a rogue, Curb, without ethics or scruples. You would be wise to keep away from Ardakkeans, henceforth."

"I didn't invite you here in the first place!" I yelled. But they were stalking through the airlock, ignoring me, dragging the lock shut behind them.

It took me a little while to recover from the experience. I kept seeing Sergia's face as she held me in the air and looked me over. And I knew that I'd be seeing it in my more dejected moments for a long time to come. But in the end I managed to put the events more or less out of my mind, and to finish my preparations. Frejji would be there soon, and it would be time to leave. And by then I definitely felt like a bit of relaxation. I'd earned it.

Finally I had shifted all the mini-devices from my headband to strategic spots on my Grislewing mask, and put it on. Which got a big belly-laugh from Frejji when she arrived. Then Posi announced that the pod had returned – with, reassuringly, no message from Mala. So all was clear at the spaceport landing area.

Leaving Frejji to it, I slid into the pod and headed down, to mingle with my enemies.

Chapter 11

As the pod slowed and the atmosphere-burn began to fade, I could see a sprawl of hazy lights coming up fast. That was Uulaa-la, the dominant city on the planet's dominant land mass. Not a city but a metropolis, with enough mazy back streets and alleys and passages to satisfy the most avid intriguer. Let any crook try to find me, I said to myself, when I go to ground in Uulaa-la.

Shortly the pod made its unceremonious bump of a landing at the immensity of the spaceport, and I stepped warily out. This was the bad time, when a host of watchers would be inspecting new arrivals. But while I spotted eighteen known spies in my first glance around, none of them seemed to be focused on me. We were, after all, in the huge Personal Carrier area, with pods, shuttles and other small vehicles coming down in a steady stream, every one of them disgorging masked and costumed revellers.

Calmly I paid for the pod's berth and walked away, neither too fast nor too slow. I couldn't resist taking a swing over towards the even huger area where full-sized ships would come down, if they did. I wanted to check on the landing patch that I keep there on a semi-permanent lease. My route drew no special attention, since many others were moving over that way to watch a magnificent Tau-cluster Megaliner thunder in, no doubt carrying another load of rich hotburners. From the crowd's midst, I glanced to one side and saw with satisfaction that my sign was still there, hovering like script in the air over my leased patch. It's a bright Flot-n-ad made by the Electroflare people, and says CURB THE COURIER with, in smaller letters, *Del Delivers*. Simple and tasteful.

I'd seen no sign of Mala, but I hadn't expected to, since she'd been right about us being less obvious if we were apart. Still, I regretted it. A return to Uulaa at festival time always brightens me up, even with danger around, and I would have liked someone to share it with. I had the crowd around me, shuffling slowly into a large ground-skim heading for the city centre, but it wasn't the same. I didn't much want to share anything with a grossly fat man wearing nothing but one of the lately fashionable cherub costumes – consisting solely of two small white wings glued to his blubbery back. Nor was I drawn to two lofty and leafy exters resembling very tall thistles on legs.

So I kept myself to myself, watching everywhere without seeming to look anywhere. The mask's eyes hid my own eyes' movement, just as a filter over the mouth would alter my voice when I spoke, in case anyone was using an audio pick-up with instant voice-print comparison. Also, my costume had discreet padding and my boots had lifts to change my apparent height and size. And I was wearing a mini-scrambler to distort any perceptor's examination of me. All standard anti-detection practice for the prudent professional.

At the city centre I slid out of the skim and moved away through the dense crowds. It soon became reasonably certain that I hadn't picked up any kind of tails or bugs, and so I could begin to relax. Around me the entertainment centres were bulging and booming as the night gathered impetus. Places to eat, places to drink, places to watch a show, places to put *on* a show, places to smoke or sniff or inject or otherwise absorb any of the various ecstatic drugs, places to find a partner or several, places to lose a partner, places to gamble, places to indulge your smallest whim no matter how illegal or depraved, places where if you wished you could simply stand and scream.

Places to spend your money.

I stopped for a bite at an eating-place that was in a huge hover-bubble, drifting slowly above the roof-tops along one of the main spiral streets intersecting the city centre. It was always a favourite place of Mala's, and I hoped to get a glimpse of her in that enticing felinoid suit, to be sure she was all right. The place seemed unusually full of lovely women, including an eight-foot mutant human with skin the colour of moonlight – but no Mala.

Still not worried, still sliding smoothly through the crowds, feeling as elusive as a shadow, I passed from night-spot to night-spot. And I began to think that if Uulaa-la was really as full of criminals as Frejji said, they were being very shy. Aside from the usual number of spies and hustlers, I'd seen only a scattering of hard-faced thugs, just low-level muscle. None of the big-name crooks at all. In fact, I may have been lulled by that into an unwise bravado.

And the bravado caused me to forget about caution and to head for a place that I'd earlier avoided – because it was my favourite night-spot in Uulaa-la. Anyone in the city who knew me also knew that I could be found there, at some time every night, if I was on the planet. It was office, meeting place, amusement centre, whatever I wanted. Or whatever the owner allowed.

The owner was a small exter named Fif, a ball of orange fur with tentacles, whom I'd known for a long time on various planets. Not that we were friends. Fif always seems a little surly with me, because he blames me for some trouble he had on another world. (But it wasn't *my* fault that someone blew up his sky-bar while trying to get at me.)

Fif's place is an energy-field structure with no visible walls (making it popular with watchers) but with only one entrance. There Fif stands guard, with a troop of armoured mandroids, checking his clientele. The structure dominates a central area of the city where developers have built a new Transi-plaza – the kind whose exterior architecture and landscaping is holo-grammic, altering entirely (but superficially) every twenty-four bio-hours. Never a dull moment, sitting around in Fif's.

I'd rarely seen the place as packed as it was when I got there. At the entrance Fif extruded a couple of tentacles – probably organs of vision, but you don't like to ask – and surveyed the large group seeking admission, which included me. The mandroids didn't stir, so we were in. I pushed past a knot of overdressed pubescent girls, each with a scarred upper lip that carried a smear of coloured grease. It was called *Frag*, and it would be giving off enough psychochemical fragrance into their nostrils to keep their minds dislocated for a week. While slowly rotting the flesh of their lips. I went looking for a quiet place to sit – while gazing with interest at the multi-armed, three-breasted Salmo'kkan dancers being sinuous on a mini-stage – when I was frozen in mid-stride.

A table nearby had erupted into a burst of crashes and screams. Then a formation of Fif's mandroids shouldered through the throng, and I followed in their wake. I saw a dwarfish exter on the floor with a nasty gash in his head, while another exter with claws and a beak looked about to disembowel him where he lay.

Clearly a momentary difference of opinion. Nothing to do with me – but useful. For the small table where the two combatants had been seated was now empty. As the mandroids calmly gassed the beaked exter and carted them both off to be flung into the street, I slid on to one of the unstained seats at the table and cheerfully looked around for a servaton.

And then nearly dived *under* the table. Except that I couldn't move.

As the throng around me rippled and shifted, I had seen the occupants of two other, larger tables. The one some way to my left contained a number of exters – some insectile and leggy, some reptilian and scaly, some piscine and finny. All were armed, with everything from blazers to vibro-knives. And in their midst, immense and motionless, sat a squat, wet-skinned, tentacled being with a trail of black mist escaping from his mouth. Ten-huc, and his pirates.

At the table a short distance to my right sat a number of bulky, cold-eyed humans with guns visibly bulging beneath their over-tunics. Black over-tunics, with a fine white stripe, and black shirts with wide white ties. In their midst was a lean and hot-eyed man toying with a glass and wearing an expression as fierce as a fusitron. Pulvidon, and his Famlio followers.

I wanted to leap up and run, but I stayed very still. If I left a table in Fif's that I'd just acquired, I might attract attention. I badly did not want to attract attention. As it was, they were all staring fixedly at the entrance to the place, so I had already been inspected by them. And by then I could see others, pirates and Famlio, circulating tirelessly through the throng, watching, waiting.

Most often the two groups ignored each other, but tension fizzed in the air around them. Now and then a circulating pirate might come face to face with a Famlio thug, and there would be some ritual snarling and glaring. Also now and then someone at one of the two tables might look at the other table with a sneer or an ugly remark.

If I hadn't been rigid with shock, I might have found it ironic. For each threatening look flung from one table to the other passed right across where I was sitting, between them. There they were, all wrapped up in their rivalry, never guessing that the object of it all was sitting in front of them.

But it was a perilous position. They had already outguessed me, by staking out my favourite haunt. The longer I stayed there the more likely it was that I'd make some betraying movement and fix their attention on me. So I sat motionless, sweating inside my costume, trying to think.

At least, in Fif's, drinking wasn't a betraying movement. When a servaton finally appeared, I ordered a goblet of the fuming Paoostyc liquor called Old Sunburst, raised my mask just enough to gulp it, then ordered two more. The first one was still exploding through my cortex as I gulped the second and reached for the third. I threw that one back even faster, because in that moment a new shock struck at me – proving that bad things *do* come in threes.

Not that the new development was entirely bad, for it certainly riveted the attention of the pirates and Famlio. But there was nothing else welcome about it.

Creating a little flurry at the entrance, in came Gharr the Gherpotean, with his Gharrgoyles. He was dressed all in white, as before, skin and hair gleaming and golden. He'd even enhanced the swashbuckler image with a slim molecublade sword – gold, of course – at his hip.

And he had Mala with him.

Around me, as the pirates and Famlio stared at Gharr, the atmosphere grew so much more charged with fury and tension that it almost crackled, like a defective energy field. But I hardly noticed, for my attention was entirely on Mala.

She was still wearing her slinky felinoid disguise, with mask, but I knew it was her. And she didn't seem to be a captive, though there were Gharrgoyles all around her. In fact Gharr's muscular left arm was clamped firmly around her waist. But the clasp was more like an embrace, with the hand sliding caressingly and too familiarly up towards her left breast. And she didn't seem to be resisting at all. In fact as I saw them she was saying something to Gharr, making him smile. I then saw that her arm was around his waist as well.

It occurred to me first that she was playing some dangerous *role* – as in her old undercover days – perhaps trying to gain some sort of information or advantage. Though I couldn't think what it would be. But then the clutch of girls with grease-smeared lips, the frag hags, stumbled past in a burst of squeals at the sight of Gharr the golden. And I realized the truth. Mala had to be *drugged*. For why else, I thought, would she be in that position, sensuously embracing a vicious criminal who had tried to kill her partner?

The realization eased my shock a little – enough to make me aware of the sense of violence building up around me. The pirates and the Famlio thugs were stirring, brandishing or fondling weapons, looking enraged by the entrance of yet another rival. The Gharrgoyles seemed to be bracing themselves, readying their own weapons. Fif's mandroids started forming up, stunners and gas-guns poised. It looked as if a four-way war was about to break out. Even the most brain-damaged of the revellers sensed it, and the noise of the place began to die away.

It was Ten-huc who defused it, perhaps showing that old age brings wisdom even to pirates. He spat out a black-misted growl, and the pirate crew sullenly began to subside. So did the Famlio thugs, after Pulvidon had snarled at them, not wanting to be outdone. And Gharr grinned his gleaming, toothy grin, and took Mala and the Gharrgoyles off to a suddenly vacated table on the far side of the place.

Everything went back to normal. The noise swelled again, now enlarged by people gabbling about how *exciting* it was at

Fif's, and wasn't that *gorgeous* man the famous Gharr, and who was the sexy little cat-person with him, and so on. And, still unnoticed, I sat and thought and had two more Sunbursts. Then, while the pirates and Famlio were staring piercingly at a new contingent of roisterers coming in, I decided to move.

It was one of my more regrettable decisions – for I got up and moved towards Gharr, and Mala.

The drinks did it, I know, and the adrenalin rush of the entire evening. Having gone that long undetected by the enemies sitting almost next to me, I'd got my over-confident bravado back with interest. I felt ready for anything, despite being a little unsteady on my feet. I felt even readier when I saw not a Gharrgoyle in sight at Gharr's table. Just the golden giant himself, still clasping Mala, but also laughingly fending off the attentions of the giggly frag hags.

Mala was looking at them in a distant and superior way when I sidled up next to her. "Come on," I muttered. "I'll get you out."

She whipped her head around, blue eyes staring from behind the felinoid mask. Then she laughed.

"Get lost, biscuit-brain," she said.

That drew Gharr's gaze. "What's this?" he rumbled in that musical baritone. "An intruder? Fly away, little Grislewing!"

Rising to his feet, grinning, he placed a large golden hand over my mask and pushed. I was flung back, flailing, tripping over my cape, into a shrieking crowd of students who were certainly mind-blasted. With more shrieks, they pushed me back towards Gharr and Mala, who were laughing boisterously.

That was when the bravado and drink and adrenalin took me further than I might have wanted to go. In a flash of over-stimulated temper, I was on the verge of silencing Gharr's laughter with one of my mini-weapons. But I wasn't that drunk. It would have been a clear giveaway. And yet I badly wanted to make some kind of personal response.

So I hit him.

At the time it seemed one of the better right hands I've ever thrown – from the shoulder, punching not at but through the

103

target, with a half-pivot that threw all my weight behind the blow.

But it had almost no effect at all.

The punch merely turned Gharr's head slightly away, while one ring left a tiny cut on his jaw-line. Then I wished I'd used the grenade in that ring instead. For Gharr, still laughing, swung a backhand that smashed into my face with the force of a Kefridian ramwhale.

That time I was lifted from my feet as I hurtled backwards. Missing the students, I crashed on to a table occupied by several globular exters with drooping antennae and startled expressions. Dazed as I was, I managed to roll on to the floor and crawl under the table as people crowded over to watch what they thought was a fight. Then Fif's mandroids pushed their way through, and in the melee I managed to scuttle on hands and knees among all the legs before getting up and getting myself and my aching face away from there.

The jutting snout of the Grislewing mask had absorbed most of the blow, or I'm sure my face would have been crushed. Even so I felt severely bruised. And I felt worse, as I stumbled away, remembering Gharr's laughter when I'd struck him. It would be different, I told myself furiously, when next we met. I'd probably been off-balance, what with the drinks and the crowds and everything.

I just wished that Mala hadn't also been laughing so hard.

I rode a half-empty ground-skim back to the spaceport. I wanted to get out before anything worse happened. I'd stay on the ship, whatever Frejji said, and wait for her to finish. And when Mala came back, I promised myself, I'd be very cool and distant until I got a proper apology.

If she came back. . . .

But those gloomy musings ended abruptly when the skim dropped me near where the pod was berthed – and when I saw the shadowy figures around it. The gnarled shapes were unmistakable even in semi-darkness. Gharrgoyles.

So Gharr not only had Mala but also knew our pod and had set a trap for me. Or thought he had.

I slid away, another shadow in my dark costume, and made a wide half-circle to an unoccupied area being prepared for new landing patches. There I fumbled under my costume for my pendant, and called Posi.

"Hello, Del," she said cheerily. "Your friend Frejji is a nice person. She has been telling me. . . ."

"Posi," I interrupted sharply. *"Later.* Is Frejji's shuttle still there by the ship?"

"Yes, Del," she said, sounding as if she'd be pouting if she had lips.

"Can your call-beam link with it and access its controls?"

"Easily."

I exhaled with relief. "Then send it down to this position to pick me up."

"The passenger pod is still down . . ." she began.

"It's not available," I snapped. "Send the shuttle."

So, before long, I was climbing into Frejji's little shuttle, stumbling through the mess of tools and equipment, squeezing into a spare spacesuit, costume and all, and finally lurching through the airlock of my ship.

There, to my surprised pleasure, I found grav and life support operating. There too I saw Frejji's ample backside jutting out of the forward workings behind the control panel. She drew back to look at me, startled.

"Y're back early. Not dawn down there yet."

"It got . . . boring," I said vaguely, as I pulled off the helmet and my mask.

Frejji grinned, seeing my bruised face. "Don't look like it was borin'. Who hit y'?"

"A little accident." I touched my cheekbone and winced. "How are you doing here?"

"Got the planetaries fixed, no trouble," she said. "Checked other stuff, an' the mechs've put on a new hull section, sealed in nice. But I got trouble with the ceptor links. Faulty interfields. Can't get 'em t' stay on phase. . . ."

She can go on like that for hours if she isn't stopped. "When will it be ready?"

"Can't say. With these interfields, could be coupla hours, couple days."

I ground my teeth as I watched her crawl back into the machinery. Two days, with a planetful of crooks looking for

105

me . . . and Mala perhaps staying on the planet, with Gharr. . . .

"You received a communicator call, Del," Posi put in. "Shortly after you left the ship. I did not acknowledge, but merely recorded it, as you instructed."

Now what? I asked myself. There were a number of people that I didn't want to hear from. At least Posi hadn't given our position away by replying.

"Play it," I said tensely. Sinking into the pouch-seat, I was aware that I was getting a severe headache to go with the soreness of my face.

Then the message came on-screen and turned the headache into a cosmic migraine.

It was Gharr, with his most arrogant grin.

"Del Curb," he said. "I have your woman, Mala Yorder. Even in disguise I knew her at once, for a truly sensual woman cannot disguise herself from my perceptions once I have seen her."

Bighead, I thought.

"She is not yet aware that I know her. Nor that she is in fact a captive. She seems very enamoured with me . . ."

Smug oaf, I thought.

". . . and so I will enjoy her this night before explaining her position to her in the morning. I intend to *keep* her, Curb, and perhaps sell her when I tire of her. Unless you wish to buy her from me now."

I sat up at that, knowing what was coming.

"The price of her freedom is the container of the Ardakkean substance."

Whistle for it, I thought angrily.

"I know you are nearby," he went on, "since she is here. I know your ship's comm will record this message, and that you will see it before long. I give you one bio-day exactly to make contact with me and give me your answer."

Chapter 12

I sat staring at the empty screen for a long time, oblivious of everything around me, including Frejji's cursing as she struggled with interfield links. My head throbbed agonizedly, and with each regular pound I could hear Gharr's voice echoing in my mind.

Worse, I could see clearly the image of Mala clinging to him within the circle of that powerful golden arm. Enamoured, he'd said.

I told myself that she *must* have been drugged. I told myself that someone like Gharr *would* imagine that all women adored him. But doubts and anxieties crept in among my thoughts, riding the cruel thumping of the headache, tormenting me with the likelihood that Mala was ... that Mala would ... that Mala had. ...

Only after a time did I force my attention on to the other problem – Gharr's demand for the phetam in return for Mala. I knew I didn't want to give either of them up. But the memory of Mala in that half-embrace with Gharr made me wonder if she had not already ... travelled beyond my reach.

In which case, if our relationship was already wrecked beyond repair, I could hold on to the phetam. I might even be able to think of an interesting way to make a larger profit than I would by tamely handing it over to the Fraxillians. The God-King and his people couldn't stop me, or retaliate, or even demand their money back. Not with what I knew about their crimes against Ardakke. And Mala wouldn't be there to reproach me for unethical. . . .

"Del, y' all right?"

Frejji's voice, making me jump, jolted my headache up on to a new level.

"No," I groaned, "but I'm going to be."

"That's good," she said vaguely. "Me, I gotta go downside, get some stuff. Those ceptor links won't hold – gotta put in replacements. Back in a coupla hours when I get the stuff together."

I nodded weakly, wished I hadn't, waved a hand more weakly. Frejji trundled off to get suited up for the short jump to her shuttle, while I walked very slowly to my cabin in search of medication.

Some time later, my headache had receded, my costume was discarded and my bunk was clasping me as tenderly as a mother's arms. And I was reaching some conclusions about the choice that Gharr had given me. It was not a choice that I would ever seek. But now that Gharr had taken Mala away – and had probably been *enjoying* her, as he'd quaintly put it – I'd begun to see that I really *had* no choice. Parting from Mala would be painful, and I would miss her. But such pain and sadness would be eased by the mega-fortune that the phetam would bring. If I could make a suitable deal. . . .

With such thoughts bringing peace to my troubled, weary being, I sank gently into sleep, to dream of the happiness to be found among the galaxy's wonders by someone who had just become immeasurably rich. . . .

"*Curb!*"

The shriek that jerked me from sleep sounded like a Lehrathghan harpy-bat. But it was on the comm, put straight through to me without warning. Because the face on the comm was Mala's, distraught and even tear-stained in the early morning light of Uulaa-la.

"Curb, I'm at the spaceport! Can't get to the pod, there are Gharrgoyles looking for me . . . I need help!"

I raised myself from the bunk slowly. "Well, well. Not so happy with the golden boy now, are we?"

Perhaps it was an effect of the screen, but I thought I saw a flush rise on her throat. "You . . . heard from him?"

"Oh, yes," I said, smiling sourly. "He was going to sell you back to me. For a ridiculously high price. Has he decided you're not worth it?"

Fury flared in her eyes. "When he told me this morning that I was his *prisoner*, not his . . . not anything else, he left two Gharrgoyles to guard me. I don't think they took the job too seriously. So I got away."

I could imagine – and I knew the guards wouldn't quickly forget her. Mala is not only FedPol trained in unarmed combat, she is one of the best naturally *dirty* fighters I've ever seen.

"But now they're looking for me everywhere," she went on. "Can we talk after you pick me up?"

I raised a cool eyebrow. "I don't recall you being so keen to leave while your lover-boy was knocking me around in Fif's last night."

Her eyes widened to their full luminous extent, and her lips fell open in an expression of total, artless surprise. "Was that *you*, Del? The Grislewing? I had no *idea*. . . ."

I stared back at her. Part of my mind was trying to point out that the facial expression was wholly unlike her, and that she never called me *Del* unless she wanted something. But the rest of me ignored those details and clutched hungrily at the reassurance that she hadn't really played a willing part in my humiliation.

"I'm glad . . ." I began.

But then she produced another harpy-bat shriek and vanished from the screen. I was looking then only at an empty stretch of spaceport beyond the comm-booth that she'd called from. But I could hear the breathy snarl that Mala makes when she is about to hurt someone quite badly, and with it a menacing series of grunts that could only be Gharrgoyles.

"Curb!" Mala shouted, off-screen. "Get me *out* of here!"

Then the dark furriness of a Gharrgoyle, limbs flailing, flew into the comm-lens with a splintering crash, and the screen went blank.

"*Posi!*" I yelled, leaping to my feet. "Get down to the planet's spaceport, *quick!*"

"Attempting a landing would be unwise, Del," Posi's calm voice replied. "The perceptors have become even more unreliable, and could go off-phase . . ."

"We're not landing!" I was spitting with fear and frustration as I yanked on some clothes and flung myself into the control area.

"Why should we go down to the spaceport, then?" she asked interestedly.

"We're going near to ground level," I snapped. "Aim for the comm-booth that Mala called from, and grab her with the Magnigrip when she's in range."

"If I can, Del," Posi said. "But many perceptors are in irregular tremor, phasing in and out. We really should wait for Frejji to come back and fix them."

I ground my teeth. "We have to get Mala *now*, Posi. Just *do* it."

A few seconds later we were plunging through atmosphere, and Posi told me cheerfully that one of the in-phase ceptors had locked on to Mala's position. At full mag the ceptor screen showed a small group of struggling figures – several gnarled and dark-furred, one bright, trim and sleek. The bright one was moving in a silvery blur, and there were quite a few dark-furred heaps lying crumpled nearby.

But my spine seemed to turn to cold stone when I saw two other groups converging on the scene of combat. One seemed to be humans dressed in black, the other was a motley group of exters. Famlio and the pirates, who had clearly learned from spies about Gharr's captive, and her escape.

Then a line of orange flame, like a livid thread on the screen, spat from the hand of one pirate towards the tangle of Gharr-goyles. I leaped as if it had been fired at me, and shrieked at Posi. Instantly the narrow-focus tractor beam called the Magnigrip speared down. It fastened on Mala like a grasping hand and snatched her into the air.

Seconds later she stumbled in through the airlock, gasping for breath, her costume ripped, her hands and face grimy and blood-smeared.

"You took enough time," she panted.

I ignored her. "Posi, take us out. Firstlight at the earliest possible moment."

"Are we not going to wait for Frejji?" Posi asked plaintively. "The perceptors. . . ."

"*Out*, Posi!" I yelled. "*Now!*"

The faint surge, as the planetaries swung us away, dropped Mala in her pouch-seat, where she slumped exhaustedly.

"Sorry," she said to me. "I should thank you."

Still I ignored her, watching the screens. We were then too high for much detail, but it looked like a general mêlée back where Mala had been. And while the crooks were fighting each other, they wouldn't be rushing off to throw ships up after us, to lock on to us before we reached Firstlight.

"Aren't you going to say anything?" Mala asked.

"What should I say? Talk about the weather? Ask you if you had a nice time?"

"Curb, stop," she said tiredly. "Gharr was at the spaceport when I landed, and he spotted me right away. He told me he's infallibly able to recognize women even if he's only seen them once. He claims it's a mutant ability. Something to do with pheromones. . . . "

"I'm sure you were giving off plenty of those," I said bitterly.

Now she was ignoring me. "I didn't know, at first, that he'd recognized me. I thought he'd . . . just picked me up. So I had to go along with it, to avoid making him suspicious."

"I saw you going along with it," I snarled. "Climbing up him like a vine."

She was silent for a moment, and my stomach clenched as I saw her face soften, her eyes grow dreamy. "He's an amazing man, Gharr," she said in a faraway murmur. "A magnetism like nothing I've ever . . . Totally overpowering. And so romantic . . . and gentle . . . and skilled. . . ."

I swallowed. "Skilled?" I repeated raggedly.

The dreaminess left her eyes as she glanced at me. "In many ways," she said quickly. "He has many abilities. . . ."

I met her glance, not sure what she was saying. "When I saw you in Fif's," I said tentatively, "you seemed . . . not under your own control. As if you were drugged, or hypnotized."

111

She nodded slowly, her mouth curving in a small, remembering smile. "Perhaps I was, somehow. In a way, I think I was."

"I *knew* it!" I slapped my thigh with delight, making her jump. "I *knew* it had to be something like that. So it wasn't your fault. You can't be blamed for . . . anything. And we should just forget it. Just put the whole episode out of our minds, pretend it didn't happen."

"Yes," she said quietly, still with the little secret smile. "Fine. We'll put it out of our minds."

"You must have been furious," I added, "when he told you this morning why he'd picked you up."

"At first." Her smile faded. "I suppose I felt used. But thinking about it – " the smile grew again – "maybe not. He never hurt me. And whatever he may have tried to gain from me, he also gave me a great deal."

I frowned. "Such as what?"

"Oh. . . ." She glanced quickly at me again, then away. "I just mean experience. A learning experience."

"Right," I said, nodding. "And the chance to flatten a few Gharrgoyles."

"That too," she said with a grin. "And it's all worked out. I'm free now, we're safely away from Uulaa, and we still have the phetam."

"I'm not so sure about *safely* away. Frejji hadn't finally rationalized the ceptor links. They're phasing quite a lot."

"You mean they might not get us to Fraxilly?"

"Can't tell. But anyway, I . . . um . . . I've been thinking. About Fraxilly."

She sat up, glowering at me. "You can *stop* thinking, if that means trying to find a way to steal the phetam and sell it somewhere else. I know you, Curb. I'm not even sure I should be letting you talk me into taking the phetam to Fraxilly rather than the FedPol. But we're certainly *not* going to play highest-bidder games. Not with some of the worst criminals in the galaxy after us."

"And the Ardakkeans," I said without thinking. Then I had to tell her about the visit – about most of it – from Sergia and her cohorts. And that made Mala even more adamant.

"We wouldn't have a chance," she insisted. "Not against all

of them. Our only hope is to get the phetam to Fraxilly, get our creds, and find a safe hiding place – until everyone's interest in us dies down."

"But the ship," I said lamely. "Couldn't we just think about my idea, while we look for a place to get the ceptors repaired . . .?"

"Posi," Mala interrupted, "what's the probability of a total perceptor breakdown, leaving you unable to navigate?"

"The perceptor links are going out of phase at random, Mala," Posi replied. "But up to this moment no single phaseout has lasted more than 4.58 bio-minutes. Nor have *all* perceptors, as yet, phased out simultaneously. The probability of a total breakdown of perceptor links, for a duration that would inhibit navigation, is 84.91 against."

"There," Mala said to me firmly. "We can make it to Fraxilly. And we're *going*, Curb. I want to get clear of this mess before anything else happens."

I hunched down in my pouch-seat, trying hard to think of a good argument against heading for Fraxilly. Then I found that something was nudging at my memory. I tried to play back what we'd been saying. That was it – when Mala said, "I want to get clear. . . ."

"*Posi!*" My yell nearly made Mala jump out of her pouchseat. "Are we *clear*? Of *bugs*? Sweep the ship, now!"

The standard security measure would have been second nature to me, on leaving any planet, if I hadn't been burdened with so many excitements and anxieties. Mala looked a little tense, showing that she'd forgotten as well. And strangely, for Posi, there was an almost measurable hesitation.

"Del," she said. "the ship itself is clear. But is it correct to include Mala's person in such a sweep?"

Mala sprang from her seat as if she'd been electro-jolted. "*Me*? There's a bug on *me*?"

"Yes, there is," Posi said primly.

"*Where*?" Mala and I demanded, in the same breath.

"On your lower back. It is one of the common forms of the brand called AdhesiMole, resembling a small skin blemish."

With a strangled cry of rage and disgust, Mala grasped the top of her ragged costume and yanked it all the way down to her waist. Then, with a furious hiss as she saw my gaze drop and become a stare, she whirled to present me with her back.

"Stop gawping and get it *off!*" she yelled.

I glanced down at the lissom length of her spine. "Can't quite see it," I mumbled. Taking hold of her costume, I tugged it farther over the firm buttocks.

"Get the *bug* off me, not my clothes!" she spat.

"*There* it is," I said at last. A small dark spot, very like a mole. I slid a fingernail under it and peeled it away, leaving a tiny redness on the skin.

Mala jerked her costume up to cover herself and swung around, glaring at the thing furiously.

"It is a simple tracer mechanism," Posi told us, "designed to transmit a thread-link along the Netlines. It is unable to gather or transmit audio-visual material."

"He must have *intended* you to escape," I said with a frown, "if he bugged you."

"Perhaps," she said icily. "Especially when I told him you were highly unlikely to give up the phetam for me."

I pretended to ignore that. "And it's odd that you didn't *notice*, when the bug was put on."

Again Mala's throat showed the faint flush. "Gharr probably put it on me when I was asleep," she said defensively.

"*Asleep?* Where? When?"

"I was his prisoner for the night," she snapped. "I was given a place to sleep."

"And did you sleep alone?" I asked harshly.

She drew herself up, looking outraged. "You have no right to ask that question, Curb. We're just business partners. And if you want our partnership to last through this flight to Fraxilly, you'd better do what you said and put the whole Gharr episode out of your mind."

I stared into her angry eyes for a moment. "All right," I muttered at last, and turned towards the disposal to jettison the bug. Aware as I went that she had dodged the crucial question. Also aware that I was happier with the evasion than I would have been with a wrong answer. . . .

"And that bug is your proof," Mala added, "of what we're up against. All those criminals with all their resources. We have to keep to the plan – get to Fraxilly and away again, fast, then lie low for as long as it takes."

I shrugged reluctantly, not having a counter-argument.

"It's the only way, Del," she said quietly.

I opened my mouth to speak, but she forestalled me. "Posi," she said, "let's start again to lay in a Netline course for a Highlight crossing to the planet Fraxilly."

Part Two

World of Conflict

Chapter 13

"Del," Posi said, "every one of the forward perceptors has gone off-phase."

The statement was unnecessary, since I was looking at the forward perceptor screens, which showed a silvery shimmer like visible white noise. The other screens showed that their ceptors were all right – but they displayed only the usual star-pitted expanse of deep space. The forward ceptors had been showing a bright little disc that was the planet Fraxilly, steadily enlarging as we crept near to it on planetary drive.

"Will we get them back?" I asked. "Or have they hit burn-out?"

"They have not burned out," Posi said reassuringly. "But the tremor has grown more erratic, and the off-phasings are lasting longer."

"Do we need the forwards right now?" Mala asked.

"I can navigate on planetary speed without them," Posi said, "so long as we do not lose others."

"That's all right, then," I said, with more confidence than I felt. "Maybe the God-King has some engineers who can fix them before we leave."

The ship slid on, minutes passed. Mala and I stared at the enlarging disc that appeared on other screens after Posi revolved the ship to bring the lateral ceptors to bear. And by the time we had butted our way into orbit around the planet, I was feeling fairly relaxed. We were in one piece, we still had the phetam, we had reached our destination, no other ships had emerged from lightspeed behind us, and the second half of that huge fee was almost in our hands.

"It all seems a bit of an anti-climax," I said idly.

Mala gave me an amused look. "I could always call Ten-huc or Pulvidon on the comm, to get a little excitement going."

I grimaced. "You'd probably call Gharr."

"*Leave* it, Curb," she said coldly.

I gave her a nasty smile and left it. As I had done several times on the journey, since I hadn't entirely managed to put out of my mind the events of Uulaa and my suspicions. Or to stop making sardonic remarks about them.

But then it was time to retrieve the cylinder from its hiding place in my cabin, and make myself ready. Since delivery only required one of us, I'd undertaken to go down to Fraxilly while Mala stayed with the ship. I had the feeling that she might be less than diplomatic when confronted by the God-King's luxurious life-style. And when I reminded her of our meeting with the Emissary, she had to agree.

For myself, I anticipated no problems. I was quite enthusiastic about the chance of meeting a God-King, perhaps establishing some useful contacts among his courtiers. Provided they weren't all as gruesome as the Emissary. All the same, with proper professionalism, I checked my weaponry thoroughly as well as my appearance. I was again in a basic canary yellow, with cerise piping and stripes of varying shades of purple on the trim at belt, wrists and headband. I liked to think that, while discreet enough for an important occasion, the ensemble made its own kind of personal statement.

Then I was ready, ignoring Mala's stifled giggles and her remark that the mauve roll-flaps topping off my boots were going too far. She was in one of her sloppy coveralls, which put her in no position to be critical.

Normally I would have gone down in the passenger pod, but of course the pod was back on Uulaa. So the ship was to go briefly near ground-level to set me down by tractor-beam. I wasn't happy about being ruffled up by the beam, and left untidy and dusty. But Posi promised to lower me slowly, to raise minimal dust from where the beam hit the ground.

Anyway, there wasn't a choice. I didn't want to try landing

the ship itself, because coming in to an accurate pin-point landing requires delicate navigation, which was impossible with the ship's erratic ceptors. It wouldn't improve my chances of pleasing the God-King if more ceptors phased out at the wrong moment so that the ship set down on top of something valuable – like the royal palace, the Divine Sanctum.

So once Posi had drifted the ship down near the surface, I prepared myself for my descent – the cylinder in a carry-net slung over one shoulder, a hand raised to hold on to my hairpiece. Soaring out through the airlock into the Fraxillian sunshine, I thought of how I must have looked to any people below. A godlike figure, I thought, descending lightly but with dignity from the sky.

It was several perceptors phasing out together, Posi later explained, that threw directional control and some other functions out of kilter. So the tractor beam set me down nowhere near the Divine Sanctum. Worse, the beam shut off while I was still four metres from the ground.

I might easily have broken a leg in that fall. But instead it was the fall that was broken – by a soft heap that was unmistakably, even to an off-worlder, Fraxillian fertilizer.

Luckily, that part of the planet is hot and dry, and the upper surface of the pile had formed a thick crust. Landing feet first, I broke only partway through the crust, so that nothing but my boots plunged down into the softer material beneath. Softer, wetter and fouler. Emitting a stink that would have made a Tyryttiaki swamp mist seem fragrant.

Slightly stunned by the abrupt landing, half-dazed by the assault of the overpowering stink, I lay still for a moment on the crust, groaning and gagging. Somehow then I found the strength to roll away, dragging my boots away from the clutch of the pile's soggy depths. As I rolled to the ground the stink came with me, from the greenish-black stains on my boots, nearly making me lose my breakfast.

"Curb, are you all right?" Mala's voice from my pendant, sounding less anxious than I would have liked. Probably distortion.

"Just barely," I said through gritted teeth as I struggled to my feet. "What happened?"

"Some kind of cross-tremor from the interfield," Mala said. "Posi's investigating." As I snarled something foul, she went on. "Be grateful it didn't cut out when you were higher. And don't worry about it. We'll try to get it fixed so we can pick you up after you make delivery."

I gabbled for a second as shock and rage choked my words. "*After . . .?*" I finally yelled. "You have to pick me up *now*! How do you expect me to get to the Sanctum from here?"

"Walk," Mala said briskly. "You're only about six kilometres from the Sanctum, and you have your personal mini-ceptor to guide you. Stop whining and get going. We have work to do here."

And though I yelled a few more descriptive expressions, neither she nor Posi replied.

So I let go of the pendant, gathered myself, and looked around. And the full awfulness of my landing hit me in a rush. There was nothing in sight but what appeared to be a desert landscape of bare ridges and hollows, with occasional patches of scrappy vegetation, close to the ground. And of course there was the fertilizer pile, next to me – beyond which was a slightly different pile, with dark sticks thrusting out of it at odd angles.

Then some creatures emerged from it, through an opening that I hadn't noticed, and I realized that the other heap was a dwelling. Of a sort that would make the word "hovel" sound too grand.

As the creatures turned towards me, I took an instinctive step back, before reaching the startled conclusion that they were human – more or less. It wasn't easy to tell, from the filthy and shapeless rags that covered their filthy and shapeless bodies, but I guessed that there was a man and a woman and some smaller ones that were children. And against all sense and credibility I worked out that I had landed in the midst of what might be called a farmstead, Fraxilly-style.

I smiled at them in friendly fashion. They stared. I wished them good day. They stared. I apologized for dropping into their fertilizer. They stared. I asked if they knew the way to the Sanctum. They stared.

Finally, in growing anger, I told them to perform an unlikely act upon themselves – they stared – and turned away. Behind my annoyance the self-preserving part of my mind was pointing out that the sooner I got going, the sooner I could be a long way from Fraxilly farmland. So I activated my headband ceptor – and, sure enough, it fixed on what seemed to be a good-sized urban area in the distance.

That, I reckoned, would be the major city of this land mass, near which the Sanctum lay in semi-isolated splendour. So I strode away, with a casual wave to the family of farmers. Who stared. For all I know, they are there yet, staring at the place where I was.

Before long, I saw more signs of agriculture, on a pathetically primitive level. Herds of scrawny little creatures, local life forms – smooth-skinned, pot-bellied, longer hind legs than fore – huddled in the gullies, gnawing at the vegetation. On some of the more level stretches rows of colourless plants drooped in the sun, scraggy and semi-lifeless but obviously tilled crops. Once or twice I saw a few other shapeless human figures prodding listlessly with crude implements at the dust among such rows. They seemed too wretched even to stare.

Pastoral life on Fraxilly, I thought, leaves a lot to be desired. This was a new definition of poor – a depth of misery more nauseating even than the stink that still rose from my stained boots. If I'd been a religious man I would have thanked one god or another for the large number of kilocreds I was soon to collect, which would keep me from any kind of poverty for a long time. But then, I told myself with a half-smile, I *would* be thanking a God-King.

That was the only light moment that came my way on that trek. Even the fact that I finally found a trickle of scummy water, which let me rinse some of the filth from my boots, did nothing to lift my spirits. I had not been prepared for a walk across a wasteland under a hot white sun. I had no way to deal with thirst, heat, dust and all the other miseries afflicting me. (I couldn't have drunk any of the foul water.) I did allow myself a Metastim tablet from my belt-pouch, but even its effect was minimal, and temporary.

Yet when I saw the city, from the top of a sun-blasted ridge, I wondered if the farmland wasn't preferable.

A long kilometre or so later, I entered the city's outskirts. Now I'm familiar with urban centres on a variety of worlds, human or exter. They nearly all have some things in common. Basic city things, like lots of people, and lots of structures to contain them. And other things that would seem basic, like modes of transport, communication centres, systems of commerce or cultural interaction.

This Fraxillian city apparently had none of those things, except objects that by a stretched definition could have been called buildings. But they were deserted. So were the shapeless spaces between the buildings, which could never be called streets. And the buildings looked as derelict as if they had all been lifted by some force and dropped again.

They were cracked and crumbling, split and broken. They leaned crazily, with large chunks of roofs or walls fallen away. Windows and entrances and other holes in their shells gaped blankly like the mouths of imbeciles. Everything about them was in a state of collapse, because everything was cheap and badly constructed – the low-grade chunki-crete of the frameworks, the corroded metal that trimmed or braced.

In the spaces among the buildings, rubble and litter of every sort were scattered and heaped, forming deeper piles here and there as if they had drifted like sand. Chunks of crumbled crete, unrecognizable fragments of low-tech machinery, crushed food containers and packaging, junk beyond description, filth beyond imagination. The stink told me that the heaps were also depositories for organic matter that didn't even have the excuse of being fertilizer.

In short, the place looked dead. Not so much what ancient writings used to call a "ghost town" – more like a *corpse* town. Lifeless, decrepit, falling apart, putrefying.

And it was indescribably eerie – so that I almost began to wonder if Posi had brought me to the right planet. Where were the people? And how could people who lived in places like this, farm or city, manage to support a God-King in limitless luxury?

But of course that was the answer. *All* the resources of the place went into keeping up the God-King's life-style, rather than improving the lives of the people. Which thought briefly led me to weave a vision or two. Of how a man might contrive to open a cylinder of phetam, and perhaps set up as a God-King himself, on a more salubrious world. . . .

Prowling on through the foul open area, wrapped in such pleasant fantasies, I almost failed to see the furtive movement on the edge of my vision. But the recognizable impulse from my headband ceptor drew my attention. Life-forms, nearby.

I stared nervously around, then saw it. A creature skulking past the collapsed corner of a building. Before it whisked out of sight I got the impression of a bloated grey body standing about hip-high to me on four thin legs. Then there was another, and others behind it, and I saw the long bare tail like a whip, the narrow head, the yellow teeth that seemed too big for the jaws, the glittering red eyes.

I nodded to myself, knowing the creature. It was no local Fraxillian life form. Humanity had brought many things along, inadvertently, when it came out to populate the stars – unseen stowaways like bacteria, flies, fleas. And this creature, which thrived, and mutated, everywhere it went. Most human worlds had eradicated it, by my time, but poor Fraxilly clearly couldn't afford to eradicate anything.

Maybe, I thought, the rats had eradicated the Fraxillians, in the city.

I moved on slowly, watching on every side to be sure some monster-rat wasn't creeping up on me. I was sure that I'd be safe from them when I finally emerged from the city on the far side – it wasn't likely that rats would be allowed too close to the Divine Sanctum – but I couldn't yet see any sign of a far side. The buildings were rickety ruins, but there were a lot of them.

So I plodded on. Growing thirstier and hungrier and wearier and unhappier, as the blistering sun edged across the sky. And growing more uneasy. The rats had not shown themselves again, but I'd begun to feel them watching me from shadowed hiding places. The feeling sent the adrenalin rushing around so fast that it threatened to wear me out before I got to my destination.

And that was another detail making me uneasy. Was I going to get to the Sanctum before nightfall? I wasn't sure how long a day was on Fraxilly – and I didn't want to be wandering in Rat City after dark.

I was lifting my pendant to ask Posi a question or two – and to get an update on the state of the ship – when I saw the girl.

I wasn't sure it was a girl, at first, what with the shapeless and grimy robe she wore – ankle-length, made of coarse brown cloth – and the heavy, oversized boots in which she was clumping along. But then I saw her face within her tangle of tawny hair – unmistakably young and female. Not far past adolescence, I guessed, but far enough. And possibly pretty, I also thought, under the dirt that smeared all of her visible skin.

She seemed to be in a hurry, striding quickly along with her hands tucked in her large flapping sleeves, boots kicking up dust. She was also looking carefully around her as she went, and watching where she put her feet. But she wasn't looking *up* high enough to see something that shifted my pulse rate along a notch or two.

A very large, bulbous rat was crouched on the half-collapsed top of a small building, and the girl was heading straight for it.

She was a few strides away, I was taking a breath to shout a warning, when unexpectedly – by some wary instinct – she looked up, and halted. I was impressed, for her only reaction was a slight flicker of her eyes. Then, to my surprise, she grinned.

"Brother Rat," she said, in a fetching accent. "Do you come to greet me? That is. . . ."

She stopped. The rat's eyes had grown redder, and its hindquarters were bunching. Then it leaped.

The girl's grin did not alter at all as she drew her right hand from her sleeve, holding a large, ancient, projectile-firing pistol, and blew off a large bit of the creature's head.

At which point two other giant rats sprang from the lower part of that building, jaws agape, and flung themselves at her.

Despite robe and boots she moved with graceful speed, and without any flicker of fear. The ancient pistol fired again, and one of the rats twisted in mid-air and fell, writhing. Then she

126

leaped away from the second rat, just in time. The rat-teeth missed her but caught her robe, slashing it open from hip to ankle, revealing a long and shapely leg.

Then the rat wheeled to attack again. And the one that had been writhing on the ground recovered itself, lunging towards her from the other side. And as she raised her pistol again, it misfired.

To my surprise, I found that I was running *towards* the battle. As the monster rats charged at the girl, I aimed my wristband blazers and blasted large fiery holes in both of them.

Chapter 14

The girl stood absolutely still as I ran up to her, staring at the
dead rats and then at me. Closer, I could see that she was
quite a big girl – maybe a centimetre or two taller than me –
and looking healthy and quite attractive under the dirt. Then
she looked me up and down, and grinned an impish, earthy
grin that would have been very appealing if she'd had all her
teeth.

"Off-worlder!" she said delightedly. "With off-world weapons!
What a *gift* you are!"

I assumed she meant the words as an expression of thanks
for her rescue. "Think nothing of it," I said agreeably, and
introduced myself.

"Mister Del Curb," she said, studying me. "I'm c'Vira. And I
do think something of it, Mister. I think much of it, and so will
everyone. Will you walk with me?"

I hesitated, about to decline, to say that I had an urgent
appointment with the God-King. But some instinct stopped
me. There was something odd about this girl with her old-
fashioned gun and her dirty robe. She seemed too aware, too
capable, too self-contained – like a totally different species
from the gaping, downtrodden peasants by the fertilizer.

So I listened to my instinct. "I'll gladly come with you,
c'Vira," I said. "I'm looking for help. My spaceship, in orbit
around your world, is damaged and needs repairs. Do you
understand about spaceships and things?"

Again she flashed her knowing grin. "I know something of

them, Mister Del. Maybe more than you know about Fraxilly. Come."

She turned, seeming unaware of how the movement caused her torn robe to fall open, revealing again the full length of her leg from rounded buttock to slim ankle. It was very clear that she was richly, lushly formed, and fairly clear that she wore nothing under the robe. But her movement, the swirl of her robe, revealed something else about her, a little less appealing. She stank.

It was noticeable despite the fouled rubble around us or the gruesome reek of the dead rats. It was something uniquely c'Vira. It was ripe and yet it was sharp – it was stomach-heavingly sweet and yet it was eye-wateringly sour. I took a hasty step backwards and started breathing through my mouth as I tried to think of a way to withdraw my acceptance of her invitation.

But my instinct still made me wary of antagonizing her. So I was committed – even when she bent to grasp the tail of one dead rat and directed me to take hold of the other two.

"For the feast we'll have," she explained. "And to prove to the Treffs what a gift you are."

"Feast? Treffs?" I asked, breathing shallowly and taking a gingerly grip on the two scabby tails.

And as we moved away, dragging the rats, she explained further, and underlined my uneasiness about what I'd got into.

It was bad enough that she assumed we – with the others, whoever they were – would be eating the rats. People mostly did, she said, whenever they could. And while she hadn't actually been hunting, she was pleased to have got lucky. With my help.

"Why *were* you out here?" I asked, trying not to think about eating the foul flesh of the monsters I was dragging. "And where *is* everybody?"

"I was visiting kinfolk, outside the city," she said. "Some years ago, there was a pestilence here. Many folk died, and the rest fled – to open country and farmland. And they never came back, though the plague has been finished a long while. Out of the city people can hope to dig and scratch and feed themselves, away from rats and plagues." She grinned. "And sometimes they can hide some of what they own, from the godlies."

I had an idea what she meant, but I was playing the part of innocent traveller, so I blinked and looked puzzled. And received in return a fairly thorough outline of the nature of life on Fraxilly.

By the "godlies" she meant agents of the God-King formally known as the Godly Gatherers of the Tithe. That meant that they regularly visited the people and took away most of what they had, to support their ruler's luxurious habits. If anyone objected, the godlies called in the "royals" – meaning Royal Guardians of Good Order. They were storm troopers with armoured vehicles and fairly advanced weapons, who liked nothing better than a little target practice on a tithe withholder.

"That's *terrible!*" I said, trying to sound as morally outraged as my role required. "I've never heard of any place so oppressed. The SenFed should do something."

She shrugged. "The SenFed authorities believe what the God-King's Emissary tells them. But there are those, Mister Del – " the wicked grin flashed again – "who are trying to do something. Here, where it matters."

Again it was clear enough what she meant in that heavy hint. And it made me all the more anxious to shake myself loose – when a suitable time came – from c'Vira and her friends. Meanwhile, I continued to look outraged and interested.

"What can anyone do, here?" I asked.

"People can band together," she said firmly, "to get ready for the day when we rise up and drag the God-King from his throne."

Great, I thought. I'm contracted to do a job for the God-King, and I fall in with a nest of zealot rebels who want to overthrow him. I reckoned they'd feed me to some live rats if they knew the truth, so I went on looking amazed and fascinated.

"You're one of them, aren't you, c'Vira?" I said, as if the notion had suddenly struck me. "That's why you don't seem downtrodden, and why you carry a weapon. . . ."

130

"It's so," she said, looking as pleased with my perception as if I'd just discovered anti-gravity. "One of the Treffs."

She told me about them at great length, including many of their heroic exploits – which were mostly along the lines of throwing dried rat-dung at royals and running away. "Treff" was taken from a word in the local dialect, meaning "unwashed young person with smelly feet", which seemed appropriate. Generations of young rebels had taken to the name with delight, partly because they could give up bathing in a place where water was scarce, also because of a dull old proverb about cleanliness being next to godliness. On Fraxilly, no young radical ever wanted to be godly.

The Treffs, c'Vira declared, were the planet's only way out from misery and slavery. It was clear to me that the Treffs had a lot of puffed-up aspirations, a few out-dated weapons and absolutely no hope at all. But her smile grew manic with fervour as she spoke, so I merely nodded and murmured and tried to look impressed rather than anxious.

Until anxiety burst through, full-force, when a sound struck at us from the near distance. The high-pitched howl of a heavy-duty skimmer.

"Royals!" c'Vira said. "This way!"

She set off at a run, with me half a step behind her and gaining. Then she shrieked and stopped and sent me back, for I'd dropped the rats' tails in order to improve my speed. But she was right – dead rats with large blazer holes would have been a bit of a giveaway. Panting, sweating, struggling, I ran as best I could with the rats jouncing behind me, catching on every protuberance. Somehow I managed to reach the twisted doorway of the building where c'Vira had disappeared, just before the big skimmer swept into view in a whirlwind of heat and dust.

I found c'Vira crouching with pistol poised next to what had been a window. She grinned at me, a more demonic grin than ever.

"If they come looking, Mister Del, you can burn them down like you did the rats."

"Uh . . . that wouldn't be wise," I suggested. Wise? Fraxillian soldiers killed by off-world weapons, and then an off-worlder

131

turning up at the Sanctum? I'd be lucky if they just executed me.

But c'Vira turned on me, scowling as if she felt betrayed, the pistol's muzzle gaping like a mouth. I flinched back, beginning to think that I'd have to take some drastic action to protect myself. Then her glare vanished, replaced by the grin in one of the fastest mood-swings I've seen.

"I understand," she said. "You do not wish to reveal your presence."

I smiled vaguely and peered out of the window. For all the concern c'Vira had shown, the royals could have been surrounding us. Luckily, the skimmer was drifting on past, its occupants apparently uninterested in the rubble around them. Probably off to some farm to molest a few peasants, I thought. I wondered if they might run into the family that had stared so unblinkingly at my arrival. But somehow I doubted that those people would volunteer, to the royals, the news of a man dropping from the sky into their fertilizer.

Anyway, it didn't matter if they did, since I didn't think that falling into fertilizer was a crime on Fraxilly. And when I finally delivered the phetam to the God-King I expected to be treated as a hero, not a criminal. If, I thought, I could get free of these clownish rebels and make that delivery.

But some time later I still hadn't worked out how to get safely away from c'Vira, and her pistol. By then we had crossed quite a lot more of the city, with our rats – until finally c'Vira led me into a large, half-collapsed building. There some rickety stairs led to the cellar and the mostly hidden entrance to a tunnel.

The tunnel was lightless and of course as foul-smelling as a sewer. But by then my sense of smell had just about gone on strike – and I dealt with the darkness by flicking on my headband micro-light, which made c'Vira clap her hands like a child. The light showed that the tunnel's low roof was wholly unsupported, which explains why I went along the tunnel in a sprint, despite being crouched and dragging two giant rats.

We emerged into the dimness of another cellar, with several other half-hidden tunnel mouths – alternative escape routes, I thought, for what had to be the rebel headquarters. And I was proved right when we went up some steps into a cluttered area holding about fifty or sixty amazingly unwashed young people, all in dirty brown robes, who turned and looked at us, open-mouthed.

Staring seemed to be widespread on Fraxilly, I thought. But then they closed their mouths and crowded around c'Vira in a flurry of exclamations and questions, with plenty of sidelong glances at me. And while c'Vira was telling them everything, I maintained a noncommittal smile and looked carefully around.

The area had a sagging ceiling and almost artistic mould-stains on the walls, but otherwise seemed solid enough. Doorways, some with ragged half-curtains, led to separate rooms here and there – probably extra sleeping places. There were many scattered, filthy pallets in the main area, much nondescript clutter, and some low-tech machinery – including, to my surprise, a small, wavery but functional galacvid screen. In another corner was a grimy collection of metal objects that seemed to have something to do with food preparation. I wasn't sure which would be worse, eating the rats or eating anything at all cooked in that place.

But then it was time to stop looking at things and turn my attention to people, for c'Vira had finished her lively account of our meeting, and the rest of the Treffs were examining me, looking even more noncommittal than I was.

"Mister Del," c'Vira said, coming back to me with her wicked grin and a leg-flashing swing of her torn robe. "This is y'Tylo, leader of the Treffs."

She also rattled off the names of a few others – c'Pexa and y'Foti and so on – but I never did bother to sort them out. My focus was on the leader, y'Tylo, a strapping youth with heavy shoulders and lank black hair who smelled as if he had just come from a long soak in Fraxillian fertilizer. He had a length of stained rope around his robe at the waist, through which was thrust an old-model therm-gun, the standard-gauge Fusofire. As he stepped towards me, with one hand resting not too idly on the gun-butt, he wore a heavy-browed expression that mingled suspicion and stupidity in equal parts.

"What you want here?" he grunted.

"It's just as c'Vira told you," I said. "My ship. . . ."

He silenced me with a brusque wave of his hand, not the gun-hand. "I heard all that. You think *we* gonna fix yer ship somehow?"

"Not at all," I replied, feeling both nervous and nettled. "I was looking for someone who. . . ."

"Yeah," y'Tylo growled. "Lookin' fer royals. Lookin' fer t' ask the God-King for help."

"That's. . . ." I was about to say "stupid", which might not have been tactful, when I was interrupted. A small youth pushed forward, chubby of face and skinny of body, but with a sharper awareness in his eyes than all the other Treffs put together. And those eyes were studying me very thoroughly.

"Off-worlders don't usually know much about the God-King," he said quietly, "or how things are here."

Big y'Tylo shifted his feet and scowled. "I don't like him, y'Wipo."

The lout's instincts were working well. Luckily, his brain hardly worked at all. No doubt he was the leader because he was the biggest and strongest and most mindlessly brave. But little y'Wipo with the chubby cheeks was probably the intelligence behind their scruffy operation – and, happily, he seemed to be on my side.

As did c'Vira, who thought the proceedings worthy of her wicked grin. "You *should* like him, y'Tylo. Without him, I'd be as torn up as my robe."

She swirled the garment as she spoke, giving us all a flash of ripe thigh within the rent, and giggled.

Little y'Wipo cleared his throat. "And he could have tried to alert the royals that they saw," he pointed out. "You don't have to like him, y'Tylo – but I think we can be friendly to him."

The big leader was still scowling – and, to my surprise, an entire thought managed to force its way through his mental undergrowth. "Some'p'n's funny, that's all." He aimed his scowl at me. "If yer ship's bust an' ever'thin', how'd you get *down* here?"

It seemed a good question to the rest of them, too – while to me it couldn't have been a better feed. I widened my smile a bit, briefly blinded them with a little science about tractor beams, then used the sort of manipulation that works well on suspicious primitives. I told them how the beam became defective and – with excellent comic timing and delivery – just how and where it had deposited me.

No vid joker could have had a better reception. All children and dimwits love jokes about excreta, and so did the Treffs. They listened to me, they looked at the stains on my boots, and they laughed till they cried. Some of them fell down and clutched their stomachs. Some of the girls, including c'Vira, rushed off to what was apparently the latrine, gasping that they were nearly going to wet themselves – which seemed a bit fussy for people wearing those robes. Even y'Tylo bellowed and roared and hiccupped and finally clapped me powerfully on the shoulder – with the hand that he'd taken off his gun.

But I didn't fail to notice that y'Wipo only tittered a little, and smiled knowingly, and kept smiling the same way while the others roared off to prepare the dead rats for the feast. And during it, y'Tylo declared in friendly fashion, he would get me to tell it all again.

"One thing, though," y'Wipo said through his smile. "This tractor beam that . . . dropped you in it. If it isn't working now, how will you get back to your ship?"

I waved a hand in an expansive gesture. "The beam won't be needed. Since I'm here on the ground, the ship can get a fix on my position, and can navigate to that fix even if several perceptors go off-phase. So when the time comes, I'll just find a safe place with lots of room, and call the ship down to make a landing."

"Will you, now," y'Wipo said very softly. "Will you."

But I only half-heard him. Because c'Vira had turned towards me, with a wilder smile than ever, and with a remark that froze me where I stood.

She said, "You know? It's just like on the vid, when the off-world hero lands on the planet that's all enslaved and every-thing, and helps to win the revolution!"

*

Chapter 15

So that, I thought, was what she meant about me being a gift. She had notions about dragging me into their doomed little rebellion. Because I had the up-to-date weapons. No doubt she saw me as one who would drop everything for a chance to strike a blow against oppression.

Well, so I will. If it's me being oppressed, and if I'm fairly sure the blow won't simply provoke worse oppression. But I wasn't about to go striding out through the ruined city leading this smelly rabble to death or glory. Between those two results, the odds favoured the former. And I wasn't interested in either.

But I *was* interested in saving my skin. So I hid my anxieties, smiled my smiles, and bided my time.

Shortly the meal arrived, and we all sat on the floor eating greasy rat stew from stained ceramic bowls. It wasn't the worst food I'd ever had to eat in the interests of tact and caution, but very nearly. Especially with the warm brackish water that was what they had to drink. Still, while we ate, I learned a few interesting things. Mainly I learned that the Treffs weren't quite as totally hopeless as I had thought.

For one thing, they had sources of information about life inside the Divine Sanctum. Not always fully knowledgeable or reliable sources, but devoted.

"Mothers," c'Vira told me, giggling. "The God-King takes girls into his harem – " as I knew, though I didn't let it show – "but he gets rid of any that start a baby. Throws them out here again, like he does with the ones getting older."

"But pregnant harem girls get well treated out here," y'Wipo added. "So they survive. And some of them tell their children stories, and secrets, about the God-King who is their father."

"So *we* know things," c'Vira said, "that other folk don't."

"You?" I said, goggling in a suitably impressed way, though I'd seen it coming.

"Many of us are children of the God-King," y'Wipo said. "Including c'Vira, and y'Tylo."

I made further noises to indicate amazement. "And what sort of secrets do your mothers tell you?"

"Mostly bits of scandal," y'Wipo said, while c'Vira giggled lasciviously. "But it was a mother from the harem who first organized other young people to form the Treffs, many generations ago. Because she was the one who discovered Fraxilly's biggest secret."

He paused, and the others smiled broadly as they watched me assume a look of eager expectancy.

"Which is," he continued, "that the God-King is no god at all."

I outdid myself with astonished goggling. The others laughed and nodded, but y'Wipo merely gave me a half-smile and went on. "That woman, the much-remembered c'Sela, Mother of the Revolution, revealed that the God-King gets his apparently divine powers from a rare drug."

For a while the others vied with each other to give details of the God-King's powers, most of which I'd heard before, while I maintained my look of amazement.

"And the drug," a girl finally said, "is an off-world substance, brought secretly to the God-King every few years by some. . . ."

Her voice trailed off as an awful thought struck her. Visibly it was also striking most of the others, except big dim y'Tylo. Just as visibly it had occurred to y'Wipo a considerable time before.

"By some off-world agent," y'Wipo said, still with his knowing half-smile. "Who would normally land at the Sanctum itself. Unless, perhaps, his ship developed a malfunction and set him down in the wrong place."

By then they were all staring at me. Some were looking shocked, like c'Vira, while others were scowling angrily –

including y'Tylo, who had finally caught on, and whose great fists were bunching like clubs.

You're sharp and quick, I thought, looking at y'Wipo. But you're still a back-sector bumpkin. It'll be a lifetime before you can hope to play in *my* league. And while I was thinking that, I was returning their stares and glares with a bewildered expression that very slowly – I was proud of the timing – changed to a mixture of understanding and indignation.

"You don't think," I said, just this side of a splutter, "that this drug . . . that *I* have anything to do with it?"

To his credit, y'Wipo's little smile didn't flicker, though many of the others began to look unsure in the face of my outraged innocence. "You carry a strange metal cylinder, Mister Curb," y'Wipo said quietly. "Will you tell us what's in it?"

I glanced in well-judged astonishment at the cylinder, lying next to me in its carry-net. "*In* it? What do you mean?"

"He means what you got *in* it," y'Tylo rumbled.

"It's a standard Bazeley-Wynd through-pass infractor unit," I said smoothly, as if such things were commonplace in every derelict cellar. "It's almost certainly the source of the disruption in my ship's interfield system. I brought it along hoping to find a repair service, to get it fixed or to get a replacement. Have a look if you want."

Casually I tossed the cylinder to y'Tylo. He nearly fumbled it, scowled, turned it over several times, then handed it to y'Wipo. The smaller youth's half-smile had begun to fade, and I felt a measure of hope. I was quite sure that even y'Wipo would have no way of knowing about the high-tech inner workings of a spaceship.

"How do you open it?" y'Wipo asked, prodding with a finger at the tiny slot that would admit the molecular key.

I smiled with just the right touch of an amused adult indulging innocent youth. "You don't *open* it. It fits into the grid-system on molecu-mag links, so that it forms the through-pass."

"Does it," y'Wipo murmured. The half-smile had returned, but I now saw in it the look of a semi-clever youth trying to impress the others by pretending to know what I was talking about. Certainly the others were looking blank – y'Tylo looked as if he'd been hit by a blunt instrument – and watched y'Wipo with humbly admiring gazes.

So it all seemed to pass off well. The cylinder was returned to me – I tossed it on to the web with apparent indifference – and the conversation went back to their main obsession, the great confidence trick played on their world over two centuries by the long-lived God-King. I learned more than I wished to know about the stages in their revolution, and how not the tiniest advance had ever been made towards victory.

And by the time they circled back, as I knew they would, to talking about how things would be different now because I was there, I was ready for them.

"You must understand," I said, looking around with earnest sincerity. "I hate tyrants as much as anyone, and I'd *love* to join your revolution. But I can't."

The first of my words had made them all look happy, the last word made them look sad. But it wasn't quite that simple. Especially when I was constantly distracted. Somehow c'Vira had shifted position so that she was directly opposite me – and every now and then she made a tiny, sinuous movement that briefly parted her torn robe to reveal a grimily luscious sweep of bare thigh and hip. The display was also being carefully monitored by most of the male Treffs, so none of them noticed my dryness of throat and occasional stumble as I explained why I couldn't go into battle, guns blazing, at their side.

It made some sense, in fact, as every good confidence trick must. I told them it was tactically absurd to think that I could blast my way with mini-weapons into what was probably a well-fortified and well-guarded Sanctum. (They confirmed that it was.) I also told them that if I didn't get my ship repaired and continue my journey I'd be reported missing and the FedPol would put out a search party. (That wasn't so – it's every man for himself in deep space – but I didn't think the Treffs would know it.)

Instead, I made some lavish promises. I would get my ship fixed and travel to the cluster-worlds of SenFed Central, where I would publicize the plight of the Fraxillian people. I spoke of having influential friends in the SenFed. I vowed that the

Federation would be forced to set up an inquiry into Fraxilly. And I added my belief that brave warriors like themselves would still be needed – to face any flurries of violence from the royals before the God-King was finally deposed.

They all cheered and yelled and waved their weapons, looking like they might rush out and shoot a few royals right then. But instead they merely rose and milled around, dragging me up for manly claps on the back and womanly embraces, while c'Vira made her eyes smoulder in my direction.

And all the while, y'Wipo was gazing at me and smiling his little smile. Which, I was sure, was to maintain his pose of intellectual superiority.

"One thing, though," y'Wipo said to me when the tumult faded a little. "How do you plan to get your ship repaired here?"

I blinked. "There must be some kind of spaceport with repair facilities, mecho-labs. . . ."

"The only spaceport," y'Wipo said quietly, "is the property of the God-King, and it lies within sight of the Sanctum."

I smiled around at them all. "Then I'll have to go there, and play the part of an innocent off-worlder with a damaged ship, who knows nothing about Treffs and revolutions."

That had them all rolling with laughter again, though y'Wipo just smiled and nodded. "I'm sure you'll play the part well," he said.

I looked at him closely, for there was a faint tone in his voice I didn't like. But I wasn't able to follow it up, for c'Vira came to wind herself about me, less than fragrantly, grinning.

"What did I say, Mister Del? You're a gift!"

As she chuckled, and hugged me, there was a faint ripping sound. I looked down to see that nearly her whole side, a curving sweep of soiled flesh from rib-cage to ankle, was wholly on view.

She followed my gaze, and chuckled again. "Well, look at me. I'd better sew up this robe before it falls off."

She moved past me, through one of the doorways that was half-covered with a torn curtain. The door was near to where I stood, so I easily manoeuvred myself a step or two nearer.

With a slight turn of my head I could see c'Vira in the other room. I could also see a few more rumpled sleeping pallets and other clutter on the floor. But I was mostly looking at c'Vira, as she kicked off the oversize boots to reveal shapely and extremely dirty feet. Then, with her back to me, she began slowly to pull off her robe. I was riveted as the hem slid slowly upwards, revealing the flowing length of both legs, then the enticing lower roundness of her buttocks. . . .

At that moment the robe stopped rising – and c'Vira, with her most wicked smile, turned her head and looked straight at me.

I was contriving a fairly wicked smile of my own, in return, when her expression changed. Suddenly she looked past me, eyes opening wide as if in astonishment.

I felt a crushing, agonizing impact at the base of my skull, and all light and sense departed.

In time – late in the day, according to the shadows in the room – I swam upwards through waves of pain and awoke. Without feeling any pleasure at the fact. My head was hurting, I felt sick to my stomach and I was goose-pimpled with anxiety down to the soles of my boots. Except, I found, I wasn't wearing boots, or anything else.

I was lying on my back, entirely naked, on one of the filthy pallets in the room where c'Vira had been disrobing. My arms were raised over my head with wrists tied, my ankles were also tied, and both sets of bonds were somehow attached firmly to the floor. In that immobile and vulnerable state, I grew aware that someone was watching me from the doorway.

It was y'Wipo, still with his knowing little smile. "Are you all right? I tried not to hit you too hard."

Lacking a suitable reply, short of blowing his head off if I'd had my blazers, I merely glared.

"You're quite a character, Curb," he said amiably. "You tell lies as well as anyone I've ever known. And I've never seen so many hidden weapons."

His eyes moved as he spoke, and I turned my throbbing head to see my clothes – along with belt, wristbands, headband, the cylinder, everything – lying in a heap across the room. It looked like my clothes, even my boots, had been shredded in the Treffs' search – no doubt warned by c'Vira – for my mini-weapons.

"What's this all about?" I said thickly. It wasn't much of a sally, but I wasn't well.

The little smile widened slightly. "*Mister* Curb, let me make things clear before you say anything that will embarrass you. First, as you should have noted, we have a vid, and a few of us watch things other than action shows and slush films. We watch for information about the galaxy, about new technology, about many things. Which is how I've acquired a fair amount of knowledge about odd matters like containers of Balbazian steel that are opened with uniquely polarized molecular keys."

I suddenly felt cold, and shrank a little.

"In short," y'Wipo went on, "you've been feeding us as much fertilizer as that pile you fell into. I knew it, and c'Vira knew it before anyone – because she says she can always tell when a man is lying to her."

I shrank a little more.

"But still," he went on, "she was right. You *are* a gift. Or you can be."

Wordless, goose-pimpled, I stared at him.

"You see, Curb, this group of Treffs is *special* – unique in the history of the revolution. We've made a breakthrough that could mean *victory* at last." His eyes were bright, as if some real fervour was shining through the cynicism of his smile.

"What could that be?" I said sullenly. "You heard that the God-King is allergic to body odour?"

He actually laughed a little. "No, no. A few years ago, a pregnant harem girl was expelled from the Sanctum with priceless information in her head. She had accidentally stumbled on a *secret way into the Sanctum!*"

"Pardon me if I don't leap up and cheer," I muttered.

He ignored me, and told me what the girl had found. The Sanctum apparently had only one entrance, he said – a well-guarded pair of massive doors. But the builders had also put in a second, very secret entrance – or exit – perhaps as an escape route if the Sanctum was ever besieged. It was located in the food preparation area, where the harem girl had been looking for a snack. By some freakish chance she had accidentally tapped out the right code to open a hatchway that looked like the locked cover of a storage space. But the hatch led into a shaft, like a metal tube or pipe as wide as a man, with another hatch at the far end. Opened to the outside.

Aware that she had stumbled on an important and scary secret, she quickly closed everything up and got out of there. No one noticed, no one ever suspected. And later, after her expulsion, she had told the story to the Treffs.

"We've never found a way to use the route," y'Wipo went on, "because it's too solidly locked to be opened from the outside. We need someone on the *inside*. But all we have is young girls going into the harem – and they're too terrified to be any use."

My head was pounding, I was sick and miserable, but even so I could see where he was heading. I moaned quietly and tried to sink into the pallet.

"But now," y'Wipo said, "we have you. An off-world messenger, who will be welcomed into the Sanctum like a visiting Emissary, because he brings the God-King's miracle drug. For that *is* what's in the cylinder, isn't it, Curb?"

I said nothing, concentrating on shrinking.

"So, when you're in, all you need to do is find the hatch, get rid of any guards that might be near it, and open it for us."

Oh, is that all? I thought sourly. What could be easier? Except I'd probably be burned down if I took one step out of bounds. I recalled all too vividly the data about the God-King's troop of ultra-modern killdroid guards.

But I was in no position to fling a refusal in y'Wipo's face. Forcing aside my pain, fear and nausea, I summoned a reasonable facsimile of a smile.

"I'll gladly do that, y'Wipo," I said with deep sincerity. "You can count on me. I know I told some stories about what I was doing here, but I thought you people would turn against me if you knew the truth."

"You got that right," he said flatly.

"I'm just a courier, paid to do a job," I said, summoning all my charm. "I didn't know anything about Fraxilly, or about what's in the cylinder, until you told me. Now that I know, I'm on your side, against the oppressor. I'll take the cylinder into the Sanctum and do just what you want. Trust me."

Trust me to disappear off this stinking planet as soon as I get my fee, I thought to myself. But my heart sank when I saw his nasty little smile reappear.

"I know," y'Wipo said. "You *will* do what we want. Once I've worked out how to get the leverage that will force you to obey our wishes without betraying us."

"No, listen . . ." I protested. But he ignored me.

"You can be sure, Curb, that I will find it, in time. And we have time. The Treffs have waited for this chance for generations. We can wait a little longer."

And with that he turned away and left the room.

Chapter 16

I lay still after he'd gone, thinking. And listening to the noises outside the room – the mutter and rustle as the Treffs talked and moved around. The shadows lengthened, darkness began to gather, and in a while – which seemed longer because of my uncomfortable position, in every sense – the sounds diminished as the Treffs took themselves to their night's rest. Once two of the young women came in with candles to collect the other pallets from my room. They paused to stare at my anatomy with considerable interest, then scuttled off without a word or a wink.

Later, when night had wrapped me in unnerving blackness, the hulking shape of y'Tylo loomed through the doorway. He was carrying a crude electro-light, and in its gleam I could see him staring at me angrily. But he wheeled and stamped away without a word, so I lay back and went on thinking.

Among other things I thought about the contradictions in the Treffs. They were more aware of life beyond their world than I'd imagined, yet they were still primitive to overlook the value of brains – y'Wipo's – in choosing the large, stupid y'Tylo as their leader. They were also all young enough, I thought gratefully, to believe that what they knew about modern life was all there *was* to know.

So they saw no risk in leaving me unguarded while they slept. I was naked and tightly bound. How could I get away?

In fact, quite easily. So easily that I was in no hurry. I was lying there waiting for all sounds of activity beyond my room to stop. And debating, in the course of my thoughts, whether to put y'Wipo out of action before I slipped away. It made sense, for without him the other Treffs would be so disorganized that I'd be in the Sanctum with my feet up before they could start a search. But it seemed a cold-blooded thing to do. Not to mention risky, if it woke the others.

I was still pondering that and other choices when I became aware that silence had descended beyond my room, save for a few snores. So I started to get into position to free myself.

But I hadn't anticipated one other factor.

A flickering light at the curtained doorway told me I was to have another visitor. Because I half-expected it would be y'Wipo or y'Tylo again, I was a little startled. It was c'Vira, wearing her neatly sewn-up robe, her outsize boots, and her most impish expression.

She stood quietly for a moment, holding a hand-light like y'Tylo's, letting her overheated gaze wander over my body till I imagined that I felt a scorching sensation.

"Mister Del," she said softly at last, "you should just let yourself be a gift."

"I want to, c'Vira," I assured her earnestly. "But y'Wipo won't listen." I gave her a full-wattage sincere smile. "But you know *you* can trust me, don't you, c'Vira? The man who saved your life? If you let me go, I give you my word that I'll go to the SenFed just as I said."

Her giggle was almost manic. "You know, Mister Del," she said throatily, "I've been lying down with men for near as long as I can remember. I'd be lying down in the God-King's harem if my mother hadn't hidden me with the Treffs when I was little. I like men a lot, Mister Del. I like you. But I can always tell, never fail, when a man's lying *to* me instead of just lying *with* me."

"But, c'Vira . . ." I gulped.

"Hush now," she said. "I've had enough of the one kind of lying. Time for a bit of the other."

And she kicked her boots off, crossed her arms in front of her as she had done before, and began to pull up her robe.

Again it rose slowly and teasingly. But this time she was facing me, and the literal disrobing left no doubt about how

146

misleadingly shapeless the brown garment made her look. Her body was flawless – full-breasted, slender-waisted, richly rounded at hip and thigh, with the taut firmness of healthy youth. I thought briefly of how glorious she would be if she could strip off the dirt as readily as the robe. For even though my sense of smell had mostly been stunned by the overdose of stinks in that place, the reek of c'Vira's nude body reached out and shocked it back to life.

She tossed the robe aside, next to my ruined clothes, and grinned. "You glad now we took your clothes off? That y'Tylo kept talking about how you only have little weapons . . . But I told him, little ones shoot just as well."

She walked sinuously towards me, knelt on the pallet, trailed a hand over my stomach. "My, my, Mister Del," she murmured. "Even being hit on the head and tied up and everything, you can't keep a good man down. You know?"

My voice creaked as if it needed lubrication. "Untie my hands, c'Vira. . . ."

She chuckled as she shifted position. "For what I've got in mind, Mister, you don't need hands."

Then her arms and her odour wrapped themselves around me, and I was lost, overpowered, engulfed.

It was an hour or two before I came back to myself, out of a sleep so heavy that it was almost as if I'd been hit on the head again. But this time my headache and nausea were gone – c'Vira having provided one of the better cures for such ailments. Even so, I felt full of aches and pains, as if I'd been in hand-to-hand combat with a wild beast. Which in a way I had.

I could only guess at the time, but it was still deep night. On the floor beside the pallet, the small electro-light flickered, pushing away the darkness. Next to me, c'Vira lay pungently sprawled on her back, in the deep slumber of the young animal whose hungers have been temporarily sated. I gazed at her awhile, enjoying her lush beauty but feeling no pangs about leaving her. I wasn't sure I could survive any more of her inventive demands.

Then I set about the simple business of freeing myself.

Though they had taken my clothes, they would have had to skin me and perform some amputations to remove *all* my little aids to survival. A cautious man tries to plan against every possibility – including the chance that he might not always be fully clothed. So it took me only seconds to twist my hands around, extrude the tiny, thread-like vibro-blade implanted in the nail of my little finger, and get to work.

I winced as I did so, for the blade's operation sends shooting pains through the tendons of my hand – some imperfection in the implant that I must get fixed when I have time. Also, the blade whines, like a persistent insect. But pain and noise lasted only briefly, for the hyper-vibrations slice through most materials effortlessly. As they did with my ropes.

Two or three instants later, I was on my feet, rummaging through the ragged remnants of my things. My clothes and boots were in fragments, my belt and headband and wristbands were ripped open and empty, my jewellery and accessories were missing. Except, I saw with gratitude, my pendant. Obviously y'Wipo had seen that it wasn't a weapon – and it was a sign of his overconfidence that he hadn't taken it anyway. Just as it was a sign of his intentions that they'd also left the cylinder. Ready for me to use to get into the Sanctum and do their bidding.

But the revolution will have to do without Del Curb, I thought cheerfully.

Behind me, on the pallet, c'Vira shifted position with a small murmuring sound. I turned quickly, but her breathing showed that she was still deeply asleep. For a moment I looked down again at her revealing sprawl, knowing that I would not forget my night with her for a long time. If only because I felt it would take a long time to rid myself of the stink of her. Then I reminded myself to hurry, before another Treff came to look at me.

I dragged c'Vira's robe over my head – holding my breath when the foul cloth covered my face – and slid my feet into her outsize boots. Then I put the pendant around my neck, picked up the hand-light that c'Vira had brought, and fled.

None of the grunting, snoring Treffs stirred as I tiptoed through the main area. Retracing the route that c'Vira had led me through before, quaking again within that unsafe tunnel, I finally reached the outside. The night was warm, the sky was clear, a moon with two coronas added its brightness to my hand-light. I moved away at speed.

The clumsy boots and the rubble underfoot made my movements a little less stealthy than I would have liked. After some minutes I heard the faint scrabble of claws that warned me I had company. But I kept well away from any shadowed areas, and the rats that trailed me didn't seem inclined to come out into the brightness of the hand-light. So, escorted but not yet threatened, I stumbled on through the Fraxillian night.

Eventually, after about two hours and a good number of kilometres, I found what I needed – a big open space clear of buildings. I stood in the middle, well away from rat hiding-places, and called the ship.

Mala had obviously been asleep, and seemed more annoyed than concerned. "You haven't even got to the *Sanctum* yet?" she asked witheringly, after I'd barely got a sentence out.

"Mala," I said through clenched teeth, "since I landed I've been assaulted, I've been taken captive, I've been . . . uh. . . ." I paused, changing tack. "I've been able to escape, and now I need you to get me *out* of here. At once."

"Tractor beam's still disrupted," she said laconically.

"Then I want Posi to *land* the ship," I snarled. "Right here. Right now."

"In that city?" Mala said, surprised. "We still have ceptor problems, in case you've forgotten. If we waver on the descent path, we could do a lot of damage."

"Listen!" I yelled. "This place is ruined, deserted, dead! You can level the whole blistering thing if you want! Just get *down here!*"

"All right," she said, yawning. "Keep your hair on. Posi has got a fix on you, so back off and we'll come down."

I bit off another snarl, realizing that if Posi's descent did waver, there *was* something on the ground that could be damaged. Me. So I backed off. That was a little worrying, for there were lots of ominous shadows at the edge of the clearing. But before any rats could creep up on me, I heard the distant thunder, rapidly becoming not too distant, and saw the growing point of light falling towards me. Presumably the rats saw and heard it too, and vacated the area.

Soon the ship's great semi-ovoid was clearly visible, gleaming softly in the moonlight, thundering like a thousand new volcanoes. I smiled to myself, thinking of the Treffs waking to that noise, finding me gone with the cylinder, realizing I was too far away to be caught. . . .

Then I stopped smiling and ran for my life. The ship *was* wavering, drifting to one side almost as if aiming at me. But at the last minute Posi regained control, as something in the system phased back in again. The ship settled in a cloud of dust only a few hundred metres from where it should have touched down.

Coughing because I wouldn't wait for the dust to settle, I ran towards the looming shape. When I came up to it, Mala had extended the ladderamp and was standing halfway down it, staring at me. Then she began to laugh, the sort of helpless giggles that infuriate me more than anything else, when they're aimed at me.

"Look at you!" she gurgled. "What the well-dressed Fraxillian is wearing this season . . . With the glimpse of hairy leg adding that extra touch of elegance!"

I glanced down, speechless with anger. All right, c'Vira's robe was calf-length, so a bit of bare leg showed above the clumsy boots. But I would have thought my appearance was a cause for sympathy, not hilarity. Though when I furiously said so, Mala's giggling redoubled.

"Stop it!" I shouted, moving towards the ramp. "All you can do is laugh? When I've just barely managed to esape from maniacs who would probably like to *kill* me?"

And then I went very stiff and silent, when a dry voice spoke from the darkness beyond the clearing. "You got that right."

I recognized the voice and the expression. I could almost see y'Wipo's smug little smile. Then I heard another familiar voice, and visualized another smile, when a second voice spoke from the darkness.

"Didn't know you had a *girl* on your ship, Mister Del. Maybe

150

you ought to give me back my robe, in case she's the jealous type."

I've been set up, I thought dumbly, as the laughter of the Treffs rang out from what seemed to be a wide semi-circle around the clear area. And I was too shocked even to enjoy the fact that Mala's giggles had been sharply silenced, replaced by paleness and tension.

"What *is* this?" she hissed at me.

"It's what I said," I growled, "if you'd been listening. These are local rebels. They know about me, and the cylinder, and they captured me to try to force me into helping them."

"Trust you," Mala said bitterly, "to stumble into trouble."

Then, without warning, she whirled and leaped for the airlock at the top of the ramp. But she halted just as quickly. A projectile gun banged from the darkness and the bullet ricocheted from the ramp just in front of her. As it whined angrily away, from the other direction a crimson bolt from a therm-gun also bit into the ramp, melting a gram or two of the metal.

"You and the lady stand very still, Curb," y'Wipo's voice said. "If either of you moves, we shoot the lady."

Silence fell, and with it a vicious glare from Mala fell on me. Ignoring it, I let my head droop forward, chin on chest, and folded my arms across my chest, letting one finger stray across my pendant. "Posi," I said in an intense whisper, directed downwards. "There are people surrounding the ship. Swing the guns around and blast them."

"I cannot obey, Del." Posi's voice sounded reproachful. "You know that the primal constraint forbids it. I can use the weapons only in defence of the ship."

"Posi," I hissed, "they're trying to *kill* me!"

"If they fire upon the ship," she said, "I can return fire. But they are not doing so."

"Couldn't you just *hurt* them a little?" I pleaded.

But it was too late. The Treffs were advancing into the clearing, weapons aimed at us, looking determined and capable. I glanced at c'Vira and her pistol, thinking not so much of her beauty – now hidden under another dirty robe – as of her cool marksmanship when she'd faced the rats. I saw

hulking y'Tylo with his therm-gun that didn't waver a millimetre as he strode towards us – not even when he surveyed
Mala and grinned. I turned away from the brightness in her
eyes as she inspected him, and noticed that y'Wipo was
carrying a pathetic little short-range stun-gun. But there was
nothing pathetic about the sharp awareness in his eyes, or
about his knowing smile.

With great distaste, I confronted the fact that I had been
outsmarted by a group of smelly, back-sector kids. The whole
thing had been set up, including my pendant and the cylinder
being left in my room, even the light that c'Vira had brought.
I thought sourly that she probably would have pretended to let
me talk her into untying me, if I hadn't freed myself. But I
didn't want to think very much about the special part she'd
played in my carefully engineered escape.

They had correctly guessed that my ship wasn't totally
disabled – probably thanks to c'Vira's uncanny, built-in lie
detector – and they'd guessed that I'd call it down. If the
tractor beam had been working they would have stopped me
before the pick-up – but they hadn't needed to. They'd been
ahead of me all along, and it had worked out just as they
planned.

I recalled y'Wipo saying that he would work out a way to
get leverage on me. It hadn't taken him long. And he didn't
take long to confirm it.

"Come away from the ship, Curb," he said as he walked
towards me, into the light. "With the lady. And let me explain
to you how it is – and why it is – that you're going to help the
Treffs win the revolution."

Chapter 17

I stood listening, in a gloom bordering on clinical depression, while the Treffs committed me to a project as pointless, life-threatening and strategically absurd as any of the wars of the Manic Age before the 21st century.

I was being guarded by several armed Treffs, including the glowering y'Tylo with his therm-gun. Some distance away, Mala was wearing ancient but effective metal manacles and was being guarded by other Treffs, c'Vira among them. With her wicked grin she was murmuring things to Mala, and I could guess what those things concerned – for Mala was staring at me with an expression that mingled startled amazement with wild laughter. I didn't see why she should want to conspire with the enemy in trying to ridicule me, so I turned coldly away and went on listening, as well as watching the activity around the ship.

Yet more Treffs were busily fixing small magnetized packets to the ship's underside, along its whole length. The packets were linked by hair-thin wiring that adhered almost invisibly to the hull. It was dated technology, but fairly sophisticated for the Treffs. And y'Wipo clearly thought so, too. He was telling me at some length how generations of Treffs had laboriously acquired, or created, their pathetic arsenal. He was also explaining in detail what they were doing to my ship.

It was a very basic linked series of hand-made limpet bombs that could be detonated by remote control. And that would then reduce every part of my ship, and Posi, to scrap metal.

Those bombs, and the guns at Mala's head, formed my commitment. They were supposed to control me and direct me as thoroughly as one of the old Hypno-lobe implants. The fact that they would probably direct me to my death seemed of little interest to anyone but me.

"In short," said y'Wipo, winding up his discourse, "if you betray us to anyone in the Sanctum, we destroy your ship and shoot your girlfriend. Think about it."

I thought about it, rapidly. The fee for delivering the phetam would buy me a new ship, but I'd have to get at least two jobs that paid as well before I could also replace Posi. As for Mala ... I glanced over at her, and saw that she and c'Vira were nearly helpless with laughter, tears streaming down their faces. They saw me look at them, and the laughter soared away to new heights.

Maybe, I thought grimly, I could do without Mala.

"Remember, Curb," y'Wipo added, "without a ship you'd have to buy your passage off Fraxilly on an official ship. And the God-King enjoys charging thousands of kilocreds for places on his ships. Though you could always stay. Maybe get a job as a godly or a royal. For life."

That chilled me to the marrow. Was my choice going to be either leave Fraxilly penniless or not leave at all? Every other consideration faded. I'd rather face all the God-King's kill-droids, I thought hopelessly, than be marooned forever amid the stink and misery of that world. Or than risk returning to civilization with no ship, no creds, no prospects. . . .

"There's nothing to be afraid of," y'Wipo was saying. "You'll be a welcome visitor to the Sanctum. Everyone will treat you like a lord. And after you open the secret entrance and let us in, you can leave the Sanctum the same way, and be free to go."

"I'm not *afraid*," I said stiffly. "I'm ... thinking about it, looking for flaws in your plan."

"Nothin' wrong with the plan," y'Tylo rumbled. "Nobody does better plans 'n y'Wipo."

The little Treff grinned, then reduced the grin to his usual knowing smile. "You have only one real choice, Curb. So choose."

"All *right!*" I snapped. "I'll do it! But I'll be running enormous risks inside the Sanctum, and I won't be hurrying. So don't get too hasty with those bombs!"

"We will give you a full Fraxillian day," y'Wipo said, "from the moment you pass through the Sanctum doors. That should be plenty of time for a man of your . . . initiative."

I glared at him, but there were no arguments that I could use against him. "I'm not going like *this*," I snarled, gesturing at the filthy robe that I was still wearing.

"You don't care for our revolutionary uniform?" y'Wipo said mockingly. "But of course not. We would hardly send you to the Sanctum wearing a Treff robe. Go into your ship and make yourself ready, however you like. *Except* – you can leave all your little weapons behind."

I heard c'Vira's voice call out something about one of my little weapons being attached. She was obviously referring to the vibro-blade in my fingernail – but the remark brought an eruption of crude laughter from all the others.

"And take your time," y'Wipo went on. "We needn't reach the Sanctum till mid-morning – which gives us hours to travel a short distance."

Not enough hours, I thought wretchedly as I clumped up the ladderamp. Still, I was at least being allowed to get rid of those ill-fitting boots, the smelly robe and all the layers of dust and stink. But I wasn't allowed to go in alone, for Mala had been sent with me, to exchange her light slippers for footwear that could stand up to a walk through a wasteland.

"What an interesting person, your fragrant Fraxillian girl-friend," she said with heavy mockery as we went through the airlock.

I scowled at her, disdaining to reply, moving away towards my cabin.

"And such amazing things she talked about," Mala added, laughter audible behind her voice. "What weird quirks you have, Curb. With your hands tied, too. . . ."

"Just *forget* it!" I shouted, whirling on her. "You shouldn't believe everything some smelly nymphomaniac says! What you should be thinking about is that we're both likely to get killed!"

155

Obviously, among her other confidences, c'Vira had filled Mala in on the Treff plan. "Don't be stupid," she said crisply. "No one wants to kill us. If you do what you're supposed to do, we'll be fine."

"You mean open a secret entrance for these lunatic revolutionaries, with about a hundred killdroids watching me?"

Her mouth twisted. "You're pathetic. The Treffs should keep you and let *me* go. They probably would if the God-King wasn't expecting *you* to make the delivery." She took a deep breath. "Listen. You're the man bringing the God-King's phetam. You'll be the most important visitor for years. No one is going to question you if you wander around the Sanctum a little. Pretend you're admiring the architecture or something. Then open the entrance, slip out through it and come back here. It's simple."

I glowered and stalked away, wishing that they *were* sending her into the Sanctum instead of me. Inwardly I cringed, thinking of all the mockery and sarcasm to come from her in the weeks ahead, until she grew tired of dragging up c'Vira's revelations.

In my cabin, I recalled y'Wipo saying that I could take my time, so I made the most of it. I had a full Omnipure combined sauna and power-spray shower with Instadri at the maximum heat I could stand. I used nearly my whole store of cleansers and conditioners and deodorants. And still, when I was done, I felt that I could detect the odour of c'Vira. (Her robe and boots had gone straight into the disposal.) But a few more dashes of personal fragrance seemed to improve things, as did my ultimate choice of costume.

It was one of my newest, worn only once, to the funeral of someone whose widow I'd hoped to impress. A high-necked tunic with discreetly padded shoulders, skin-tight leggings with codpiece and equally subtle padding for thigh and calf, low boots with furled uppers, and a short cape that swept handsomely over one shoulder. I'd chosen it because I wanted to convince everyone in the Sanctum that my purpose was noble and my heart was pure – and nothing exuded nobility and purity more than the exalting sky-blue of those garments. With a strawberry stripe down the legs, echoed in the trim of collar and cape. As a contrast, I chose an understated ultramarine for the usual accessories – while feeling a renewed stab of misery at having no weapons in headband, belt and so on. I also regretted having to leave my jewellery behind – though I did wear the pendant, since it wasn't a weapon.

Then finally, reluctantly, I had to admit that I was ready. I swung the carry-net with the cylinder over a shoulder – not the one with the cape – and strode out of the ship. On the ladderamp outside, I paused for a moment to stare coldly down at the assembled Treffs – and Mala, still manacled, freshly booted, with c'Vira again.

"You took long enough," y'Wipo complained as I strode down the ramp.

"Then let's get going," I said brusquely, before wheeling and stalking away. The effect was diminished a little when y'Wipo pointed out that I was going in the wrong direction. But then we all sorted ourselves out, and set off.

It was not an enjoyable journey. The sun rose not too long after our departure, and the morning became hot quite quickly. And I was travelling in the midst of some sixty odorous youths. At least they weren't crowding me – probably because they knew about the vibro-blade – and they spoke only seldom. But they stank.

And dust from the ruined city's rubble swirled around us in a choking cloud, making it even less enjoyable to breathe. Nor did the dust, or heat, or stink, grow less when we finally left the city. We entered what looked like a bleak and empty desert, with only rare patches of the scraggy weeds and no sign at all of the primitive Fraxillian agriculture. I guessed that when the plague drove the people out of the city they had all gone to settle on the *far* side – not the side nearest the God-King's Sanctum. That revealed a little more about the relationship between ruler and ruled on Fraxilly.

Eventually, when everyone's senses were dulled and energies dropping, we came to a halt at the foot of a stony ridge, which sloped steeply up for several metres to a ragged crest. One of the Treffs scrambled up, very carefully peered over, then grinned and nodded down at us.

Little y'Wipo seemed more weary than any of us, after that

157

trek, but his eyes remained clear and watchful. "Over the ridge," he told me, "you'll see the Sanctum's spaceport on the right, and the Sanctum itself in the distance. There shouldn't be many guards in the port buildings, so if you stay on its edge you should get to the Sanctum unchallenged. We'll circle around to the far side of the Sanctum, to where the secret entrance opens." His gaze grew more intense. "Remember your ship and the girl, Curb. Don't let us down."

I looked at Mala, who pushed her hair back from her sweaty forehead and stared expressionlessly at me. So did all the Treffs, except c'Vira, who gave me her impish grin and a wink.

"I'll do my part, friend," I told y'Wipo in a voice made husky by dryness and dust. "You make sure you do yours."

It was a line I remembered from one of the great old vidfilms about the Wars of the Rim, starring everyone's favorite hero-actor, M. M. Morrison. The Treffs clearly hadn't seen it, for they all looked startled and slightly impressed. Mala, of course, just grimaced.

Then, with dignity and care, I made my way alone to the top of the ridge.

Shortly I was moving with some wariness past the expanse of the God-King's spaceport. It was huge, larger than some on major trading worlds – another monument to mindless ostentation. And it was empty, except for a couple of small passenger pods and what looked like a strato-shuttle partly disembowelled outside one of the port buildings. That building had to be some kind of mecho-lab or repair centre, and I watched it carefully for signs of life, human or artificial. But no one seemed to be at work on the port that day. And if there were any killdroids or royals on guard, they weren't watching the perimeter.

Nonetheless, my nerves twitched all the way past the port. And I grew even more edgy as I approached the side of the Divine Sanctum. Looming over me, its immensity looked like a gigantic, slightly flattened globe, which was supported about two metres from the ground on several faintly fizzing energy-field pillars. The outer shell of the building was smooth, pure white, and more glassy or ceramic than metallic. The surface would have been entirely blank, featureless, if it hadn't been for the graffiti.

Some were raggedly painted, some were burnt on even more raggedly, while attempts had been made here and there to wash or scrape them away. The surviving bits were mostly misspelled innuendo about the God-King's ancestry, or suggestions about what depravities he should perform on his own person. Typical of the Treffs in every way. One or two of the more graphic suggestions, in fact, made me wonder if c'Vira had been their author. And scattered among those items was a repeated slogan – "Killdroid Was Here" – which made no sense to me at all.

Then I rounded the structure, from the side to the front, and saw a glowing ramp leading up to two giant, glistening-metal doors. And killdroids definitely *were* there.

They look fairly human, though buyers can ask for superficial variants. These were big and bulky, in not-too-glamorous green uniforms. And naturally no visible weapons. Killdroids have built-in armaments – a blazer bolt in one index finger, a para-laser in the other. Psychologically it's effective, that they can kill by pointing an accusing finger. They're also heavily armoured and shielded under the uniforms, and immensely quick, strong and deadly with their bare hands.

So of course they're painfully expensive, for these reasons and one other. Because they are able to bypass the primal constraint imposed on artificial intelligences – against killing real people – they have to be counter-psyched with every available form of cut-off, fail-safe, check and balance. To keep them from killing everything, at random, during a malfunction. So one top-quality killdroid is worth as much as, say, a four-cabin infra-system shuttle. Yet the God-King, preferring to entrust his security to such incorruptible mechanisms, had more than a hundred of them on guard in the Sanctum.

And I was looking at four of them.

Aside from their battle reflexes, killdroids are designed to respond to stimuli like cops always have, everywhere. That is, to be stolid, humourless, reactionary – and above all, darkly suspicious of any kind of behaviour that doesn't fall within their own impossibly narrow view of normality. The four guarding the great metal doors were no exception. I was an off-world stranger who was *walking* out of the wasteland towards the Sanctum. It's a miracle that they didn't dismember me on sight.

But they did cluster around me at once as I came up the ramp, pinning me to the wall next the doors, demanding to know who I was, where I'd come from, where my ship was, and where I thought I was going.

When I explained that my purpose there was to deliver a valuable article to the God-King, they nodded grimly. As if to say that while it wasn't the most inventive lie they'd ever heard, it was passable enough for a moment's interest. I brandished the cylinder, and they took it away from me. I grew agitated, and one clamped a hand under my jaw and nearly lifted me off my feet. Then they searched me, seriously disarraying my clothes, before pointing their lethal index fingers at me and saying that I was under arrest as a suspected thief and/or assassin.

"Just take me to someone in *charge*," I pleaded. "They're expecting me. The God-King's expecting me."

One of them laughed mirthlessly. "The God-King is always expecting you – or some kind of killer like you. Several have tried to reach him in the past, to their cost."

"After the trial," another of them said, "the God-King will want to break your bones himself before you are nailed to the outer wall. It is a special honour, reserved for would-be assassins."

"But I'm *not* . . .!" I howled.

As if my cry had angered them, two of the killdroids abruptly seized me again, while the others stood back with fingers aimed. I was lifted so that my feet dangled, and propelled towards the tall metal doors, which began slowly to open – on to darkness, like the entrance to a tomb.

Chapter 18

It wasn't really dark, beyond the doors. It just seemed so, compared to the mid-morning glare outside. I might have enjoyed the gentler light, the coolness, the flowery fragrance carried on the air. I might have been impressed by the arch and sweep of the entrance hall around me – the domed ceiling, the gleaming mosaic floor, the profusion of works of art, the graceful ramps and balustrades, the many symmetrically placed doorways with decorated surrounds ... Well, I *was* impressed, later. But right then I was focused mainly on rough killdroid hands clutching me, and muzzle openings on killdroid forefingers seeming to enlarge, hypnotically.

Then there was a squeal – it's the only word – of outrage, followed by the four most gratifying words I'd heard since I landed on Fraxilly.

"*Stop* that at *once!*"

The speaker, or squealer, was descending from a personal floater, richly cushioned, that had silently entered the hall, attended by athletic-looking young male servants – perhaps mandroids, I wasn't sure – in light tunics. The floater's occupant was a small round person with a small round hairless head jutting from a fluttering froth of light robes in a variety of colours. On a taller, graceful figure in repose, the inter-leaved drapery of the robes might have been attractive. On this chubby person scuttling towards me with very short steps, the effect was comical. But I was too busy fighting back tears of gratitude to see the humour.

"That is Mister *Curb*!" the person squeaked at the killdroids. "An honoured visitor whom His Mightiness has been *expecting*! Your whole troop has been *instructed*!"

The killdroids had released me at the instant of the first squeal. They now stood unmoving, their faces wearing that distant blankness of the cop who is being reprimanded by someone he must obey but does not respect.

"He has no ship, lord," one said.

"He walked, lord," another said.

"He's all alone, lord."

"He had this, lord. Could be explosive."

"This" was the cylinder, which the small round person snatched with a shrill cry that was almost ecstatic. Then he whirled back to me, robes flapping.

"I can never apologize *enough*, Mister Curb. Though I came as swiftly as I *could*, after being alerted that a stranger had. . . ." He halted, as if he had suddenly taken in what the killdroids had said. "Mister Curb? You *walked*?" And his little eyes widened as he finally noticed my sweaty, dusty, dishevelled condition.

I started to gabble my prepared explanation about disrupted ceptors on my ship, having to land some distance away so as not to risk damaging the Sanctum. But he stopped me before I was fully through it, with squeaks and moans and flutters of over-acted sympathy.

"How *terrible*! Out in all that *dirt*! Come with me at once, we shall slake your thirst and provide cleansing and tend your *every* need!" The last phrase was accompanied by an arch little smirk that oddly reminded me of something I couldn't quite place.

After dismissing the killdroids with much flapping of robes and wrists – "Back to your posts, begone!" – he bustled to the floater, drawing me with him by the arm. On that silent, hovering conveyance we swept through a high-arched doorway, through a series of interconnecting areas and passages, and finally into a small antechamber set to one side of a larger space like a reception area. The antechamber was round as a globe, with the same translucently glassy walls and ceiling as the other rooms and halls, and held a scattering of rich furnishings. While the floater and its young attendants waited outside, my guide ushered me to a pale soft sofa where the cushions moulded themselves to my shape and began delicately to rub my back. From a nearby table poised on an energy-field pedestal he produced a large beaker, beaded with its contents' coldness, of what proved to be Cratifarin fogapple juice, as gently cooling and invigorating a stimulant as you would wish for. I drained every drop without pausing, while my tormented throat sobbed with relief.

Meanwhile, the little fellow in the robes sat himself beside me and decided to improve my appearance, by rather ineptly dabbing with a chubby hand at the dust on my leggings. On my upper thigh, to be exact. With that, the nagging feeling of familiarity congealed into memory.

"Are you," I asked, trying to shift myself away despite the fondly massaging clasp of the cushions, "related in any way to the Emissary, y'Fiprehaude?"

The chubby hand stopped dabbing, and its owner did a great thresh of robes as he emitted a high trill of squeaks that was probably laughter. "Oh, how entirely *thought*less of me!" he squeaked. "Not to introduce myself! And how perceptive of you, to see the family resemblance!" The hand returned to my leg. "I am the Emissary's elder brother – y'Bagnehaude is my name. I have the joy and honour to be the Most Sacred Body-Servant of His Immensity the God-King."

I blinked, and stared. Some of my awareness registered that I was in the presence of the person who was supposed to receive the cylinder. But mostly my mind had fixed on one word.

"*Elder* brother?"

That produced another glissando of squeals. "Yes, in*deed*! In my position one's appearance counts for so *much* – and His Superlativeness has in his goodness recently provided me with a full Rejuve Programme by some simply *marvellous* Guáfák-kán technicians, in their own laboratories." The fat hand tightened insistently on my knee. "I feel they have quite *restored* me, don't you agree?"

I stared again at his shiny fat face, which resembled that of a hyperthyroid fourteen-year-old eunuch. Then the word "restored" showed me a useful diversion.

"Presumably the God-King," I said innocently, "is himself never in need of things like a Rejuve."

The hand drew back from my leg as if scalded, and y'Bagnehaude's little eyes flickered to the cylinder lying on the sofa next to him.

"No, no," he said uneasily. "His Toweringness requires no such aids to godliness. . . ."

Then his gaze swung suspiciously back to me again. I had no doubt that his brother the Emissary would have reported my guess about the phetam in the cylinder, which had made me impose the surcharge. So y'Bagnehaude was clearly wondering what was coming next. But when I smiled disarmingly, he became chubbily jolly again.

"Now, my dear Del – I hope you will allow? – we should attend to business before . . . anything else." His gaze strayed down to the vicinity of my leggings, then back to my face.

I nodded encouragingly. "Business, of course. There is the . . . cylinder, safely delivered. Which raises the matter of the fee."

I had nearly said "there is the phetam" and y'Bagnehaude was sharp enough to note the hesitation. He went silent, watching me – perhaps waiting for me to make some further demands. But that would have been a mistake. You don't try to pressure someone when you're sitting in their palace surrounded by their killdroids. So I also remained silent, trying to look guileless. And he eventually exchanged his thoughtful expression for a small smile and a nod, seeming to say that while I was obviously no more trustworthy than anyone, it was good of me not to be more greedy.

Suddenly then he was all efficiency, in a storm of robe-swirling. Clutching the cylinder, he touched something on the table that summoned a servant – like the floater attendants, a well-built youth in a skimpy tunic. With a proud leer, y'Bagnehaude told me that all the Sanctum servants were the latest state-of-the-art serviloid. Which, I knew, were far costlier than the non-humanized servatons that most wealthy people own. And, y'Bagnehaude added proudly but unnecessarily, he himself had chosen the design of his *personal* attendants.

The boyish serviloid was directed to guide me at once to

some guest quarters, and to take my clothes for cleaning while I prepared myself. For, it seemed, I was to be presented to the God-King – in his private chamber, called the Personal Haven – later that day. Or, y'Bagnehaude said with a faintly unsure flutter, maybe the next day.

That gave me a troubling mental picture of Mala, my ship and the Treffs. I knew that I would soon have to make some kind of move. But another important item had to come even before that.

"It will be a great honour," I said, as enthusiastically as I could. "But forgive me for raising again, lord, the matter of the *fee*."

He produced another trill of squeals. "What an *effect* you have, dear Del, that I should forget such matters! I have of course made your fee ready in the holding facility of your bank. To be released to your account as soon as you return to your ship and make the necessary confirming call."

"To my ship," I echoed resignedly.

"Indeed." He held up one of the plastiform wafers that recorded such transactions. "Here is the certification."

I took the wafer and checked it, but I knew it was all there. The God-King and y'Bagnehaude would have no interest in cheating me – not with what I knew, or guessed, about the cylinder. At the same time, they were sensibly making sure that I would be staying around the Sanctum, to be "presented", until they'd checked the cylinder's contents.

"So you need be concerned no longer, dear Del," y'Bagnehaude went on. "Go now and refresh yourself, relax, indulge in whatever enjoyments appeal to you." He produced his arch smile. "But do not *over*-indulge, dear boy. For I hope you might spend some time with *me* before you leave."

I assured him that such a prospect filled me with expectancy, while privately wondering if I couldn't find a way to strangle him before making my getaway. If I could get away.

Then I walked off – y'Bagnehaude kept the floater – in the wake of the silent serviloid, into the bowels of the Sanctum.

*

As the serviloid led me from the antechamber back into the series of interconnecting passages and chambers, with doorways on every side indicating more interconnections, I suddenly realized what the building was, within its massive outer shell. Each separate area had curved walls and ceiling, with no angles, like an oversized tube or globe. And they were all made of that glassy, translucent material that allowed in a diffuse, lambent light. Those were the main elements of the architectural style first popularized in the bureaucracies of SenFed Central and commonly called Maze-web.

Every tube-like passage or spherical chamber in the Maze-web led to more and more intersections, more branching corridors, more chambers or clusters of chambers, along with ramps or stairways or hyperlifts to other levels. Seen from above, I'd heard, the effect could be very beautiful, like the magical web-weavings of the Mivtakean sea-spider. But I'd never seen it. The necessary glassteel, and the demands of the shaping, made Maze-web buildings almost impossibly expensive even for the more spendthrift planetillionaires. And SenFed Central had abandoned the style and demolished the buildings – because it was easier to find your way around a four-dimensional labyrinth designed by a lunatic.

My heart began to sink. I suppose I'd anticipated some sort of overstuffed mansion or castle, with clear indications of where a food preparation area would be located. But in the Maze-web, with all its linkings and branchings and crossings, I'd be lost in seconds. For a moment I thought of asking my serviloid guide for directions. But he had been told to take me to guest quarters, not a food preparation area. He might ask some official, even y'Bagnehaude himself, for permission to change the route. No, I thought, I was on my own.

Which meant I had failed before I'd started.

As that bleak thought began to build tensions within me, the journey came to an end. By then I was entirely lost, as I'd expected to be, though at least I knew that we'd moved up a couple of levels, and some distance towards the heart of the Sanctum. We walked finally into another sort of antechamber, with tables and cabinets, and then into a huge globe-chamber beyond it. The chamber was clearly some kind of lavish recreation room – and its contents showed that, in the Sanctum, your recreations weren't expected to be spiritual or contemplative.

Food enough for thirty people, hot and cold, sweet and spicy, from more than a dozen worlds that I could identify, lay heaped on groaning tables. Containers of drink – from delicate fruit-wines to a smoking flagon of the Rale-byssan liquor called Skinpeeler – crowded more tables. Other serviloids stood by, ready to offer helpings.

And the lush sofas and divans were crowded as well – with minimally clad persons of various genders, ages, sizes and shapes, all smiling hopefully. They had with them a variety of objects – assortments of drugs, vials of unguents, collections of implements. For the jaded pervert who has had everything. They were even accompanied by two well-fed examples of the small, pot-bellied native beasts that I'd seen on the wasteland. I didn't let myself think what their function might be.

"Your guest quarters, sir," murmured my serviloid guide.

Perhaps it was the shock of what had been provided for me – catering to *any*one's every need – but something just then galvanized my thought processes. A solution to my problem leaped fully formed into my mind.

"No!" I said sharply. The word stopped the serviloid in his tracks. "I want this chamber cleared, at once. I want to be *alone*, to rest and ... and to prepare myself to meet His Overpoweringness."

"As you wish, sir," the serviloid replied, and gestured to the underdressed throng. One thing about the God-King and his life-style, he knew how to keep people in their places. There were a few pouts and grimaces, but all of the throng leaped up at once and filed out. I felt a twinge of regret as I studied one or two of the pertly rounded young girls among them. But such matters as life and death took precedence just then.

I ordered out the other serviloids as well, then sent my guide away with my outer garments, for cleaning. Because y'Bagnehaude might be keeping some sort of watch on me, I wanted to behave as expected. For the same reason I had a quick sluice-down in a fricti-rinse shower that I found in the adjoining bedchamber, and emerged to pour myself a snifter of vintage blister-water from Pyrylllyp. By then the serviloid had brought back my sky-blue outfit, as good as new.

Dressed again, I lounged on another of the back-massaging sofas, nibbling at a pastry, drink in hand – the very picture, in case anyone was looking, of a man who had completed a difficult task and was awaiting an audience with a grateful divinity.

In fact the little wafer confirming my fee – tucked safely inside my tunic – was all the gratitude I wanted. And being left alone for that time was all the chance I needed.

If I was going to get to the food preparation area, find the secret entrance, and make my way out of the Sanctum and out of trouble, I had to get going.

Chapter 19

I toyed idly with my pendant, kept my face blank, and called Posi with minimal lip movement.

"Do you have any ceptors working," I asked her, "to get a fix on my position?"

"Certainly, Del," she said cheerfully. "Several perceptors are in phase."

"Good. Can you tell if my immediate area is bugged in any way?"

There was an infinitesimal pause. "My perceptors can locate no spy devices in your area. But there is a mandroid very near to you who seems to be in a listening mode."

She had barely uttered the last word when the serviloid appeared silently. "Did you speak, sir?"

"Speak?" I said, trying to sound surprised. "No, I was ... I was singing."

"Singing, sir." He managed to inject a wealth of doubt into those two impassive words.

"Yes. I always do, when I feel happy." I smiled brightly at him, and hummed a bar or two of the theme from a popular galacvid game show.

"Very good, sir," he said, still with an edge of dubiousness, and withdrew.

"Posi!" I hissed. "I want you to access that serviloid's memory bank for the location of the food preparation area in this building!"

Another tiny pause, which seemed to last an age, while Posi set up her call-beam connection with the serviloid's circuitry.

"I have it, Del," she said, with a touch of smugness.

"Good. Keep your fix on me and guide me to it. But first, shut off the serviloid."

"Del!" Posi sounded shocked.

"I don't mean *kill* him," I said exasperatedly. "Shut him down for a little while, so that ... ah ... so I can make an adjustment to his programme."

Posi still seemed reluctant, but finally she did as I asked. It's quite simple for a high-powered Intelloid with a call-beam facility to manipulate simpler mechanisms. A lot like some human relationships, I always say. In an instant it was done, and my way was clear.

Then I had another thought. "Posi, within this structure there are a number of killdroids. Can you shut them down too?"

"Are you making adjustments to all of their programming?" Posi asked innocently.

"No," I said through clenched teeth, "I simply don't want them shooting me by accident on the way to the food preparation area."

"I am sorry, Del," Posi said, not sounding very sorry, "but killdroids have built-in barriers against interference, and can only be shut down by means of a coded instruction. The code is chosen at random and personalized to the owner."

Oh, well, I thought, it was just an idea. Anyway, if I did meet killdroids, it was no longer likely that they'd shoot first and interrogate later. Not now that I was to be presented to the God-King.

And with that hopeful thought in mind, I set off.

It should have been simple. The serviloid's memory would naturally contain clear maps – pictorial, schematic, three-dimensional – of the Sanctum's interior. Posi knew just where I was and just where the food area was. She should have been able to direct me in a straight line, or as near to a straight line as a Maze-web allowed.

But when Posi started making demands on the ship's perceptors, to monitor my progress, their instability started getting
worse. It seems to be just my luck, provided by some perverse
galactic fates that have taken a dislike to me. Those dysphas-
ings mostly chose moments when I was reaching an intersecting node that linked many passageways. Then Posi would be
helpless for a while, and I either had to wait where I was,
sweating and chafing, or choose a route at random.

If I chose at random, I almost always chose wrong, and had
to retrace my steps when the ceptors phased in again and Posi
could get back to guiding me. And if I stayed still, exposed and
lost, I moved fairly close to the edge of panic.

But at least, mercifully, nothing too upsetting happened
when I was on the move in the right direction. At least not at
first. The areas around me were deserted, as if they were
other, unoccupied guest quarters. Though I did wonder idly if
the God-King kept a crew of people with goodies – and animals
– in every guest-chamber, all the time, in case a visitor arrived
with one or another unsatisfied longing. But I never found out.
I merely walked on, sweating, limply relieved when every
passage or chamber proved as empty as the ones before it.

That quiet time, however, came to an end – as I was led
down a level, then another, getting closer to the operations
areas and servants' quarters. Or so Posi told me. She was also
telling me about other areas of the web, but I wasn't really
listening – except when she revealed that the God-King's
private place, his Personal Haven, took up the entire *top* level
of the web. So if the God-King's headquarters were in the
head, I was down among the internal organs, you might say,
the Sanctum's life support area. Which meant that I was
making progress. But then it also started to mean that I had
encounters.

Most of them were with mandroids, of one sort or another.
There were plenty of the boyish serviloids in skimpy tunics,
gliding along on various errands, eyes on the floor. Among
them, other mandroids wearing coveralls in pastel colours
hurried past, clutching objects and tools, which told me they
were engineering and maintenance staff. There were also a
good few of the half-dressed and heavily made up creatures

171

hurrying past – part of the recreational staff – which made me realize that probably few or none of those who had been in my guest quarters had been human.

Not that I'm prejudiced against servomechanisms, in bed or anywhere. It just was another indication of the *control* that the God-King seemed to like to have, and to offer to his guests, over his workforce.

That control also showed in the attitude towards me of all those mandroids. Which was non-existent. They glided or strode or scurried along, looking down or straight ahead, apparently not noticing the presence of a blue-clad, off-world human with a hunted expression who was talking into a piece of jewellery. I worried briefly that one of them might report my presence to some official, but Posi monitored a few – when she could – and said not.

"You are none of their concern, Del," she said. "So they cannot be said to be truly aware of you."

I suppose it shows that working mandroids are just like folks. Or maybe more so. They do the job they're supposed to do – and not a step, a nudge, a millimetre more. You never see a mandroid doing unrewarded overtime to finish up a piece of work, or taking work home, or volunteering for anything. I respect them for it.

Once in a while I'd spot a human in among the passing mandroids, and my heart would try to jump up into my throat for comfort. Not that it's always easy to tell the difference, for humans can also have blank eyes and fixed expressions. But in the Maze-web I could tell every time. The humans – mostly wearing loose robes like understated versions of y'Bagne-haude – would gape at me. They would look me up and down. And then they'd look away, their faces would tighten up, and they'd scuttle off at speed.

I didn't need Posi or anyone to access their minds. I knew the type. Minor civil servants, data processors, that sort. Narrow little folk in narrow little jobs. And there was I, an off-worlder in the Sanctum, looking as if I knew what I was doing, looking interesting and important. They had no idea who I was or why I was there. Which was further proof, to them, that they were uninteresting and unimportant.

And since that's always a painful thing to have proved to you, they pretended that they hadn't seen me, I wasn't there, it hadn't happened.

So, as I went along, since everyone in the place seemed content to ignore me, I began to relax. I even began to smile and nod at the tight-faced humans, who would flush and walk on even faster. And I would grin to myself and continue on my way, having fun.

Until I met the killdroids.

It was another squad of four, and for all I knew they might have been the same ones I'd met at the Sanctum entrance. Or their replacements. It didn't matter. Unlike all the other passersby, they looked at me, sized me up – and by a neat manoeuvre blocked my way and stopped me without quite touching me.

"Sir?" one said, looming. "Have you lost your way?"

"Not at all, I know just where I am," I babbled. "I have an excellent . . . sense of direction."

They studied me with those glassy mandroid eyes as I blinked and tried to smile. At least it seemed that they knew about me, unlike the first four I'd met. They weren't actually arresting me, and they seemed to know where I was supposed to be. But they were doing their job, which was to assume guilt until innocence had been unarguably proved. So they looked at me in the true police style, with a heavy politeness masking a much heavier menace.

"Could you tell us why you are in this area, sir?" another of them inquired.

I tried to look worried. It wasn't difficult. "Why – am I trespassing? Is this private, an exclusion area?"

Cops don't like you to answer a question with a question. None of them moved, but I gathered that they would have liked to bang me against the wall several times and then ask *their* question again. I managed, effortlessly, to look more worried.

"It is not an exclusion area, sir," one of them finally said. "But it is an area where guests do not usually enter."

There was my crime, or anyway the root of their suspicion. I was being unusual. Presumably if I'd been back in my quarters rolling around on the furniture with all the half-naked people and both animals, they wouldn't have thought twice. That was usual.

"I see," I gabbled, trying to think. "Well, it's because . . . I'm here because. . . ." My mind was as blank as their threatening eyes – until fear gave birth to inspiration. "Because I'm *exercising*. Going for a little run, along the passages. Keeping fit, you know."

I was bouncing up and down on my toes and flapping my elbows to illustrate my meaning. They watched, managing to emit from their impassive mandroid faces a clear sense of disapproval. As mandroids always can.

"Exercising, sir."

The flat echo of the word was equally full of disapproval, and doubt as well, a general mandroid commentary on human behaviour – like the serviloid's response to my supposed singing.

"Yes – to pass the time usefully, before I meet the God-King. His, um, Gloriousness."

And after that stress on my divine connections I nodded and smiled and did a little light jogging on the spot, while they reluctantly came to the conclusion that they had no grounds, just then, for tearing my head off.

"Very well, sir," one said at last, doubt and frustration seeming to resonate behind the toneless voice. "Please return to your guest quarters as soon as your . . . exercises . . . are complete."

"I will, I will," I said. And I smiled, and nodded, and waved, and jogged away along the passage. Behind me, I knew without looking, the killdroids were watching me go. I could feel their gaze on my shrinking back as sharply as if they were firing their blazers.

I half-expected them to follow me. I more than half-expected them to report my *unusual* activity. And y'Bagnehaude might wonder why I was out running around, getting all sweaty – as I was, though mostly from anxiety – just after having cleaned myself up for the meeting with the royal divinity.

"Posi!" I panted quietly into my pendant. "I'm running out of time!"

"I am sorry to hear that, Del," she said brightly. "You do seem to be moving more quickly, though. At the next globe-chamber, take the first exit on your left."

"Where does that lead?" I gasped, slowing down as a stitch cramped my guts.

"Your speed has diminished, Del," Posi pointed out. "But it does not matter. The small exit leads to a passage that will bring you into the first of the main food preparation chambers."

"Is it occupied?" I asked.

"The serviloid's memory had no data on that," Posi said.

Oh well, I thought, probably not. The harem girl had found the secret entrance without being stopped by anyone. And the opening wouldn't be a very well-kept secret if killdroid guards were posted outside it.

So I jogged painfully on. Through the food preparation chambers, where my mouth watered a little. I hadn't eaten for some time, except for a bit of pastry, earlier, and some mouthfuls of stewed rat the night before, which were best forgotten. And in those chambers I think I could have helped myself to a ten-course feast. There were a few mandroids tidying up in the first chamber, who ignored me, but I assumed that it was between mealtimes because the other food chambers were deserted. As were the passages that linked them.

And in the last of those passages, just as y'Wipo had told me, I found a plain metal hatch-cover on one wall. The only hatch-cover in any of the passages. So it was what I was looking for – and it certainly looked big enough to allow a normal human to pass through into the supposedly secret shaft beyond it. It was also unguarded and isolated, which was such an unexpected benefit that it drove away my stitch.

Then I looked at the electronically coded locking mechanism that opened the hatch-covers at both ends of the secret shaft. I remembered that the harem girl had found the code by accident, at random.

"Posi," I said urgently, "can you reach this lock with your call-beam and break its code?"

"I'm sure I could, Del," she replied. "But at this moment,

several of my perceptors have gone simultaneously into off-phase. I can still locate your position through the comm-link, but I cannot pinpoint the lock in order to make call-beam contact."

My whole body twitched, as if going into some off-phase trauma of its own. I yelled aloud in a wild mixture of fury, frustration, fear and a lot more. Then in rage I slammed the side of my fist against the locking mechanism.

That made me yell again, with pain. The sounds echoed along the passage. And so did the muffled clang as the hatch-cover slowly swung open, crashing back against the wall.

Staring, astonished, I thought that I'd heard a second clang, in the distance. Was that the second hatch-cover at the other, outside, end of the secret shaft? If so, I'd done it. The way was open – my escape route. No wonder the harem girl had found the shaft, I thought, if the hatch lock was so vulnerable.

I looked around, but no serviloids were coming to investigate the noise. I held my breath and listened as the echoes died away, and realized that I could hear sounds that were not echoes. Sounds from beyond the open hatch – from the shaft, whose dark gaping mouth had been exposed. Faint scrapings and slidings, a dull clank. . . .

Someone in the shaft.

I wanted to look, but I wasn't going to offer a target to some trigger-happy Treff. Carefully, I slid one eye past the edge of the hatchway, and peered.

I couldn't see too much in the dimness. But it seemed that the shaft sloped away and down at a fairly easy angle. And down at the far end of it I could see a shape. The foreshortened shape of a human, moving up the slope in a kind of crouching slither. It looked like a large shape, with shoulders that threatened to become wedged.

So, I thought, big y'Tylo is being a good leader and coming up first. And the other Treffs would be right behind him. I was moments from getting out – if y'Wipo was going to keep his word.

And if the food chambers behind me weren't filling up with killdroids, right then, alerted by the unusual sounds.

I pulled back from the hatch and crept away along the

passage, listening hard, sweating harder. But I heard no indications of danger. And at the end of the passage, when I peered through the doorway into the food chamber beyond, it was wonderfully, heart-warmingly, empty.

Then I heard the footsteps behind me, in the passage, and turned to greet y'Tylo and the Treffs, and to receive their gratitude for a job well done.

But my smile fled. I may have bitten a knuckle. I may even have made a shocked sound resembling a whimper.

The person I was looking at was not big y'Tylo – but bigger. He was not a smelly Treff in a brown robe, but a golden-haired, golden-skinned giant wearing white clothes and a big white grin.

With a gun in one hand and a golden molecublade sword at one hip.

Gharr the Gherpotean.

Chapter 20

My first instinct was to get away from him. Slowly I backed away, through the doorway, into the unoccupied food chamber. But Gharr, still grinning, sauntered forward to keep pace with my retreat. As I looked wildly around for a place to run to or hide in, he lazily lifted his gun, aimed it at me, and held me fixed like an insect on a pin.

I would have given the whole Fraxilly fee, at that moment, for one of my own wristband mini-blazers. So I could have wiped away that insufferable grin.

"Kind of you to let me in, Curb," he drawled.

I clenched my jaw, aching with hatred. "How did you get here?"

"Sweet Mala led me," he said merrily, "as I'm sure she has led many a man."

"Impossible!" I snapped. "We found the bug you put on Mala."

His laugh was rich baritone music, discord to my ears. "You found the bug that I intended to be obvious. The second one, which eluded you, I put in . . . a more intimate location. With a special sheathing to deflect perceptors." He laughed again. "Suitably high-tech, for a high-quality lady."

I sagged against a food counter, swearing in a steady stream under my breath. I cursed Mala for having been set up, I cursed Gharr for merely existing, I cursed Posi – unfairly – for not spotting the second bug. And I cursed my perverse fates as

178

well, for having thwarted what should have been a simple getaway.

"Where's Mala now?" I finally asked, when I'd regained some control.

"Outside and unharmed," Gharr said lightly. "My Gharr-goyles are looking after her and all the smelly youths." He laughed again. "She was beautifully enraged when I told her how I followed her. Stamped and swore and promised to take vengeance. But I find that women need these little emotional storms now and then, do they not? And are all the sweeter, afterwards."

"Spare me your philosophy," I snarled. "What are you doing here?"

"Don't be naïve, Curb," he said. "I am here for the Ardakkean phetam. I would have had it on Vadinamia, and Mala with it, but you proved harder to kill than I had guessed. And I might have taken it on Uulaa. . . ."

He paused. Beyond the door of the food chamber, back along the passage, we could both hear a sliding and a scraping, coming from the open hatch.

"That will be the Gharrgoyles," he said, keeping his gaze and his gun fixed on me. "Bringing in Mala and the brown-robes. I understand the youths are local rebels of a sort, so the Gharrgoyles will release them into the Sanctum – to create a diversion, while we seek the phetam."

As I rummaged around in my mind for a suitably sharp answer, we heard heavy footsteps coming towards us along the passage. Holding the gun steadily on me, Gharr turned towards the doorway.

And froze. And lost his grin. While I jerked as if electrified, and uttered a gasping shriek.

A monstrosity stood framed in the doorway. Squat, sleek, grotesque, fully armed in both senses, terrifying.

The tentacled pirate chief, Ten-huc Blackbreath.

Gharr began to turn, to swing his blazer around towards this new threat. But the exter pirate, despite his age, was too quick. Ten-huc's eight shorter tentacle-arms held an assortment of ugly bladed weapons, but the two longer tentacles were free. One of them lashed out like a whip, struck at Gharr's gun hand, and the blazer fell with a clatter.

"Too many women, Gherpotean," Ten-huc said in a voice like metal cutting stone. "They slow you down, so even an old one can disarm you."

Gharr's face darkened to deep bronze. "It is you, Black-breath," he growled furiously, "who will be dis*armed*!"

And he snatched the golden sword from his belt, the mole-cublade hissing with deadly power.

The change on the pirate's face might have been a grin or a grimace. Either way, it was appalling. And from the slit of his mouth, a trickle of black began to seep, like sooty steam.

"It pleases me that you will fight with a blade," he rumbled. "Now at last I can be rid of you. You have been in my way too many times. You will not interfere with my plans here."

He lumbered forward, squeezing his bulk through the door-way into the food chamber – as Gharr moved back, his blade weaving a golden pattern in the air. I moved back too, at some speed, to a side of the chamber well away from the two of them. It occurred to me only later that in that moment I could have fled, and neither of them would have noticed. But my thought processes were too overwhelmed, and my knees made too rub-bery, by the unexpected arrival of them both. So I merely stood and stared, while Ten-huc raised his writhing tentacle-arms, gripping eight cruel blades, then . . . blew out his breath.

It poured forth in a roiling cloud, as lightlessly black as space beyond the Rim, stinking like a tomb-full of mouldering corpses. It swirled around Gharr, extinguishing his white-gold brilliance like a blown-out candle.

Then, with a ghastly hissing battle-cry, Ten-huc leaped forward, blades whirling around him, and vanished into the blackness.

Just as another blackness swept across my vision, my legs seemed to liquefy, and I crumpled to the floor.

Mala claimed that I must have fainted, but I can't accept that. I have never fainted, except perhaps once or twice from over-exertion and a lack of oxygen. I believe that as I tried to move further away from the unseen combat going on inside that black cloud, I must have lost my footing and struck my head as I fell.

Anyway, Mala was there with me when I awoke. In fact she woke me, by fiercely pinching my earlobes. And though I was dazed and confused, I came awake swiftly enough to see the livid fury in her eyes, and to know that I should handle her gently until she had got over the effect of what Gharr had told her.

"What happened?" I mumbled as I tried to sit up.

"Disaster," Mala snapped. And in her crispest manner, she told me. Which made me think that "disaster" was an understatement.

Outside the Sanctum, some while after I'd been taken away by the killdroid guards, the Gharrgoyles had suddenly come from nowhere and had taken the Treffs without a shot being fired. Gharr had then released Mala, seeming to enjoy himself greatly when he told her how he came to be there. Then, when I had opened the way into the secret shaft, Gharr had disappeared into it. Almost at once, the exter pirates appeared – also from nowhere – overcame the Gharrgoyles and took everyone prisoner. Ten-huc seemed taken with Gharr's idea of creating a diversion, and told the pirates to get both the Treffs and the Gharrgoyles into the Sanctum, with their weapons. But first old Blackbreath had gone in ahead of them, to dispose – as he said – of Gharr.

"And me as well, I suppose," I said.

"He didn't mention you," Mala told me coldly. "Everyone had pretty well forgotten about you."

Oh, fine, I thought bitterly. If it wasn't for me and the risks I'd run, everyone would still be out in the wasteland taking each other prisoner. But I could see from the tightness of Mala's jaw that she wouldn't be interested in that point.

"So after a while," she continued, "the pirates started herding the Treffs and the Gharrgoyles into the shaft, one at a time, with weapons, so they could go and fight the killdroids or whatever. It was a crazy mess, everyone screaming and shouting and swearing, some of the Treffs crying. Though your bedmate c'Vira was laughing herself silly."

She would, I thought sourly.

"The pirates pushed me into the shaft last of all, and started to come in after me. Then I heard other pirates yelling, outside, and some shooting in the distance. And the last few pirates who came up the shaft said that a troop of killdroids had come out of the main doors of the Sanctum to attack us, but had been driven back."

I blinked, puzzled. "By the pirates?"

"No. The killdroids were attacked by armed humans who seemed to come from nowhere." She shook her head wearily. "Famlio."

I goggled, while my stomach seemed to try to take up residence in my boots. "That's . . . it's . . . how. . . ."

"I suppose," Mala went on emptily, "that when Gharr bugged us . . ."

Us? I was on the verge of furiously reminding her who it was got herself into a position to be bugged, whose fault it was that all the crooks were on Fraxilly. But another look at the frozen-steel expression in her eyes made me decide that it would be unwise.

" . . . Ten-huc had also bugged the Gharrgoyles, and maybe Famlio bugged the pirates. Anyway, they're all here, all after the phetam."

"*Where* are they?" I croaked.

She made a vague gesture. "In the Sanctum somewhere. They all just rushed through and scattered, especially when they'd heard about Famlio. No one noticed when I dropped back and stayed here."

"What about Gharr and Ten-huc?" I asked. "They were here, fighting. . . ."

She shrugged. "They weren't here when the others came in. If they're still alive, they'll be somewhere in the Sanctum too. It'll be chaos in there, a lunatic war with three criminal gangs and the Treffs and the killdroids rushing around trying to kill each other. All we need now is a FedPol detachment."

"Don't say that!" I leaped up, galvanized. "Let them kill each other! I've been . . . *we've* been paid for the delivery, so we can get *out*, now!"

"Not that way," Mala said as I started towards the passage

leading to the hatchway. "The pirates destroyed the shaft. To keep killdroids and Famlio from coming up behind them."

I felt the blood draining from my face, and rational thought fleeing from my mind

"We'll have to make for the main entrance," Mala continued. "Famlio will certainly be trying to fight their way in through there. So it shouldn't be too long before the entrance is clear, one way or another. If we can find the way to it."

"Posi can guide us . . ." I said, lifting my pendant. Then I felt as if my spine had been removed without anaesthetic.

The pendant must have swung under me somehow when I'd fallen. The front of it was crushed, and within it small bright edges of metal and silicon revealed breakage beyond repair.

"Come *on*, Curb," Mala said tautly, and I stopped the high keening noise I'd somehow begun. "We'll have to take our chances. We can't sit here."

Why *not*? I asked myself wildly. It was *safe* there. But Mala was already striding determinedly towards the far door of the chamber, and I didn't much feel like being left there alone. Stricken with stress and misery and deep psychological pain, I gathered a few bits of strength and blundered after her.

Unfortunately, what Mala had called the lunatic war in the Sanctum was not concentrated in one place. Everyone had scattered everywhere – looking for the phetam (Gharr and Ten-huc), looking for the God-king (the Treffs), looking for intruders (the killdroids) or just looking for a fight (the Gharrgoyles and the pirates). At that time I believed that the Famlio thugs would be still trying to blast their way in, and I was fervently hoping that they and the killdroids opposing them would fight to the last man and mechanism, leaving the entrance clear.

I hoped, as I often do, in vain.

The first bit of the free-for-all war that came to us took the form of two Treffs, running along a passage that we had just entered. One was a fat boy with a rusty stun-gun, looking combative. The other was a tall girl with a gashed arm and a long knife, looking even more combative.

Seeing us, the boy slid to a startled halt and fired at Mala (who was ahead of me). But she had already flung herself forward in a smooth dive, and the flash struck the wall above her. Acrobatically, Mala turned the dive into a shoulder-roll, came smoothly to her feet, kicked the boy in the crotch with perfect precision, plucked the stun-gun from his hand and dropped the girl while the howling boy was still doubling up.

Then she moved on, light-footed as ever, without another glance at the fallen youths. I stumbled after her, looking down at the boy who was clutching himself in purple-faced anguish. "You were going the wrong way anyway," I told him pleasantly, and hurried on.

Until I reached the end of that passage and saw Mala crouching by the doorway, holding up a hand to stop me.

"Killdroids," she whispered, gesturing at the area beyond the doorway.

I didn't want to stop. By then my sense of self-preservation had made it clear that safety lay in getting *on*, and *out*, as fast as possible. Creeping around and lurking and hesitating would only mean that I would be inside the Sanctum longer. Yet I didn't want to expose myself to killdroids, either, who would be shooting strange humans on sight. Almost gibbering with frustration, I stared around, hoping that another route would appear.

But then Mala jerked back from the door as the area beyond it erupted with a deafening burst of blazer fire and grenade explosions. I flung myself down, arms wrapped around head. But the noise stopped almost at once, and when I looked warily up I saw Mala peering through the doorway.

"Famlio is inside," she said tersely. "That was them and some Gharrgoyles, caught the killdroids in a cross-fire. Come on."

I lurched to my feet and followed her through the door. The chamber beyond was littered with disrupted killdroids, along with a few black-clad humans and dark-furred exters. Mala picked up two Famlio blazers, tossed one to me, and discarded the stun-gun. Then we plunged onwards, through other doors, along other passages. . . .

I felt as if I were in a high-glaze fever, the adrenalin almost

184

lifting me from the ground. And the situation had clearly taken hold of Mala's emotions as intensely. We fled like berserk phantoms through that labyrinth. We hardly broke stride when Mala whirled to blast two Gharrgoyles that somehow appeared behind us, or when my blazer cut down a Famlio thug and a killdroid who were locked in combat. We hardly seemed to slow down as we sprang away from a passage suddenly filled with pirates, yet Mala dropped two of them almost without looking. We sprinted at top speed through a cluster of chambers with fights going on all around us, unnoticed by any of the fighters – even when we actually hurdled a Gharrgoyle who was disembowelling a pirate with fierce concentration. We ran, and dodged, and shot, and ran, and some of the time Mala was shrieking aloud in sheer battle-maddened excitement. Which frightened me as much as anything during that flight.

Then suddenly our flight came to a shattering end. It was in another chamber, perhaps another large recreation area, where some unarmed serviloids cowered against a wall. Before we could dash out again, a reptilian pirate burst in through another door and flung what looked like a handful of sparks at Mala. She collapsed at once, as if boneless.

My blazer blew a hole in the pirate wholly by reflex. Before he hit the floor I was kneeling beside Mala, tearing her coverall from her body. The handful of sparks, I knew, was an ugly weapon known as digger-darts. Little needle-pointed, self-powered projectiles that inject a knock-out drug into the victim – and then, vibrating, slowly burrow into the unconscious body and tear holes in vital organs. So far Mala was only drugged, and I was moving with frantic speed.

I'm pleased to say that in the circumstances I was thinking only of her survival as I stripped her. Then I started plucking out darts. It was like pulling thorns from someone who'd lost an argument with a Fhrytokan whip-cactus. Except that these thorns were digging in, trying to get beneath the skin. By the time I'd removed eleven of them, there were no more to be seen. I re-checked every centimetre of her body, then sat back, twitching and sweating, praying that no other darts had already burrowed deep into her flesh, on their way to kill her.

But a minute passed, then several more, and nothing happened except that her eyelids fluttered as her system tried to fight the drug. After a few more moments – while I grew quiveringly aware of how vulnerable I was, kneeling there – she was still alive. Any darts in her flesh would have killed her by then, so there weren't any.

I breathed easier, but only a little. She would still be unconscious for some time. And my sense of self-preservation told me that my survival would be seriously threatened if I tried to make my way through the Sanctum carrying Mala. She was slim and small, but not that small.

Anyway, I told myself, she has always admired professionalism in others. And the professional thing for me to do, surely, would be to go on alone, swift and unencumbered.

But I couldn't just leave her where she was. That would have been a coward's trick. So I stood up and called to the group of serviloids still cowering on the other side of the chamber.

For all their fear, their programmed responses were in good working order. They padded across to me, eyes downcast.

"I am leaving this woman with you," I told them. "You must look after her and protect her. For I shall return for her very soon."

They murmured obedient affirmatives and gathered around Mala. I glanced down once more at her nudity, and briefly formed an interesting comparison between her graceful slimness and c'Vira's more exotic lushness. Then I forced my mind back to the task awaiting me.

I did have every intention of going back for Mala – when things had quietened down, when the warring groups in the Sanctum were no longer in the way. But then it seemed that Mala was the lucky one, being out of the action and tended by serviloids. While I still had to make my way, perhaps fight my way, to the only exit and what safety could be found beyond it.

But, I always say, a man has to do what's there to be done.

Beckoning to one of the serviloids, I directed it to lead me to the Sanctum entrance hall. As it moved off in silent obedience, I was right behind it, watchful and ready, blazer poised.

Chapter 21

As we progressed through the passages, I began to feel slightly better. I believed – naïvely – that the serviloid could get me out of the Sanctum in more or less a straight line. I also believed that he would be a useful shield if I ran into any opposition along the way.

Now and then I could hear bursts of noise as some of the various battling groups crossed paths and opened fire. But the interlinkings and overlappings of the Maze-web made it difficult to tell exactly where each burst was coming from. Or even which level they were on. Still, it all seemed to be happening elsewhere – so I began to feel hopeful that I could bypass the main areas of violence.

Then the serviloid led me into the first of a series of chambers like elongated domes which formed interconnecting exhibition areas, clogged and stacked with art objects and other exotica. When I questioned the serviloid, he confirmed that we were moving steadily away from the centre of the Sanctum, and were nowhere near the God-King's Personal Haven on the topmost level. I had checked that point because I wanted to be high enough to approach the entrance hall from one of its upper balconies, a vantage point from where I could look for killdroids or other armed obstacles in the hall. But I didn't want to climb up too many levels, and risk getting close to the God-King's Haven. That's where all the phetam-hunters would be heading.

So it seemed to be going fairly well. I was even taking an

interest in the no doubt valuable art works around me, wondering if it would be possible to tuck one or two of the smaller ones under my arm. As a kind of bonus, which I felt I'd earned, seeing what I'd been through.

But before I could make a selection, half a dozen wild-eyed Famlio thugs burst in through a door at one side and started shooting at me.

Since they were running at the time, and fairly over-excited, their blazers missed. So did mine, because I was firing back at them while sprinting headlong for another door on the opposite side of that gallery. I had a glimpse of the serviloid leaping to safety behind a heavy plinth, in the midst of crackling streamers of blazer fire that was blasting several hundred kilocreds worth of art into rubble. A final hasty glance back, as I plunged through the doorway, showed me that the Famlio half-dozen had been diverted by three Gharrgoyles who had popped into the chamber, yowled, and leaped out again through another entrance that was suddenly in flame from blazer fire.

Even so, I was still running as I crossed the chamber that I'd entered. And I was running full-tilt into nightmare.

Somehow all the combatants seemed suddenly to have converged on that area – perhaps drawn to it by the sounds of gunfire. And there were far too many entrances into that cluster of art galleries. As I hurtled across the adjoining chamber, some pirates came through a door and shot at me. In the next instant some killdroids came through another door and shot at them. They continued to exchange fire, ignoring me, as I crashed through yet another door. There a group of Gharrgoyles whirled and fired at me. They then fled when I fired at them, and ran headlong into more Famlio thugs. That developed into bloody hand-to-hand combat, while I scrambled away on hands and knees.

At one point I ran along the entire length of one enormous hall – with countless holo-portraits ranged on the walls – with armed killers crowded in every one of an endless series of doors. Here were Gharrgoyles, there killdroids, there pirates, elsewhere Famlio, all leaping out from their doorways, firing, then ducking back as the others fired at them. Popping back and forth like mechanical dolls. Not one of them, as far as I could tell, fired at me or even noticed me as I sprinted, shrieking, through their midst. And by some miracle reached the far end unscathed.

Then I was lunging up a spiral ramp to the level above, away from that mêlée. Only to be fired at by killdroids coming down a hyper-lift, opposite. The next level seemed more peaceful, until a Gharrgoyle and a pirate appeared at the same instant at opposite ends of a narrow anteroom and shot at me. I was by then nearly exhausted, so I merely cried out and fell to the floor. The two fired again, at each other, both hitting their targets, both toppling.

For a long moment I lay as still as their two corpses. I was unhurt, but I was trying to get my breath and some strength in my legs to continue my flight. By then I was close to panic – being lost again, and realizing that I hadn't by-passed all the scattered warring factions. Somewhere, I told myself, I had to find another serviloid guide – and a nice safe roundabout route to the main entrance.

I was gathering myself to get going when I heard a noise behind me. Fear clamped down on me where I lay, halting any movement I might have made. And that sudden paralysis saved my life.

Through slitted eyes I peered up from the floor at two pairs of legs moving towards me, wearing the white-striped black of Famlio. And I heard voices, one of which was familiar enough to immobilize me all over again. The unmistakable cold snarl of Pulvidon.

"I was hoping to find Curb alive," he said, prodding me with a toe. "Wanted to kill him myself, and take a while doing it."

The other one grunted. "Looks like he died hard, anyway. All blue in the face like that. Prob'ly got a poison blast from a needler."

Pulvidon laughed. "Kind of matches his outfit, doesn't it?"

I may have been a little flushed, at that, from holding my breath and playing dead. Certainly I had no illusion that I could suddenly spring up and shoot both of them with my blazer. Not when one of them was Pulvidon.

A toe prodded me again, and then to my immense relief they

189

moved away, muttering about rounding up the boys. Seconds later, with an explosive release of breath, I was scrambling up and hurling myself towards a door in the opposite direction.

Seconds after that, I was howling with terror as blazer fire from three killdroid forefingers scorched the air around me. They missed, because I'd flung myself desperately on to a nearby hyper-lift. But they kept firing, upwards, having jumped on to the next magno-disc, rising up beneath mine. Their guns had chipped and melted quite a bit of my disc before something else must have drawn their attention. Suddenly they were gone, all was quiet, and I lay huddled and trembling on the disc until it finally juddered to a halt.

I stepped off it to find myself in an apparent area of peace, the eye of the hurricane. A short, broad, blessedly deserted corridor lay ahead of me, and I sidled carefully along it, crouched by a doorway at its far end, and listened.

I heard definite sounds of life beyond that doorway. They were fairly noisy sounds, human voices that were resonant in a hollow, echoing sort of way. But that's not what swamped me with amazement.

In the middle of a major assault on the Sanctum by several well-armed and ruthless forces, the voices beyond that door were being raised in *laughter*.

Against a background of sweetly harmonious music and other sounds that my startled ears only slowly recognized as birdsong.

Through my amazed disbelief, I slowly guessed the truth. There was only one possible place in the Sanctum where people might be laughing and birds singing. That final escape on the lift had brought me to some kind of entrance into the God-King's Personal Haven.

I knew I had no business there. I didn't even want to be there. But I couldn't resist the sudden tug of curiosity. Cautiously, in a low crouch, I slid partway through the door – and simply stared.

The voices were coming from below me, for my doorway led out on to a decorated balcony looking down on an immense

190

chamber. Its floor was oval-shaped, so that it lacked corners, and there seemed to be three separate, ornate entrances at floor level. The widest part of the oval looked like being about a hundred and fifty metres across. My balcony was about twenty metres from the floor, and the walls soared up about the same distance again above me, to a domed ceiling, pale blue, with a good-sized artificial sun at its centre.

The narrower ends of the huge area each held an idealized woodland scene, with birdsong. But they proved to be Illuso-chambers, as on the Emissary's spaceship. As I looked, they shifted to become scenic mountain meadows, complete with flowers and colourful flying insects, not to mention a fresh breeze. But I saw all that on the edge of my vision. My close attention was on the central section of the oval, almost directly below me.

The central part was dominated by a limpidly blue pool of water, almost a small lake. Connected to it were secondary pools, small rivulets, waterfalls, graceful little bridges, water-side glades where small trees drooped, and much more along those lines. At one side of the waterways lay a wide stretch of artificial parkland, holding a few trees but mostly offering a rich carpet of grass and flowers. At the centre of that grassy expanse was a small hillock, a gentle sweep of grass sloping up to a broad, flat top.

All that natural lushness, the sparkling water, the rich grass, the colour and fragrance of trees and flowers – the entire scene could not have been more wholly the opposite of the arid, stinking desolation that was Fraxilly beyond the Sanctum. For all the near-perfect beauty of the scene, it was repulsive in what it revealed of wealth and absolute power turned gluttonous, megalomaniac, corrupt.

Or it would have been repulsive, had I stopped to think about any of that at the time. But as I stared down from my balcony my thinking had been a little short-circuited by sheer dazzled astonishment.

For nearly every part of that lovely setting – the waterways, the grassland, the hillock – was populated with young, nubile and unclothed women.

Theirs was the laughter I had heard, as they splashed

merrily in the water – or played bouncy little ball games on the grass – or sat around in conversational groups – or simply reclined and presented their unashamed nakedness to the sun. And, if they'd known it, to me.

I looked at them closely, one at a time, for some while. They were not entirely naked, for as well as plenty of make-up and jewellery they wore tiny swathes of something mostly transparent around their hips. Or most of them did. I couldn't be sure about those bobbing in the pool.

I knew perfectly well that I was gazing at the God-King's legendary harem. I thought at the time that it said something positive about the God-King. At least, unlike his Emissary and Body-Servant, his tastes ran to females. But naturally, like any thinking person, I generally disapprove of the idea of harems – or any of the other forms of servitude that some sentients impose on others. And yet it has to be said that the girls didn't look all that troubled or unhappy. And I was studying them closely enough so that I would have noticed.

At least, they didn't until the first interruption.

It took the form of an enormous bass male voice bellowing an impressively searing collection of expletives, some of which I took to be Fraxillian dialect. Which was followed by a meaty thump and a shrill shriek.

All the naked girls went instantly still, some looking tense and uneasy. Then there was a small burst of tittering, followed by the big bass voice bellowing again, but this time with laughter, to be followed by a relieved outburst of giggles from most of the other girls. I slowly tore my gaze away from the delicious movements that giggling produced in all that firm flesh, and looked towards the top of the hillock.

It held a platform, a kind of overdecorated dais, resting springily on small versions of the energy pillars that held up the whole Sanctum. The top of the dais was deeply cushioned, strewn with rich fabrics and also with a few more naked harem girls. And in their midst was the focus of all their attention and now, at last, mine.

The God-King of Fraxilly, y'Iggthradgipile the First.

No part of him was lovely to look at. Yet it was hard to avoid looking at all parts of him, since he wore nothing but a frothy half-robe slung over one shoulder. If standing, he would have been short and wide. His head was hairless, and there were only a few clumps of sparse white hair elsewhere on his body. His face was grotesquely wrinkled and sunken, save for a large snout of a nose. His flesh and skin had lost all elasticity and hung wrinkled, puckered and flabby from his frame as if he were made of half-deflated balloons.

As I gazed distastefully at him, I noticed the glint of metal among the cushions beside him, and recognized the cylinder that I had delivered. It seemed intact, unopened, which I thought was strange. From the look of him, the poor, old, drooping God-King was in considerable need of phetam.

That was when the thought came to me, again, that if someone *else* had the phetam, all that abundance might be his. And with the upheaval in the Sanctum, someone might get his chance ... So I stopped simply ogling the girls and started considering my position.

Which brought me a new clarity of vision, so that I noticed, with a start, two special individuals among the unclad crowd below me. I'd half-expected to see some courtiers keeping the God-King company, but perhaps they weren't allowed into the Haven. Or perhaps they were hiding, elsewhere, from the battles below. Anyway, the two persons I noticed were startling not because they were strange, as courtiers might have been, but because they were familiar.

One was a small round figure on hands and knees, who came into view on my side of the dais. The rainbow swirl of robes identified it as y'Bagnehaude, though all that I could properly see of him was his sizeable rump. It was raised in the air as he crawled slowly along, apparently searching for something in the grass. And when the God-King idly reached out a leg and swung a kick against that rump, I recognized the meaty thud, the shrill shriek and the widespread merriment that I'd heard a moment before.

The other startling, familiar figure caused me to lean forward, at the very edge of the balcony, to be sure I was seeing properly. It was one of the girls on the dais, lying on her side, looking as round and delicious as any. But she was lying rigidly still, as close to the edge as she could get.

I saw the magno-fasteners on her wrists at about the same time as I clearly saw her face – when she jerked away from an idle squeeze by the God-King.

Mala. My own partner. A manacled prisoner in the God-King's harem.

I realized at once what had happened. I had left her, unconscious and undressed, in the care of some serviloids. But they were Sanctum serviloids. They knew just what they were supposed to do, usually, with strange, unconscious, naked girls.

So they took her to the harem.

Knowing Mala, I guessed that she had been manacled after trying to escape, or perhaps after trying to inflict some lasting injury on His Godliness. Lucky for her, I thought, that she was attractive enough to make the God-King want to keep her, not kill her.

And that was the moment of the second interruption.

Through the nearest one of the three floor-level entrances – violently through it, blowing it away with the crash of a grenade – came a leaping storm of dark-furred Gharrgoyles. It seemed that they had found their way to the Haven by accident, for it certainly took them by surprise. As they burst in, they halted for an instant and gaped.

Not that they were affected by all the sumptuous femininity that confronted them. As far as I knew, those exters didn't find human women appealing, except as potential victims of criminality. It was the sight of the Haven itself that stilled them, as they took it all in.

Only they didn't have the time. One of the groups of beautiful young women who had been standing around chatting – or so I'd thought – stared at the intruders with oddly empty gazes. Then they raised their slender hands – and from their extended forefingers blasted streams of blazer fire that fried the Gharrgoyles to a crisp.

And the God-King's bass laughter seemed to shake the walls of the mighty chamber.

"Don't look like that, girl," he boomed, and I saw that he was talking to Mala, who looked as shocked as I felt. "I may be two hundred and fifty-three years old but I'm not senile. Aside from the killdroids stationed throughout the Sanctum, I keep a *special* form of them here, as a more personal guard."

The laughter rolled out again, while I watched the group of what still looked like harem girls resume their casual gathering.

My hands were shaking a little, and my sudden sweat was clammy. To think I'd actually been considering going *down* there, to take the phetam away from the flabby old man. And to rescue Mala, naturally. But now. . . .

I began to back slowly away from the edge of the balcony, thinking that there was something truly perverse about having killdroids in the shape of naked harem girls. Such delectable shapes, too, all of them. But I told myself it was nothing to do with me. And if the armed gangs were getting that close to the Haven, it was time for me to be somewhere else.

I felt a pang of regret at having to leave the phetam, when I'd been so close. And another pang, almost at once, at having to leave Mala. But I felt that she wasn't in any immediate danger, in the Haven, with the female killdroids to protect everyone. In fact she was still safer than me, for I was about to plunge back into the murderous tumult of that free-for-all war.

I suppose I was backing away from the balcony's edge because I didn't want to tear my lingering gaze away from all that girl-flesh. Even from the disguised killdroids. It was unprofessional, I know, but I don't think many men could have turned away sooner.

Unfortunately, I backed into trouble.

I knew it when powerful hands gripped me and jerked me up off the floor. I yelled, glancing wildly back, and saw that I was in the grip of two tall, well-rounded, unclad young women. But not women – as the strength of their grip and the oddly blank expressions revealed. I didn't have to see their gun-muzzle forefingers to recognize them.

Clearly I'd leaned out too far, to watch the goings-on, and these two killdroids had spotted me. So, trying not to struggle, which would have been pointless, I forced a note of outrage into my voice.

"I don't know what you think you're doing." My voice trembled, as if with anger. "I am Del Curb, an honoured guest of His Worshipfulness. . . ."

Silently, one of the two pulled me back against her, breasts hard against my back. But before I could begin to enjoy the sensation, the other one reached slim fingers to my throat.

With the pressure on my carotids, I slumped into the darkness that welled up around me.

Chapter 22

The good thing about being knocked out that way is that there are no side-effects, as there are with drugs or blows to the head. The bad thing is that prolonged pressure on the arteries can cause brain damage. But then so can drugs and blows to the head. And as far as I could tell, when I swam back up to full awareness, my brain was in working order.

Not much else was. I felt bruised where killdroid hands had gripped me, I had been very roughly searched so that my clothes were in serious disarray. Thankfully, though, the little wafer confirming my fee still lay safely inside my tunic. But I was manacled, with magno-fasteners clipping my hands together in front, as Mala's had been when I'd seen her. And I was lying face down in warm and perfumed grass, while someone with a bass voice was having an angry conversation with other people.

". . . bound to know how to open it, when he wakens," the bass voice was saying. I recognized it as the God-King, talking probably about me. "He brought it. He may have opened it already and stolen my property."

"He hasn't," said a wearily exasperated voice that I knew very well. Mala wasn't sounding too impressed with the God-King. I wished that I could quietly tell her to inject some humility into her tone. "No one can open the cylinder, I've *told* you. Not without the unique, specially attuned molecular key."

The God-King snorted. "So you have said. The key which my Body-Servant has idiotically managed to drop into the grass, and lose." I heard another meaty thwack followed by a squeal that was definitely y'Bagnehaude's, giving me a pleasant mental image of a godly foot being applied to an upturned rump.

"I *will* find it, Your Magnificence!" I heard y'Bagnehaude babble, apparently from the far side of the hillock. "If I could send for serviloids to *assist*. . . ."

"You sent for some, and they have not arrived," rumbled the God-King. "They have no doubt been delayed or destroyed by the fighting. So *you* find the key that you lost, and swiftly, before I have you melted down for cooking fat."

"Your Benevolence," y'Bagnehaude squeaked, "the fault is not *wholly* mine. So much violence sweeping through the Sanctum . . . so alarming . . . my nerves. . . ."

"You mean your sweaty little paw started shaking," said the God-King, chortling. "Yet you know there is nothing to fear. This attack is merely an amusing interlude, a relief to boredom, and I shall put an end to it as soon as the cylinder is opened." His voice altered to a commanding bellow. "You, killies! Wake this skinny peasant up! Cut something off him — that will bring him round!"

My self-preserving instinct told me that "killies" was a pet name for the female killdroids, and that the other reference was to me. In the same instant I had leaped to my feet – a little awkwardly, with hands fastened – and was backing away from two empty-eyed killdroids.

I found that I was standing on top of the hillock, next to the dais where the God-King lounged with some of his girls. And with Mala.

Whereupon, with a palely murderous expression, Mala sprang lithely from the dais – not at all impeded by her fasteners – and swung a vicious kick at me. If I hadn't been on a high level of awareness from the killdroid threat, I might now be singing coloratura in the massed choirs of Harle's World.

Instead, I twisted away in time to catch the kick on my thigh. But the force of it, from Mala's small bare foot, sent me tumbling backwards down the slope of the hillock. Perhaps I was already off balance on the uneven footing. And Mala was screaming at me, a remarkable stream of invective, which had mostly to do with her outrage at my having deserted her.

The God-King was laughing, deep booming belly-chuckles, with a revolting display of joggling flab. "Spittle-spined puke-bellied scum-pod!" he spluttered. "Very *good*, for a girl!"

And, I was happy to see, he was waving away the two killdroids.

But I was mostly looking at Mala, who was again advancing towards me, wearing on her face the pure fury of an avenging angel. The trouble was, she wasn't wearing much else. And as I backed away, I may have let my gaze slip down from her face to her appealing nakedness. Automatically she moved her arms to half-cover herself – which brought ribald laughter from the God-King and the other girls.

Flushing, Mala stopped her advance, her enraged expression shifting to a grimace of contempt. "Curb – you're *disgusting*."

"I can't help it," I said defensively, as she turned away. "I can't help any of this. You can't blame me."

She wheeled back, eyes blazing. "*Can't* I? I can blame you for leaving me! Dumping me, without my clothes, unconscious, in the middle of this filthy place, while you slithered off to save your own skin!"

"Mala love," I said, feeling deeply hurt. "I was going to come back for you. . . ."

"I'm sure you told yourself that, so your conscience wouldn't trouble you!"

"I *would* have come back," I insisted. "And I *did* get the digger-darts out of you."

She hesitated, then nodded reluctantly. "Yes, you did, I suppose. . . ."

"And also," I rushed on, grasping my advantage, "I left you safely in the care of serviloids. . . ."

"Who brought me *here*!" she spat, looking as if she might kick me again.

I took a quick step back. "But, Mala," I said, as reasonably as I could, "where could you be *safer*, in the whole Sanctum? There's a *war* going on out there! But here you have killdroids to defend you, and all these other nice girls to keep you company. . . ." I tried a small smile. "And it's not as if you've been in danger of being *raped*."

She flicked a quick glance at the God-King's drooping flesh, and amusement tugged at the corners of her mouth. "No," she agreed. "He likes to finger and squeeze, but he . . . can't get up to much else."

Till then the God-King had been enjoying our exchange, as if we were a mini-drama being acted for his pleasure. But that remark brought him roaring up from his cushions.

"Silence!" he bellowed. "You forget where you are! I will have your insulting tongues ripped from your mouths, your skin flayed from your flesh, your flesh charred from your bones . . .!"

"Quite right, quite right," y'Bagnehaude squeaked in counterpoint.

I turned suddenly cold, realizing we had gone too far. For a second I poised myself to begin a series of placating and flattering apologies, mixed with abject pleas for mercy. You learn to do that sort of thing when you've dealt with some of the major tyrants in the galaxy. But then, by inspiration, an alternative occurred to me. A bluff.

The God-King was still roaring, the killdroids were advancing, Mala was bracing herself for a glorious, go-down-fighting last stand. But I put a firm clamp on my terror, affected a cool and untroubled expression, and stepped towards the dais.

"If you do all those terrible things to us, Your, uh, Overwhelmingness," I said, "you will never get at your phetam."

That produced a thunderous silence. Mala gave me a puzzled frown, but sensibly said nothing. The killdroids halted at a gesture from the God-King. Everyone else simply stared.

"Then you know what is in the cylinder," the God-King said, his scowl tinged with weariness.

"It has been obvious to me for some time," I said airily.

"And you can *open* it?" The God-King's voice was filled with doubt and suspicion but also with a desperate hope. So I knew I had him, if I played it right. The ideal target for a confidence trick is someone who is desperate.

"He has found the *key*!" squealed y'Bagnehaude, glaring. But he subsided as I shook my head.

"I haven't," I said. "Anyway, it might not work even if it was found. The extreme delicacy of molecular keys means that they're easily damaged – by, for instance, being dropped. Probably stepped on, by now."

There was some truth in that. Molecular keys *are* fragile, and could be distorted even by a fall into soft grass. But it didn't really matter. The God-King was glowering, y'Bagnehaude was cowering, and I was centre-stage, starting to enjoy it.

"The fact is, I may not *need* a key," I went on. That startled everyone, including Mala.

"So the cylinder can be opened another way," the God-King rumbled hopefully.

"I believe so, Your Awesomeness," I said. "I have not tried to do so, of course, for as a professional courier I would never tamper with my clients' possessions when they have been entrusted to me." Only I noticed Mala's faint grimace. "But I usually carry many small devices, miniaturized implements. . . ."

"Weapons?" the God-King interrupted.

A bosomy killdroid stepped forward. "Sire, the off-worlder was thoroughly searched. He carried no weapons that could endanger you."

I smiled thinly. "I speak of *use*ful devices, Your Incredibleness. Such as this."

I activated the vibro-blade in my fingernail, smoothly cut the fastener from my right wrist, then arched my hand over and cut the other from my left wrist.

The God-King had tensed a little, glancing towards the buxom killdroid.

"Sire," she said impassively, "all his subcutaneous devices are proximital, harmless at any distance. But we can take him to surgery and remove them if you so desire."

She had a good point, I thought. My implanted weapons *are* all harmless at a few paces. Something to consider later. If there was a later.

"And that blade might cut *some* metal," y'Bagnehaude squeaked, "but not the Balbazian steel of the cylinder!"

"That is true, Your Illustriousness," I said quickly. "It is also

201

true that I intend you no harm. But among my *other* implements – " I held up my ten fingers – "is one that can function as a molecular *lockpick*. It can open any cylinder."

And that was a good idea too, I thought. If such a lockpick could be made, it would be a useful addition to my armoury.

"What do you propose, then?" asked the God-King. His voice was still full of suspicion, but also of hungry eagerness. I saw that he had dug out the cylinder from the cushions, cradling it as a mother might cradle a sick infant before handing it over to the medics.

I moved closer to the dais, with a reassuring smile. "Why, merely give me the cylinder, Your Grandiosity, and in moments the phetam will be yours."

His face trembled, and I saw the full extent of his desperation. Phetam would mean, for him, a return to health, firm-muscled vigour, potency . . . not to mention super-strength, invulnerability, the power of flight and all the rest. If Mala and I had been right about Ardakkean phetam. And the God-King's desperate craving told me that we were.

But he couldn't get at it without the lost key. Nor could I, worse luck. I could have done with a few super-powers of my own just then. Because before long my lie about the lockpick was going to be exposed. Unless I could continue running the bluff, playing for time, in the hope that a means of escape might appear.

Still, it was a fairly strong hope, even if it did depend on a lot of murderous thugs.

After the Gharrgoyles had burst in, earlier, I'd known it was only a matter of time before the other criminals found the God-King's Haven. When that happened – if I'd strung out my bluff that long – I had a chance to get out, with Mala, while the harem killdroids were battling the invaders. I might even manage to take the phetam. If I could just convince the old man. . . .

Then I tensed, for the God-King was scowling at me with mistrust – perhaps because the wrong things were showing in my face.

"What are you thinking?" he rumbled.

"How I may serve you, Your Incomparableness," I lied

swiftly. "And also, in truth, whether it might not be wiser for me to open the cylinder on my spaceship – where I have other implements. . . ."

A distant explosion thumped its shock wave into the great chamber, making the floor tremble faintly. It was the first sound from the Sanctum war to penetrate the Haven since the Gharrgoyle attack. Harem girls gasped, y'Bagnehaude squeaked, the God-King glowered.

"We cannot simply stroll out to your ship, fool. Not till my killdroids have swept away all the intruders." He gestured to the killdroid women. "To the entrances, my killies. Let no others enter here."

They moved away, some to stand in tight knots before the three floor-level doorways, others to climb up to guard balcony entrances like the one I'd found. And the God-King sighed as he watched them.

"Had I some part of the phetam in the cylinder," he said, half to himself, "I could clear the Sanctum unaided. No intruder would escape my wrath."

"You will have the phetam, Your Vastness," I assured him. "Just let me have the cylinder. . . ."

"No." The bass rumble was harsh and hostile. "I still do not trust you. Perhaps I will wait till the key is found. Perhaps before the cylinder is opened I will have *you* opened."

I felt my smile wobble as cold sweat drenched me. "That would be unwise, Your Loftiness," I quavered. "I am your only hope of getting at the phetam."

"Then prove it." The God-King's suspicious glare was aimed at my hands. "Show me this thing you have hidden in your fingers. This lockpick. Explain its workings to me."

"It . . . it would be clearer, Your Enormity," I gulped, "if I explained it with the cylinder in my hands."

"*No.*" Growing suspicion darkened his voice. "Show me first."

I glanced wildly around, aware of my own rising desperation. I looked at Mala's tense frown, y'Bagnehaude's nervous twitching, the alarmed gaze of the girls, the blank menace of the killdroids . . . And as I struggled to think of a response that would convince the flabby old fool, part of my mind was simply crying for help.

And help arrived.

In a shattering eruption of shock-wave and flames, the three floor-level entrances to the Haven were blasted open. The blasts smashed many of the killdroids to the floor, and many more fell in those first explosive moments. What looked like maniacal demons came charging in through the entrances, howling, blazers flaming.

They were all there, all three criminal gangs, each one pouring through one of the entrances. Not as many as there had been, but enough. Presumably the male killdroid guards of the Sanctum had been wiped out. Now the surviving criminals had reached the Sanctum's heart, to get what they had come for.

There was a small knot of leaping Gharrgoyles – and Gharr himself, looming and golden, blade in hand. He had a makeshift bandage around his head, a few gashes reddening his shirt, but was otherwise regrettably intact. The second entrance filled up with exter pirates, Ten-huc in their midst, with a tentacle or two missing but otherwise in good shape. Probably the chaotic inpouring of all the others had interrupted his and Gharr's personal combat, earlier, before either could win. And in the third doorway, a sizeable handful of hard-faced Famlio thugs, with Pulvidon looking carnivorous at their head.

No Treffs had reached the Haven – understandably, against that opposition – except one. That was c'Vira, amazing and unpredictable as ever. She had somehow managed to attach herself to Gharr, adhesively. He had one arm possessively around her waist, in the way that he had clutched Mala, and she seemed to be enjoying it. She had also managed again to get her robe artfully torn – down the front this time, from neck to navel, exposing most of that ripe cleavage.

For a terrible silent fraction of a second, the firing stopped and all the opposing forces stared at each other. Then it seemed, still in that frozen fragment of time, that the criminals all turned to stare at *me*, as if with a promise of unimaginable torments to come.

At that point the remaining killdroid women opened fire.

Gharr roared, Pulvidon yelled, Ten-huc bellowed, and the

three gangs fired back. Death and destruction filled the room – blazer bolts crisscrossing in the air, grenades bursting and blasting. Harem girls ran shrieking to find safety, and y'Bagnehaude's terrified squeal rose beyond the threshold of hearing as he tried to burrow into the hillock. Mala dropped into a crouch, her manacled hands twitching in their hunger for a weapon. The God-King cried out in fear, struggling flabbily to heave himself from the dais.

And I flung myself at him.

My weight slammed him back on to the cushions, as I clawed at the cylinder that he still clutched. He cried out again and threshed, clinging to the cylinder with manic strength. But I was close to manic too, and a lot younger. I struck at him, struck again – and as his fingers loosened I snatched the cylinder away.

Still he came at me, howling and frantic, hands clawed, flailing at me like a wild beast. Around us, the battle was reaching equally demented heights, and too many of the blazer bolts were sizzling too close to the dais. In fury, I raised the cylinder and smashed it into the God-King's face.

To my unending astonishment, the shiny perfection of the Balbazian steel shattered, like antique and paper-thin glass. In an incredible burst of noise.

I stared stupidly as the God-King fell back unconscious, his face smeared with blood. Impossible, I was thinking. It's unbreakable. So it couldn't have broken. But it did. And with such an enormous, terrible sound. . . .

Then a slightly less appalled part of my mind produced the idea that the smashing of the cylinder had coincided with some *other* explosion, which had produced that monstrous sound.

Slowly, dazedly, I turned my head.

Most of the harem killdroids had fallen. So had quite a few of the criminals. The rest had stopped firing, and were staring as stupefiedly as I was.

The sound that I'd heard had been created when the entire, immense domed ceiling of the Personal Haven had been ripped away and flung aside.

By, apparently, a small group of blue-caped figures who were now hurtling down towards us.

The Ardakkeans had arrived.

Chapter 23

They were, beyond any doubt, flying.

The terrifying noise of the dome's removal had silenced the entire chamber. In that ghastly stillness, all of us – attackers and attacked – stared up. It was . . . staggering.

The Ardakkeans swooped down as if on mighty, invisible wings, capes billowing behind them. Sergia was of course at their head, bosom jutting, with eleven other men and women following behind her. Even before they landed, Sergia's fiery dark eyes sought me out with a withering glance that made me flinch.

I was lucky that it was just an angry look.

As the twelve caped beings touched down, one of the more dimwitted of the pirates reacted to their strangeness in what was probably his normal way of dealing with strangeness. He tried to kill it. Opening fire with a blazer, he aimed the bolts at the two Ardakkeans nearest to him.

The shots triggered a reflex response in the other armed groups. Suddenly they were all firing at the Ardakkeans. For a second the twelve were no longer blue but orange, as the blazer fire enveloped them.

Then the firing dwindled and died away, and everyone fell into an awed silence, save for a whimper from y'Bagnehaude. For the Ardakkeans were uninjured. Not a hair, not a thread, had been singed by that flaming onslaught.

"You cannot harm us," Sergia said in her most commanding voice. "But we can harm you. Put down your weapons."

In the ensuing silence, I heard Gharr quietly murmur some remark to c'Vira. I could imagine the nature of the remark when c'Vira responded with her lewd chuckle. But Ardakkeans included super-hearing among their powers. Sergia stiffened, wheeled, and hurled another furious glare in Gharr's direction.

But that wasn't all she hurled. From those luminous dark eyes, two narrow scarlet beams scorched out – twin heat rays, lancing across the chamber.

They struck the molecublade in Gharr's hand and transformed it into a dripping lump of molten metal. Gharr screamed and doubled up, clutching his ruined hand – while c'Vira shrieked and flung her arms around him protectively.

"I could as easily have removed his arm," Sergia announced sternly. "Or his head. So could any of us. Now put down your weapons!"

As she barked the last command, the Haven filled with metallic clanks and clatters as all the criminals, looking fearful as well as awed, dropped their weapons on the floor. Then, leaving her people to keep their potentially lethal eyes on the throng, Sergia stalked towards the dais. Towards me.

Her gaze flickered over the scene on the dais – the slumped figure of the God-King with blood-smeared face, the fragments of the cylinder. She curled her lip in distaste, then curled it further as she fixed her gaze on me. I may have quailed a little. Anyone would have.

"Curb, you are a liar, a thief, a scoundrel," she said. "You had our phetam all along, as is now clear. Yet you would not return it to us, seeking your own squalid profit from it. As all of these are seeking. Creatures of greed and evil."

"No, you misunderstand," I said, improvising quickly. "Just as you arrived, I was trying to get the cylinder *away* from the God-King. I'd realized at last how wrong it was, that he or anyone should have your phetam. I would have returned it to you if the cylinder hadn't broken."

"I do not believe you," she said contemptuously. "You have consistently proved to be a liar and a cheat. With a dirty little mind. But you will be punished – as will the ruler of this world, who has been robbing us for so long."

I may have quailed a little more, for she smiled grimly. "The

207

police of your Federation," she said, "have been made aware of the violence brought to this world by these criminal elements." She glanced at Mala. "Your friend Chertro kindly alerted us. He and a large detachment are already landing here."

Behind her, a ripple of alarm and fury shook the gathering of criminals. They might have tried to get away, but for the threat of the Ardakkean heat-ray eyes. Instead, they merely shifted and growled and glanced fearfully over their shoulders, awaiting the inevitable.

Except for one. Pulvidon stepped forward, and if he'd had his gun he would have blasted me where I stood. Instead, he merely fixed me with a furious glare. As everyone else was, just then.

"Curb," he snarled, "I blame *you* for all this. And I'll fix you for it. There's nowhere in the galaxy you can hide from me. Whatever happens now, I promise you, I'll find you."

With that, I did a bit more quailing. And wishing that I was a long way away. But Sergia still held me pinned with her gaze – and I stayed pinned even when she turned to look again at the dais and the God-King.

He seemed to be slowly coming around, groaning, stirring his flabby body. But Sergia seemed more interested in the splintered cylinder.

"I suppose it was Balbazian steel?" she said idly, to Mala.

"It was, yes," Mala said. "But it broke, like glass."

Sergia shook her head slowly. "You people . . . So sophisticated, out among the galaxy's worlds. Yet so naïve. Even we on Ardakke have seen the galacvid advertisements for this indestructible steel. But, knowing something about indestructibility, we have *tested* the metal." She looked fiercely at me. "We found that the advertisements lie, and the Balbazians are cheats. Like so many of you. They hide the fact that their steel develops intro-molecular metal fatigue after about fourteen years, which renders it brittle and fragile. This cylinder had obviously passed its crucial point."

I could have wept. You can't trust anybody. If I'd only known, the phetam could have been mine, much earlier, without *any* pain or danger or violence. . . .

But then I jumped, as did everyone standing nearby. The

twin heatrays had burst forth again from Sergia's eyes, stabbing down at the dais. They struck the fragments of the cylinder, and the wet patches where spilled phetam had dampened the fabric. Smoke and flame erupted around the God-King as those last remnants burned and vanished.

An instant later, Sergia blew out a powerful breath, like a millisecond burst of gale-force wind, and the flames vanished as a candle is quenched. With a quick nod of satisfaction, she began to turn back to me.

But whatever she was planning to say or do was interrupted.

Beyond the entrances we all heard the clumping of booted feet, the clank of metal. Then what seemed to be about two hundred FedPol Forcibles crashed into the chamber, weapons held at combat readiness. They slid to an abrupt stop, staring around – especially at the criminal gangs, the weapons on the floor, the apparently unarmed Ardakkeans in control. I spotted Mala's friend Chertro at their head, just as he – looking astounded – spotted us.

A second later, we were all looking astounded.

The God-King came fully awake, groaning. As he sat up, his eyes widened and the blood drained from his face. He obviously knew what the Ardakkeans were – and he needed only that instant to realize what had happened, and what was likely to happen.

Staring around, he weakly raised a hand to paw at the blood on his face, while licking with a sloppy tongue at the smeared wetness around his mouth.

The truth hit us – some of us – only in that moment. I had smashed the God-King in the face with a cylinder full of phetam. Not all the wetness on his face was blood.

He was, in an instant, transformed. It was a change worthy of a shape-shifter, though his outward form didn't alter. Clearly he hadn't had enough phetam to improve his flabby old body. But you could see it in his eyes, his movements – the immense vitality that suddenly surged through him, new strength and life and power.

Super-power.

He sprang up, just as Sergia leaped forward and clamped a hand on his wrist. I had felt the awesome strength of Sergia's grip – but the God-King jerked his arm free as easily as I might have broken the hold of a harem girl. Well, one of the smaller ones.

Then he leaped into the air, accompanied by a chorus of astonished cries. His flabby nakedness lacked the grace of Sergia and her comrades, but he could fly. And he did – at considerable speed, straight out through the wrecked dome without looking back.

"After him!" Sergia shouted. "He ingested only a small amount – it will wear off soon!"

Two of the Ardakkeans obeyed at once, hurtling upwards like blue missiles, vanishing beyond the dome. The newly arrived FedPol stared after them, looking numb with wonder and disbelief. But so did everyone else.

It was Chertro who first pulled himself together and began to organize things. Soon the criminals had been herded together with magno-fasteners on their wrists, and the FedPol were relaxing, grinning and leering at the huddles of naked harem girls. By then Sergia and Chertro were having a quiet word, which involved some nodding in agreement and much unpleasant staring at me.

Finally Sergia shook hands with Chertro, looking stern and determined. "Our minds are nonetheless made up, friend. Ardakke was always mostly a closed world, but we allowed some contact with other planets, some off-world workers. We will do so no longer."

"I understand you have officially informed the Federation?" Chertro said.

"We have," Sergia replied. "The entire galaxy is to be alerted – Ardakke is now wholly closed to all off-worlders, and will be defended with every means. Never again will a drop of phetam be taken from our planet."

Chertro nodded. "Just as well. Makes a lot of trouble for everyobdy."

"As long as everyone realizes," Sergia added fiercely, "that any spacecraft entering Ardakke's territorial space, for whatever reason, will instantly be destroyed."

"Ought to do the trick," Chertro said dryly.

"And the rest of these . . . creatures?" Sergia said, glancing

210

darkly around, then settling her gaze on me. "They will be dealt with?"

"Count on it," Chertro said.

Sergia nodded, glanced around once more, then gestured to her people. Effortlessly, gracefully, the splendid figures rose from the floor and sailed through the open dome, quickly disappearing from sight.

Nearly everyone watched them go in silence. But Chertro was marching grimly over to where Mala and I were standing, by the dais. Mala turned towards him, drooping a little with the after-effects of that violent day. I realized that she was still wearing her fasteners, and might have cut her free, except that I was drooping quite a bit as well. Anyway, Chertro was in the way.

"Sorry, Fuzz," he said, stern-faced. "I have to take you and Curb in, as well."

She nodded, gave a small sigh, then turned to look at me. Disturbingly, there was no anger in her eyes. Just weariness, and something that might have been utter dismissal.

"You pathetic dribble-brain," she said emptily. "What a mess you make of everything."

That really hit me hard. I felt crushed and shaken – and then I began to feel resentful. She wasn't being fair. Nor was it fair that everyone else in the place should also be looking at me with one kind of dislike or another.

"*Me!*" I said. "Why blame *me*? *I'm* not the person who's been stealing phetam for two centuries! *I'm* not one of the people who invaded the Sanctum with a small army? I've just been doing my *job!*"

They won't have an answer to that, I thought – and I straightened up, crossing my arms and looking dignified. As I did so, I felt a sharp sting of pain. I lifted my hand and saw a small gash on the pad of my right thumb, still oozing blood. Obviously I'd been cut when the cylinder broke on the God-King.

"And look at that!" I snarled at Mala. "Look! On top of everything else, I've been *hurt!*"

Then I put my thumb in my mouth, as one does with such a cut, to soothe it.

211

An astonishing sensation flooded through my entire body. As if microscopic nuclear explosions were happening in every cell. But those mini-bursts were spreading a feeling of immense well-being. And vitality. And strength.

Phetam, I thought dazedly. Some must have splashed on my hand when the cylinder broke. I've had phetam.

The feeling was magnificent. I felt there was nothing I couldn't do. No weight too heavy for me, no force too strong. I felt a kind of . . . yes, *divinity* flowing through me.

I glanced around, seeing Mala and Chertro beginning to frown slightly at the changes they saw in my expression. I also found that if I wished I could see through things, like an X-ray. Not all that useful, there, where all the girls around me were already nude. But I could also feel the other super-powers gathering within me. In that moment, I had become a god.

Godlike, I seized Chertro with terrible strength and flung him aside, so that he bounced with a helpless yell on the dais and then on to the cushioning tubbiness of y'Bagnehaude. Godlike, I swept Mala up in my arms, weightless as a feather, smiling reassuringly as she gasped and tried to struggle.

Godlike, I leaped into the air, and flew.

It was beyond description. I soared and glided, laughing aloud with the overwhelming feeling, the intoxication, the liberation. I felt that I looked something like an Ardakkean myself, in my blue outfit, my own short cape fluttering behind me. I swung high towards the broken dome, then swooped down again, over the appalled faces looking up at me.

But as I laughed again, one of the more stunned-looking FedPol men, reacting as the pirate had before, raised his gun and shot me.

The blazer bolt hit me squarely in the chest.

And bounced off, doing no more damage than a moon-beam.

"Hold your fire!" Chertro roared, climbing to his feet. "You could hit the girl!"

Trust him to be so concerned about Mala, I thought irately. For a moment I was tempted to dip lower and teach both him and his trigger-happy policeman a lesson.

But, instead, I gave in to a different temptation.

I sailed across the crowd that was still goggling up at me. And before anyone could react in any way, I swung my right hand down in a sweeping backhand blow.

It was very like one that had been swung at me, among the motley crowds at Fif's, on Uulaa. But my blow contained a huge amount of stored-up ill-will, from a great number of insults and outrages that I'd suffered. And it was phetam-powered ill-will. Though I held back a little, not seeking to kill, my hand smashed with a satisfying impact – full into the handsome, golden face of Gharr the Gherpotean.

I felt his nose flatten, his cheekbones crumple, his teeth splinter, his jawbone crack. The powerful golden body was flung backwards, limp as a discarded cloth. The face so admired by women was a mask of blood. The Gharrgoyles howled, c'Vira screamed. And I grinned contentedly and flew away, through the open dome.

I expected – after everything Gharr had done – that Mala would be pleased by my revenge. Instead, oddly, she turned her face away, looking shocked and disapproving. But I didn't let it spoil the moment. I soared away with her, across the wasteland, to rip the bombs from my ship and get us, at last, away from Fraxilly.

Chapter 24

"Reckon that's about it," Frejji said as she came through the airlock, carrying her space helmet.

"Good," I said.

"Y'r Posi's got the mechatons tidyin' up. Should be good as new by t'morrow."

"Fine," I said.

"Y'r a lucky fella, Del, havin' that Posi. Wish I c'd afford one half as smart."

"Mm," I said.

"Course it all woulda been easier on the ground. Cheaper, too."

"Right," I said.

"S'not as if the place's still fulla people tryin' t' find y'," Frejji said with a laugh.

To that I said nothing at all.

Frejji peered at me thoughtfully. 'Y' sure got tight-mouthed since Mala took off. What y' gonna do – sit up here an' stare at the stars till she comes back? *If?*"

I shrugged.

"C'mon, Del. She'll be back. When she said she had t' go away an' think, it was jus' a way t' make y' sweat, get back at y' fer somethin'."

I thought of the distance that had grown between Mala and me, on the flight from Fraxilly, when she had slowly and coldly enumerated all the things in which, as she saw it, I was lacking. "Maybe," I said.

"Sure," Frejji went on. "Mala's not really gonna marry some FedPol creep. Not her style. An' she knows you two got a nice little number with this business. She'll stay away long 'nough t' make her point, then she'll be back. Y' know what females're like."

"Frejji," I said, *"you're* a female."

She grinned. "That's why I know what I'm talkin' 'bout. I mean — what's Mala gonna do? Set up on her own or somethin'?"

I sighed. "Maybe."

For a long moment Frejji studied me shrewdly. "So that's it," she said at last. "Y're not miserable 'cause she's gone, or 'cause this Chertro lunk asked her t' marry him. Y're worryin' 'bout the competition!"

I scowled. "That's not true. I *miss* Mala. I'm . . . fond of her. And there are lots of other things worrying me."

Frejji would be worried herself, I thought, if she knew that one of the things troubling me was the question of how I was going to pay her bill.

But she didn't know that, so she could cheerfully hand me the plastiscrip printout that itemized her repairs to the ship. "Don't give in t' worries, Del. They eat at y' like rust. Me, now, if things start pressin' on me, I count up all the good things happenin' at the same time. You try that. Count y'r blessin's."

"I could get more original philosophy from a mechaton," I snarled. But Frejji just gave me a grin and marched off to the airlock, refastening her helmet.

And I went back to staring into space. Literally, since the ship was in high orbit around Uulaa. Figuratively, because I'd been in a mood for inward-looking ever since Mala had left.

At least she had waited until all the dust had settled.

The FedPol had launched a major investigation — headed by Chertro — of the whole fracas on Fraxilly. Including Mala and me, not as witnesses but as suspected perpetrators. The FedPol had caught up with us fairly quickly, thanks to Mala. Not too far from the Fraxilly system we had a fairly extensive percep-tor breakdown, leaving the ship half-crippled, and Mala simply ignored my protests and put out a Netline SOS. The FedPol arrived within a bio-day, and arrested us.

But I'd been sure that Chertro would arrange for Mala to be freed, and I'd been right. She was deemed to have been innocently caught up in the whole mess, and discharged. Meanwhile I clung to my statement that I'd known nothing about stolen phetam and was on Fraxilly merely doing my job as a courier. I'd also hired an expensive lawyer with a smile like a M'farquan shark-eel, who implanted plenty of doubt in everyone's minds about my involvement.

Added to that was the increasing embarrassment among the SenFed authorities, as lip-licking galacvid reports piled up the details of life on Fraxilly and the corruption and venality of the God-King. In the end I was released, my record unblemished, as part of the swiftly begun offical cover-up.

The SenFed sent a commission to Fraxilly to organize a new government, and to channel some of the God-King's wealth back to the people to ease their misery. At that the galacvid lost interest, since the easing of misery isn't such hot news as corruption and venality. They turned, instead, to a fictionalized series about an intrepid space adventurer who crash-lands on Fraxilly and uses his combat skills to lead Treff rebels to victory. It was low-budget, far-fetched, short-lived and above all poorly cast. The people playing the Treffs were all smooth, glamorous and freshly bathed, while the oversize blank-wit who played the hero wasn't right at all.

Anyway, the last I heard, the restoration of Fraxilly was going ahead smoothly. The wasteland was being reclaimed, towns and cities were being rebuilt, most Fraxillians were eating regularly. They'd also gained a new government. It seemed to be fairly oligarchic – the SenFed didn't like to dictate forms of government to member worlds – and I was not surprised to learn that among the dominant figures was a clever young man named y'Wipo.

Meanwhile, I heard other things.

Most of the criminals who had survived to reach the God-King's Haven, at the end, had been carted off to various FedPol prisons. But, as usual, the big fishes got away. They had lawyers with even sharper smiles than mine, who found nice big holes in the official net.

It worried me enormously at the time, since I expected them all to come after me. Oddly, that didn't quite happen.

The pirate chief, Ten-huc, had gone straight back to the Alkaline Asteroids. He had suffered a large loss of men, and also of face, on Fraxilly. It was rumoured that those setbacks had finally made him feel his age, edging him into retirement. It didn't look like he'd be coming after me or anyone, ever again. Which would be good news for potential piracy victims everywhere.

Similarly, Gharr the Gherpotean was not quite the man he had been. The plastic surgeons who'd rebuilt his face hadn't got it quite right. I saw pictures that showed it to be slightly, weirdly, out of kilter. And that plus his ruined right hand seemed to have taken most of the swash out of his buckle. Anyway, it was being said that he was completely besotted with c'Vira, never apart from her, totally under her control. Which would be good news for husbands and lovers everywhere. And for me – since I like to think that some left-over fondness for me, in c'Vira, is what has kept me safe from Gharr.

As a footnote, I hear that while c'Vira has abandoned the Treff robe for more stylish garments, she still has never been known to wash. Apparently Gharr won't allow it. Which ought to throw interesting sidelights on the chemistry of pheromones.

But, aside from all that, there was Famlio.

They had been especially angry with me. More than anyone. I'd failed to pay "protection" at Vadinamia, I'd crippled one of their ships, I'd been involved in getting lots of their thugs killed and lots more jailed, I'd helped to prevent them getting the phetam. There was going to be no hiding from them – as Pulvidon himself had warned me, on Fraxilly.

Rumour told me later that Pulvidon had sworn an ancient Famlio oath committing him to having my liver removed and fed to me, among other delights. When I was in custody in a FedPol pre-trial facility he apparently tried to penetrate it, to get at me. And as a failsafe, I learned, he put out a very costly contract with the galaxy's most lethal hit-men, two poison-skin exters from Kalkovia, to have me tracked and killed if I managed to get away.

All this information reached me as soon as I was released. I then suffered a near-total nervous collapse, and in my terror and despair I thought about going to find Pulvidon and getting it over with. Luckily, though, a lot of time had passed. Just as luckily, Famlio is a *business* organization, first and above all. Its top executives don't like to break wind if there's no profit in it. And the same applies to breaking necks.

I had already cost them a great deal. During my time in custody I was costing them more – because one of their top enforcers, Pulvidon, was running crazy risks and spending kilocreds trying to get at me. So the Famlio patriarchs did some costings, and decided that I wasn't really worth all the trouble and expense. Nor the greater trouble that the FedPol might cause if I was murdered too soon after the events on Fraxilly.

It wasn't, in their view, as if I'd won any kind of *victory* over them. That would have been unforgivable. But no one had won a victory, on Fraxilly, except maybe y'Wipo. So in the end Famlio decided there was a better way to deal with me.

Pulvidon contacted me – I could see he hated it, but he obeyed orders – to tell me the better way. I could stay alive, he said, if I could *pay*. Credits. For everything that Famlio had spent on the whole Fraxilly venture. Even including the cancellation charge on the Kalkovian contract for my own murder.

The total amount came to quite a few more kilocreds than the whole of my fee from Fraxilly, plus surcharge. It even took most of what was left of my previous earnings from Ixyphal II – after I'd renewed my lease on Uulaa, replaced some lost mini-weapons and paid my lawyer. It left me nothing to pay Frejji with, and not much even to live on.

But at least I was going to live. Though one or two oblique remarks from Pulvidon indicated that he was never going to develop kindly feelings towards me.

All that business was finally concluded shortly after my release, and two bio-weeks before the day when Frejji finished repairing my ship. At the time of my release, Mala had left. To go somewhere and be alone, she said. To think about Chertro's proposal, or whether she'd stay on her own, or whether she could put up with me for any further time. I did a bit of pleading, made some promises, but even so she left. With the final chilly warning that the odds were strongly *against* the third of her alternatives.

So I was alone, orbiting Uulaa, with an emptied Fedbank account and an all-time low of spirits. On the "counting of blessings" side, as Frejji would see it, I had a restored ship, and no killers were aiming to do unspeakable things to my inner organs. That was something, I told myself. But not a lot.

In the days after Mala had left I'd sometimes idly wondered whether she would have stayed if I had managed to keep the phetam for myself. She might have liked being the consort of a new God-King . . . But at heart I knew what a foolish dream that was. I could never have kept the phetam while Sergia and her Ardakkeans were out on the Netlines looking for it.

At least I hadn't had to face Sergia's wrath any further, after my escape from Fraxilly. She and the others had gone home as they said they would, and had kept their promise to close Ardakke entirely, as if it was no longer there. And all the wild stories about super-beings that were pumped up by lurid documentaries on the vid would ensure that they would be left alone. Even by other criminals drawn by the phetam. No one was going to try to take on a planet that held several million people, any *one* of whom could fly up to meet your ship, withstand all your weaponry, and blast you out of the sky with their eyes.

But someone else *did* have to face Sergia's wrath.

I got some satisfaction when I learned what had happened to the God-King. As Sergia had said, the few drops of phetam he'd ingested wore off in a short while, so the Ardakkeans captured him easily. Sergia and company then took him back to Ardakke, and imposed their punishment. He was put to work as a labourer, tending the phet bushes. It was said that he was much thinner and healthier, but aging fast. And with no luxuries or harems. But the worst torment of all, for him, must have been to be surrounded by super-people taking phetam, with never a drop for him.

That news came out of Ardakke when the FedPol contacted the planet, asking for the God-King to be turned over to their custody. Apparently the reply was that y'Iggthradgipile was an imprisoned criminal, that Ardakke was now a closed world, and that if the FedPol wanted to make something of it they could come ahead. Wisely, they never did.

I smiled a little to myself, then, sitting in my ship above Uulaa, as the thought of all those events brought back the memory of my own brief time as a phetam-powered superman. Of course the effects of the droplet I'd ingested wore off in less than an hour. Before Posi had got us out of Fraxilly's territorial space, I'd returned to normal.

And while it had been a magical, unforgettable time – flying, being invulnerable, smashing Gharr's face in – I wasn't too unhappy that it had ended. I knew that I wouldn't have wanted to go through all the huge life-changes that would be involved in becoming a super-hero. All those expectations, demands, responsibilities . . . I was better off with just my ordinary human abilities, being just an ordinary sort of hero. I was better off. . . .

I smiled a little wider, then, with the realization that Frejji had been right. It did help to count your blessings. And perhaps I had more blessings than I'd thought.

If I admitted it to myself, Mala's absence was something of a liberation. I may have missed her obvious charms and attractions, but I didn't miss her usually sharp tongue and critical tendencies. In fact, I began to see that I was beneficially free in many ways. I was young and healthy, with lots of capabilities and a marvellously equipped spaceship. If I was impoverished, it was a temporary condition. There was a galaxy-full of creds to be earned, jobs to be undertaken, cargoes to be carried.

I rose and stretched, feeling suddenly, amazingly, better. And my next move, I thought, might be to change into some more lively clothes and to take the pod down to Uulaa-la. To see if any attractive young lady tourists might like to buy me dinner, in exchange for the *inside* story of what happened on Fraxilly.